Jill Tipping has recently discovered a love for writing fiction and this is her second novel. Her first, *Beyond Fragile Boundaries*, was published in November 2012. Jill lives in Kent with her husband and has two daughters and a son. Alongside her writing, she runs her own PR company.

www.jilltipping.co.uk

Follow @JillTipping

by the same author

fiction

BEYOND FRAGILE BOUNDARIES

The Hidden Depths of
HAYDON ROUSE

Jill Tipping

First published in Great Britain in 2013
by Kavanagh Tipping Publishing,
www.jilltipping.co.uk

All characters and events in this publication other than those clearly in the public domain are fictitious and any resemblance to real persons, living or dead, is purely coincidental.

Copyright © 2013 Jill Tipping

ISBN: 978-1-906546-13-7

All rights reserved. No part of the publication may be reproduced, stored in a retrieval system, or transmitted in any form or by any means, electronic, mechanical, photocopying, recording, or otherwise, without the prior permission of the publishers, nor be otherwise circulated in any form of binding or cover other than that in which it is published and without a similar condition being imposed on the subsequent purchaser.

for Jane Rutherford

Chapter 1

It really did not smell like home any more. The empty rooms with scrubbed floors and bleached paintwork had changed the feel of the place, and Diane's footsteps echoed as she moved desolately from room to room. So many memories.

It was early summer but she shivered as she stood and allowed herself to experience crushing regret. She was not one to give in to emotions easily, but she felt she had to fully immerse herself in this acute sadness to make sure that she could always recall the feeling – never allowing something like this to happen to her family again. In James' bedroom, she remembered him as a four year old standing next to his bed, dressed for his first day at school, big, serious eyes looking at her as he prepared himself for the ordeal ahead. He disliked change, unlike his older sister, Christie, who embraced each challenge with remarkable zest and vigour.

Diane sighed as she shut the bedroom door for the very last time. Every room had now been checked, double checked and checked again until she could not even remember what she was checking for. Maybe, she felt, if she kept looking around the house she would eventually wake up and realise that it had all been a dream: a door would bang, voices would ring out calling for tea or clothes not yet ironed. She stopped and waited to see if that would happen, but the only sound was that of the car running outside on the drive. She walked down the stairs, setting her shoulders back and shaking her head as if to clear maudlin thoughts. Grabbing her bag and keys, she walked out of the front door, shut it behind her and walked purposefully over to the car, where her family were waiting for her.

'Ready?' Pete asked, his hand ready on the gear stick to select reverse.

'Let's go, Pete. Let's just get going'.

She looked at her husband, who had hesitated and turned to her. 'I'm so sorry.' His voice cracked and she touched his cheek, knowing she had to be the strong one.

'Pete, it's a house. It used to be our home, but now it's just a house. That's all. Just bricks and mortar. Nothing else. So, come on! We're on an adventure; we've got a new life to start!' She looked behind at seventeen year old James, slumped in the back seat and staring listlessly out of the window. 'All right, son?' she asked and gently shook his knee. He looked at her from under an untidy fringe. His expression didn't change – he just looked at her and then back out of the window – and her heart twisted with hurt at his apparent callousness, and then with sympathy for his teenage confusion and fear of change.

The coach driver smiled at the young woman who was about to board. Working in a university town he saw many young people at this stage of their lives. Christie handed him her suitcase and hold all. There were tears in her eyes as she looked back at her two housemates and best friends, who were standing arm in arm waiting to wave her off. She had no idea when she would see them again and it seemed so strange to be going in a completely different direction.

The driver checked her ticket. 'Off back home to Penzance, then? All finished at uni now?'

Christie just grinned and nodded. So many emotions were coursing through her: an ending and a beginning all in one day. Her mother had sent her pictures of the cottage they were moving to: one of a row, all painted white, which seemed to be perched on a hill side. You could hear the sea from the house if all was quiet, her mother had said, trying to sound bright when they were talking on the phone. But Christie knew how hard her family was taking the enforced move and her heart lurched with pain as she thought about the countless hours, including weekends, her dad had put in over the years, running his own business. The economy had not been kind to small construction companies, though, and after one of his major customers had failed to pay, it was easy to understand why her dad had had to make the unwelcome decision to put his company into liquidation.

Her mother was a freelance journalist and could work just about anywhere via email and phone, so moving house was not such a problem. Although she would certainly have to adapt to a slower pace, she had called a few contacts and could probably get some work with one of the Cornish local newspapers. It was her dad that Christie really worried about. He had no job to go to and they would be living on the money they had made on the sale of their four bedroom house in rural Cheshire. It would just be for a while, though, Diane had assured her on the phone, just until he gets a job.

The coach pulled out of the station and Christie craned her neck to see if her friends were still there. She could see them doing the same: peering up into the high level windows to catch a glimpse of her. Waves and blown kisses came her way and Christie felt a sob rising in her throat as a magical and inspirational three years came to an end. Settling down into her seat, she rummaged in her handbag and pulled out her earphones. How did they get into such a tangle? Then, to the sounds of *Coldplay*, she allowed the city to drift by and her mind to wander over what had been and what was to come.

Pete sat in the car with the windscreen wipers on. A damp drizzle was misting his view of the Penzance coach terminal and he wanted to see the Bristol coach the minute it came in. He was excited about seeing his daughter. She always saw the sunny side of things and he felt in great need of some sunshine right at that moment. The drive down from Manchester, earlier in the day, had been pretty miserable: it had rained the whole way and there had been long silences. Diane had tried to ease the gloom with random comments about the passing countryside, but eventually even she had given up and a heavy blanket of regret seemed to fill the car, with no way to shift it.

Diane had said that no one was to blame for what had happened to the family business: it was just 'one of those things'. But it had prospered for eighty five years, the last twenty of which it had been in the care of Pete Styles. So what had gone wrong? Pete felt not only his own disappointment but that of his father and grandfather. One word encapsulated the whole gamut of his feelings: guilt. There was no one else to blame except himself: he made the decision to borrow more, and then more and more, thinking that it would always get better. But it hadn't and here he was – no longer a business owner or a home owner. Everything he had worked for had been taken from him in one fell swoop – wiped out as though it had never existed. He sighed and reminded himself, as Diane often did, that ultimately it was family that really mattered. He had to admit that she had put it all very much into perspective when she had said: 'You'd give it all up in an instant if it meant saving one of our lives, wouldn't you?' He had, of course, agreed, but that wasn't what had happened. He found it so very difficult to feel comforted by such comments, even though they were well-intended, because that scenario wasn't real. The life he was living was real, and the feeling of ultimate failure was painfully real.

A coach pulled into a bay on the far side and he could see his Christie waving frantically from the window. He flashed the car headlights and, even from this distance, he could see her wide smile. It had been a long three years. She had come home for holidays but he had never felt that she was fully there: she had always seemed to be wistfully looking forward to the next term and getting back to her friends. He got out of the car to go and hug his sunshine child.

'Daddy!' She flung her arms around his neck and he was transported back in time by his daughter's customary greeting of a huge hug. He loved it.

'Hello, my precious. How was your journey?'

'Well, quite long it seemed but it was fine. I spent most of it asleep leaning against the window with my mouth open – dribbling I expect.'

'A charming sight I'm sure,' said Pete as he took her case from her and she linked her arm through his to walk the short distance to the car.

'How far is the drive to our new mansion then?' she asked, a moment later, as she fastened her seat belt and relaxed into the warmth of her father's company.

'Oh, not more than twenty minutes or so. Mum's getting in fish and chips tonight. There are two chippies in the town.'

'That's handy because I'm starving. Dad, how are you? I mean, how are you *really* – no bullshit.'

How was he? he thought. Numb! That just about summed it up. So how did he explain that?

'Well, sweetheart,' he began, giving it a go. 'I'd say it hasn't really sunk in yet. It's a difficult time but you know how positive your mum is, so I'm just trying to keep up with her really. To be honest, I don't feel much of anything right now, except happy to see you. It's a new start, Christie, for us all, and that's the way I am looking at it. The cottage is nice – small, but really cosy. I think you'll like it.'

Christie looked at her father's profile as he drove through the drizzle. It was the oddest of sensations to be going to a new home. They had been in their previous one for fifteen years so it had been the only home she had ever really known. Now she had a new one in a place she had never even visited before. It was a small fishing town on the Atlantic coast, with a rocky shoreline and a harbour full of bobbing fishing boats and little wooden dinghies: that was how her mother had described it. They were renting the cottage from a former work colleague of her dad's who had used it as a holiday cottage. He hadn't visited for some years and was anxious to have it occupied, so it was an ideal opportunity for both him and the Styles family. 'That's good Dad. Can't wait to see it,' she replied encouragingly. Her mother had told her that it needed some work – mainly decorating and possibly a new kitchen and bathroom – so the owner had given it to them rent free for six months and Dad had the job of getting it up to scratch.

A short while later Christie entered Porthtreval for the first time. In the early evening rain it looked dismal but she could see it might have potential on a warm, sunny day with throngs of holidaymakers enjoying the mild Cornish climate. The main road led straight down to the town, which encircled the harbour in a U shape. The car rumbled along a narrow cobbled roadway alongside the harbour wall and then, after a sharp u-bend, travelled uphill alongside the shingle beach. Apart from several people braving the rain with their dogs, the street was deserted.

'Here it is,' said Pete, nodding up to a house at the end of a terrace perched on the corner with a steep hill rising up on its right hand side.

'It looks very cute, Dad.'

Christie, the forever optimist, thought her father. The salt in the sea wind had all but stripped the white paint from the plaster clad walls; a long, rust stain streamed unattractively from a cable fixing point on the front wall, and some of the gutters were blocked, causing water to pour down the side wall. 'I've got my work cut out, but at least it will keep me busy. It'll be a bit grim living here for a while, though, I'm afraid.'

'No worries! It's the start of the summer, Dad!' laughed Christie, indicating the now deluge of rain coursing down the windscreen.

At the rear of the house was a tumble-down shed with a parking space alongside. It was a tight squeeze but her dad managed to reverse the car effortlessly into it, and Christie marvelled at how men always seemed to be so adept at parking cars in tight spots. So far, it was not something she had mastered during her short driving life. Getting out of the car she was hit by the force of the wind gusting along the hilly street and driving fiercely into the little parking area, almost knocking her sideways. Above the roar of the wind, she could hear waves crashing just yards from where she stood and as she breathed in the smell of salt in the air, she felt exhilarated. There was magic here; she could feel it.

'We're back, love,' Pete called as he pushed open the back door. It was sticking and he had to give it a good shove.

'Another job for you there, Dad!' Christie giggled.

'One of many!' he replied with a nod.

'Where's my little girl?' Diane was running down the stairs and into the narrow kitchen to greet her daughter.

'Hi, Mum. How are things?' She put her bag down beside the floor-standing-boiler and gave her mother a much needed hug.

'I really think they're okay, Christie. It was hard leaving home – the old house, I mean.' She glanced at her husband as she corrected herself. 'But we're all right, aren't we Pete?'

He was moving through the kitchen and taking Christie's case upstairs. He answered with a small, unenthusiastic shrug. 'Sure, love. We'll be great.'

The two women looked at each other as he made his way up the stairs and out of sight. Diane shook her head anxiously. 'He's not right, Christie,' she whispered, 'and neither is your brother come to that. They're both a couple of miseries, I'm afraid. You have no idea how lovely it is to see you.' She hugged her daughter once more with renewed vigour.

'Mum, we're all here together and that's what matters. Things will look different when the sun shines. It looked a bit miserable as we drove through just now, but just wait until the sun comes out and you'll see: it's magical!'

Diane's eyes brightened as she smiled, grateful for the supportive optimism of her daughter.

Christie and James had the two tiny rooms facing the roadway and the rooftops of the houses opposite. As Christie looked out of her window she could see right into the kitchen window of the house opposite. *No careful planning here obviously*, she thought, turning to survey her room and putting her hand on the radiator, expecting it to be warm, but it wasn't, which was odd because the room seemed warm compared to the rest of the house. She looked around for hot water pipes or something similar that could be causing the warmth, but there was nothing to explain it, and her room was on the corner of the house so it couldn't be coming from outside. As she stood pondering this anomaly she had the first of many unexplained sensations that were to come: it was as if a pleasant energy ran through her body, accompanied by a bubbly excitement in her stomach, and she felt something like an inner shift. She knew with absolute certainty that she had 'come home'.

Chapter 2

The smell of recently purchased fish and chips drifted up to James as he lay on his bed in his new, minute room. There was only just enough room for his bed, a chest of drawers and a miniature joke of a wardrobe. Mercifully, he didn't own many clothes that needed to be hung up. His parents had said he would need to scale down but he hadn't realised it would be to this extent.

He had heard Christie arrive and he hadn't come out of his room to greet her, which he felt a mite guilty about, but being pleasant to his sister did not form part of his silent protest. He was nothing like his bright, funny, energetic sister. In fact he was almost the direct opposite: dark to her blonde, slim to her rounded shape, and enigmatic to her forthrightness. The only likeness was in their facial features, which were almost identical. They had never been close but she had always been affectionate towards him, which infuriated him even further. He would rather she be argumentative and obnoxious, then he could really let rip at her; instead, her constant understanding and forgiving nature drove him insane, as did her attempts to cheer him up, like the last conversation they had had in the old house.

'I know it's sad that we have to leave here,' she'd said, looking around the familiar kitchen, 'but I think we could all do with a new start.'

'It's all right for you: you've already left once.'

Christie had looked at him sympathetically, which he hated. It was 10pm and she had joined him at the kitchen table where he was sitting nursing a glass of milk. 'But Jay, look at it this way: you're not exactly leaving anything much behind here, are you? It's not like you have loads of friends or a dream job or anything. What are you really leaving behind?'

He had continued to stare down into his glass, saying nothing. She'd got up and moved round behind him to give him a sisterly hug and a kiss on the cheek, which he'd squirmed away from.

'Cheer up Mr Grumpy Gills,' she'd sighed. 'Who knows, you could fall into the life of your dreams and find a nice girlfriend. She could be there waiting for you, right now.' Then she'd given his shoulders a squeeze, saying, 'I'm off to bed. See you in the morning.'

He'd watched her walk along the hall and up the stairs. *What the hell did she know? Little Miss Perfect with her predicted first class degree.* School had always bored him. He just wanted to draw, loving nothing more than to sit and sketch. He had doodled and drawn his way through secondary school, coming out with GCSE As in art and technical drawing, but just scraping Cs in his other subjects. His parents hadn't actually said they were disappointed, but they hadn't needed to: he could see it in their faces, and he could imagine them looking at each other and raising their eyebrows in frustration.

The day that his parents had informed him that they would all be moving down to the West Country, James had silently got up and left the house. He did not make friends easily and the thought of being thrust into a new life was almost more than he could bear. That day he had walked down to the canal and sat on a bench. With shoulders slumped and head down he remembered feeling as if all his energy had seeped out of his body: his head had felt thick and heavy; his eyes had ached. Was this what life was supposed to be like? he had wondered. He was seventeen; shouldn't he be feeling on top of the world, hanging out with friends, learning to drive, listening to music, having his first fumble with the opposite sex? Then again, nothing that he thought he *should* be doing at his age felt right to him: it was as though he was the wrong person in the wrong body. That day at the canal, he had had a strong desire to simply topple in and allow the water to enter his body, fill his lungs and send him into the peace of oblivion. He had played the scene over in his mind – his body being found – and then he had imagined his mother's face: hand clasped over her mouth in shock and eyes screwed up in pain. No, he couldn't do that to her. So he had walked back along the high street, pushing past people who had no idea how he was feeling, and gone back home to his family who, of course, had had their own dilemmas to deal with.

Sitting at the kitchen table after Christie had gone to bed, he'd felt a little better. Maybe she was right and this was just what he needed, he'd thought, although at that moment his life could not have felt more empty – not since Vince had emigrated. Vince was a friend of the family who used to work for his father. He had started as an apprentice and ended up being the manager of the small workforce. He was single, had no dependents, and when things had started to look bad for the business, he had made Pete's job easier by offering to take redundancy. But James had relied on Vince. For as long as he could remember, Vince was the only person with whom James had felt totally at ease. He was the only person who understood that James' need to draw was like a drug for him and, although Vince was ten years his senior, they'd had an easy friendship that didn't need explaining; it just worked. They shared a similar taste in music, art and films, and James had spent most of his weekends at Vince's bed-sit on the edge of the town. It had overlooked the supermarket car park, it had been noisy and draughty, and James had loved it. He and Vince would sit together on the old sofa with their feet up on the coffee table, smoke roll ups and drink cheap red wine while they chatted and laughed. Then had come the moment when Vince told him he would be going away. James had just stared at him in disbelief. 'Why, man? Why?'

'I need to, Jay. I can't stay here. Things are too complicated.'

That had puzzled James, at first: he had thought he knew Vince so well and had wondered what was so complicated.

Something had told him not to push Vince for more information, though, and he had settled for the thought that maybe there was a side to Vince that he wasn't privy to.

The last night with Vince had been so painful, but it had awakened something in James that he had not fully understood or accepted until then, and had confirmed for him that he was to travel a different route to most boys of his age, if he was to be true to himself . He had also realised what the complication was that Vince had to run from...It was him.

Lying on his bed in his tiny bedroom, James now felt that his misery was complete. No Vince, no familiar surroundings and to top it all, virtually no mobile phone reception. As far as he was concerned life could not get much worse. Right up until the moment when the van had arrived to take away the bulk of their belongings for storage, followed within the hour by a smaller one to take what was left down to their new home, he had not really believed that it could happen. He had kept thinking that something would crop up, someone would offer to invest in Dad's business to keep it going, or someone else would find them a place to rent for a while in their home town. The problem, he had been told, was that his mother's work was just as unstable as his dad's, most of her freelance consignments coming from local papers which were in a decline and fighting a losing battle with the digital world. This was what had finally made them choose the option of a complete change and a move to what seemed to James like the edge of the civilised world. He could hear the sea, the wind and the lashing rain, and found it hard to imagine why anyone in their right mind would choose to come here on holiday, let alone to live. It was mid-June, but the grey skies made it feel like mid-November

His mother called up the stairs that tea was ready. With a sigh and a shrug he opened the bedroom door and met Christie on the landing. They looked at each other and communicated something without a word being spoken, as often comes naturally to siblings. Christie put her arms around her young brother and hugged him close. She smelt of fruit body spray and felt warm and welcoming. At least she was familiar. Holding onto his shoulders she looked directly into his eyes.

'Broadband?' she asked, grimacing.

He shook his head. 'Nothing. Can't even get a phone signal. No, tell a lie, I can if I press everything against the window to speak, or I hold the phone up in the top left hand corner of the room. It's shit, Chris! Shit!'

Christie sighed and rolled her eyes in sympathy. 'Come on! At least we've got fish and chips for tea!'

Diane spent the evening putting things away in the limited space of the fitted kitchen cupboards. After emptying the last box, she looked up at the one strip-light, which was flickering as though it was about to give up the ghost, only to light up again and stay on, faithfully emitting a gentle buzzing sound. Pete had arranged the lounge furniture and then gone off to explore the workshop, which was the one area of the house with which he was pleased. He was best off out there in his man's world, Diane mused as she boiled the kettle and made a cup of her favourite green tea. She then sat down at the dining room table with pen and notepad to make a list of what would need to be done to make the cottage liveable for the long term. Frank, who owned the cottage, had given them a ten thousand pound budget to upgrade it. Anything over and above that, they would have to pay for themselves.

She wrote: kitchen, bathroom (there was the ten thousand gone, then); decorate all rooms; paint outside of house; renew windows and doors; fit broadband and digital TV. She would have to look into the last two items sooner rather than later since they were a priority as far as their son was concerned; she underlined them. James was a concern to her. He had not really been himself since Vince left. They had been such good friends and although he did spend time with other boys, she didn't think he felt close to any of them. He certainly didn't seem interested in girls, although he had always had friends that were girls at school. She couldn't really believe that James was approaching manhood: he seemed so young in so many ways – more like a fourteen year old really. With the hopeful thought that the change might eventually improve his mood and manners, she got up from the table and spent the next hour going round each room and listing, in detail, everything that needed to be done. This would be Pete's 'To Do List', and would keep his mind and body occupied. They had decided that he would advertise his services in the town as an odd job man, and the plan was to eventually get a little van. Until then, he would have to use the family car.

Christie had finished unpacking her bags into the drawers and wardrobe and now had a large bag of dirty washing. She took it down to her mother who was inspecting the fireplace to see if an open fire might be on the cards.

'I wonder if this needs a sweep first,' she said, hearing Christie approach. 'It looks okay to me, though.'

'Mum, how on earth can you tell from just looking? Please don't do anything until Dad has had a look. The last thing we need is smoke billowing all over the house.' Christie knew how impulsive her mother could be. It was one of the things she loved about her, but it could also lead them into all sorts of trouble. 'Mum, I've got loads of washing. Is there a machine?'

'There is Chris, but it's not plumbed in and may not be for a while. How much have you got?'

'This.' She held up a large carrier bag, stuffed to capacity and spilling over.

'Ah! Well, I noticed a launderette in the town, so I suggest you get on down there with it.'

Christie wasn't fazed: she'd become very familiar with launderettes while at university. 'Okay,' she said. 'It's stopped raining so I'll go down now. Have you got any you need doing?'

'No, I got it all done in the last few days. Don't worry about tumble drying though: Dad has set ours up in the shed at the back.'

'Okay. Which way do I go?'

'If you go up the hill and past the pub, there are lots of ways of getting down to the town. It'll be good for you to have a look around. Have you got lots of change for the machine?'

'Change, I have lots of; paper money, not so much,' laughed Christie, grabbing her handbag. 'See you soon.'

Heading up hill as her mother had instructed, she smiled as she passed several small groups of people who seemed to be very jolly and obviously in holiday mood. When she reached the pub and the road evened out, she gasped in awe: there to her left was the Atlantic Ocean, stretching out to the horizon, where the mottled blue and pink sky met the sea. She could see a couple of fishing boats making their way back to the harbour, and right in the distance the silhouette of a large cargo ship. A seagull landed on top of a car just a few feet away from her as she gazed at the spectacular view, and squawked rudely at her, demanding attention. Christie stuck her tongue out at it and giggled when it flung a squawking retort in her direction and flew off towards the town.

About to carry on walking, she suddenly had a strange feeling that she was not alone and that she was being watched. She looked up towards the pub, but saw no one there paying any attention to her. Looking all around she searched for a face behind curtains or from within a nearby vehicle. Nothing. But then, as soon as the feeling had come, it was gone, so Christie thought no more about it and continued on her way. When she turned the corner, the view changed dramatically: she was looking at the harbour with the town snuggled around it. From her high viewpoint she could see roof tops with seagulls sitting on top of chimney pots. Electricity and phone wires ran crisscross, to and fro, between houses and poles installed impossibly in the cliff side. People smiled at her as they passed and it felt the most natural thing in the world to return their smiles and say 'hello'.

The harbour was alive with people who were now sitting outside in the pleasant evening sunshine, which had finally made an appearance. Stopping to ask someone directions to the launderette, she walked away from the harbour up what seemed like the high street, and found it at the top of yet another hill. Pushing the door open, she looked around and it seemed that she was the only person in there.

Ten minutes later, accompanied by the sound of the two machines going through wash cycles, she was reading a downloaded novel on the reading app on her phone, when the feeling that she was not alone once more crept over her, causing the back of her neck to bristle. She looked up and met a pair of dark brown eyes belonging to a man who had been sitting at the back of the launderette all the time she had been in there. She gasped and instinctively put her hand to her throat in shock. He was unkempt and hunched forward, his hands on the slats either side of him and his feet tucked underneath the bench. He was staring and Christie, feeling distinctly uneasy, immediately looked away and tried to focus on her novel. Concentration proved impossible, however: she could feel his eyes burning a hole in the top of her head. She braved another look and decided she had had enough. 'Er ... excuse me, but you're making me uncomfortable, staring at me like that.'

He shrugged and continued to stare. What an incredibly rude person, Christie thought, although her main concern was not his rudeness, but the fact that she was alone with him. Not really knowing what to do for the best, she put her phone into her pocket in an exaggerated fashion, sat back, crossed her legs, hooked her clasped hands over her knees and matched his brown-eyed stare with her own blue- eyed one. It was an instant challenge and an immediate stalemate, as neither of them was prepared to look away. It gave Christie ample time to take in his appearance. Deeply tanned, he was unshaven and his thick, dark, untidy hair was matted and dull. He was wearing jeans and a parker type jacket, which was totally inappropriate for June, even though it had been raining earlier. His hands, still clasped on the bench, were filthy, with unclipped, black finger nails. And he was ageless: underneath the dirt and hair he could have been twenty or fifty; there was no way of telling which.

As Christie looked into his eyes and tried to read his expression – was he simple ... not quite the full ticket? – she began to realise that what she was seeing there was pain. Her brow crinkled with natural concern and she felt something happening to her as she was looking at him: it was as if he was a book she was reading and his eyes were telling the story; they were communicating, but instead of words she was receiving his emotions.

Suddenly, he stood up, making Christie jump. He bent down, picked up a can of beer that had been standing at his feet, took a long swig out of it, raised the can to her by way of a salute and walked towards the door. As he passed her she could smell the sea and salt and damp clothes that had not quite dried. After he left, she stood up and peered through the window, down towards the harbour, but there was no sign of him – the street was deserted apart from a middle-aged couple with their dog.

Christie was shocked and exhilarated at the same time. Something was happening to her in this odd little town. Those few minutes had been the strangest she had ever experienced, and the image of the brown eyes would not leave her mind: in such a grubby, unkempt face they had seemed quite beautiful – sensual even. *How ridiculous!* she chided herself; now she was letting her imagination run away with her. The odd thing was, though, that she had not actually been frightened of him or remotely threatened by him; if anything, she felt drawn to him.

As she sat in the steamy little launderette with machines whirring around her, she felt again the sensation of warmth that had enveloped her in her bedroom. And once more, she felt she was not alone.

As she made her way back to the cottage an hour later, the brown eyes still stared into her inner vision. Was he a troubled spirit? Was he even real? He certainly smelt real! Flinging her heavy bag with its wet contents over her shoulder, she became aware of a new sensation stealing over her: this strange little town, perched precariously on the side of a cliff, seemed to be the catalyst for an overwhelming urge in her to write. All of a sudden, she could not wait to get started.

Chapter 3

Diane woke to the sound of people in her room, talking, laughing, their rounded, singsong accent different from that to which she was accustomed. Through her sleepy haze she couldn't fathom what they were talking about, but then she heard a car door slam and an engine fire up. What was happening in here? A cacophony of screams seemed to be coming from just above her head. Who was that? It brought her to full wakefulness with a start. 'Gosh it's so noisy!' she muttered, grimacing in her husband's direction as she remembered they were in a little fishing town on the south Cornwall coast. She was not used to living right by the side of a road, and seagulls were a new experience that would need to be endured.

    She turned to look fully at Pete who was lying next to her on his back, staring at the ceiling. He nodded agreement and rubbed his eyes. Pulling the quilt back he spun his naked body round and sat on the edge of the bed, his back hunched. How she loved that back! Years of physical work as a builder had given Pete strong broad shoulders and muscular arms. She rubbed him, hoping to ease the strain she knew he was feeling. He loved to be touched and she knew just how he liked it. The feel of his skin under her fingers made her feel warm and sensual and she welcomed with slight surprise the return of familiar feelings, that she had not experienced for some time, trickling through her body. She moved her body alongside his and pressed her naked breasts against his back. Still he just sat. Kneeling up she put her arms around his neck and held him close. She wanted to make love but she knew this man so well. Sex was the last thing he wanted, right now, and she could sense it. Pushing him any further would only increase his feeling of inadequacy, so she just kissed his cheek and got up, pulling on her dressing gown and slippers to go down to make the tea.

The little galley kitchen was dim as the sun had not fully risen above the buildings that were all jostling for position in a higgledy-piggledy fashion on the hill side. Diane shivered and pulled her gown closer around her. After filling the kettle and switching it on, she turned to examine the ancient boiler that stood in a space that would have once been an open fireplace. The lights were on and it was making whooshing noises so all seemed to be in working order. That was a blessing. Running the hot tap confirmed this and she smiled: simple things made such a difference.

Opening the back door she took her tea outside into the tiny backyard. A small patch of earth ran along underneath the kitchen window, but apart from that, the yard was crazy paving dotted with seagull mess. Dragging out one of the plastic chairs that had been stacked in the corner the previous evening, she sat in the patch of sunshine that had seeped into one of the corners of the yard, stretched her legs out, leaned back and closed her eyes, listening to the early Saturday morning sounds.

Pete came and stood in the doorway holding his mug of tea and dressed in shorts and a T-shirt. She opened her eyes and looked up at him, smiling and thinking that something about this place was making him look younger.

'You look like you're on holiday,' he said.

'Well, we may as well be – everyone else around seems to be.'

'Yes, but they've all got jobs and homes to go back to. This is it for us.' He sighed and looked around at the peeling paint and overgrown hydrangeas that were butting their blue and pink heads against the kitchen window.

'Come on, Pete! At some point, my darling, you're going to have to stop punishing yourself.'

He huffed and pulled over another garden chair to share in his wife's patch of sunlight.

Christie had been awake since the seagull chorus had begun several hours earlier. Her dreams had been full of dark eyes and sadness in tandem with an acute feeling of inexplicable sorrow, but six hours of sound sleep had, nonetheless, left her feeling fresh and invigorated. After pulling on joggers and a sweatshirt, she had crept silently downstairs and made herself a cup of tea. With her laptop under her arm, she had then unlocked the back door and with a mighty heave managed to open it, after which, she had picked up her tea and left through the yard gate to re-trace her steps along the top road; she wanted to find a bench she had spotted the previous evening

From her position on the bench, she overlooked the waking harbour: several fishing boats were getting ready to go out for the day, some of them taking holiday-makers out with their rods and hopes of the big catch; little vans buzzed about; a few early morning risers were enjoying the sunshine, and a man walked briskly along the harbour wall with a newspaper under his arm. It was a busy but tranquil scene.

Christie regarded the blank document page on her laptop with some trepidation: she had no idea what to write about. Finally, after some minutes of unproductive pondering, she decided to just trust that whatever the force was that had brought her to this point would show her the way. Almost as soon as she disengaged from conscious thought, she started to type.

To my darling daughter,

I love this town, especially early in the morning. This is the best time to be out and about, when few others share my Atlantic bliss. The

air is so clear, the sounds are so bright and shiny and the sun's warmth is but a promise away.

My story starts many years ago in this beautiful Cornish haven, when cars were few and I was young, carefree and in love, or so I thought. To me, at the tender age of sixteen years, every man who spoke to me was a potential lover, so why should Alan Gilmore be any different?

We were inseparable, walking hand in hand through the town, sharing ice cream or a newspaper package of the bottom of the chip pan, whilst dangling our legs over the harbour wall. Our life was innocent and beyond reproach.

But others thought differently. You see, Alan was the vicar's son. He had 'standing' in the community and was expected to follow in his father's footsteps. Everyone thought he would, and even Alan himself assumed that that was his lot. But I knew he was not a man of the cloth. I knew he was an artistic man of passion and romance, of colour and texture, of something far more ethereal than either of us could have imagined, at the time.

I was the local coal merchant's daughter, and of low standing. My future was to be in nursing or working in the fields, neither of which appealed to my romantic heart. I wanted to travel, to learn a different language, walk in the desert, swim in huge lakes and climb snow peaked mountains. But instead, I created you, my darling: a tiny human being with ten fingers and ten toes, with Cornish blue eyes and a rosebud mouth; I created perfection.

But perfection rarely lasts and no sooner had I brought you into this world than you were taken from me. Men in white jackets and nurses trussed up in blue starched linen, held me down as someone I had never even met stole you away when you were not even three months old. You cried as they took you; you screamed as if you understood the tragedy of our separation. We had a bond you see, my darling; a bond so strong no human hand could break it. Your cries echoed in my dreams as I sunk helplessly into a drug induced slumber, aware but unaware, asleep but awake, fighting while yet in surrender.

I remember the first day that I was told you were no longer mine and that I had to continue my life as though I were a childless virgin.

They could have changed my name and my heritage for all I cared, for I no longer wanted to walk this earth. I was now only half a person.

But I survived, as many of us child mothers did. We lived half-lives, pretending we were untouched, chaste and desirable. For my part, I felt soiled and worthless. I had lost the only man whom I felt I would ever love, and the one precious part of me that made me feel whole – you.

My parents sent me to Penzance, where I served at the tables of the rich and glorified. I existed on a daily basis, living only for the time, each night, when I could sink into mental oblivion and block out the sounds of your cries. So accusing. So raw.

After two years of a seemingly pointless life, I met John; dear dependable, solid, handsome John, who worked as an accountant's apprentice and was so very clever. Some people said he was boring, but I loved his clever mind and his slightly skewwhiff view of the world. He said that our paths were all mapped out for us before we entered the womb and that we had no control over what happened to us. It just had to be endured and there were always reasons for things that happened. I was honest with John and told him about you. He accepted my news with grace and we started a regular courtship, going to the cinema, the tea shop and to dinner at his parents' home. I rarely saw my parents – your grandparents, my darling – because although I wanted to forgive their actions, I could not. I was unable, as I am even now, to understand why they took us away from each other. I have never been able to allow the action to pass. It was done and I with it.

My life and love progressed with John and we were soon married and living in Penzance. My truce with your grandparents was stiff but tangible – just. I was not born with the kind of character to constantly punish others, whatever the crime, but our relationship was never the same as it had been in my growing years.

Our children, Doreen and Steven, came along within five years, and so I had my family. But I didn't have you, my darling. Nor did I know where you were, who your guardians or new parents were, or what they had named you. I called you Kathleen. Whether they kept your name or not, I never knew, but I thought it was such a wholesome yet delicate name. Each day my heart longed to hold you, hear your voice, share your dreams and be the mother to you that I know I would have been.

> *I write this to you now, my darling, because I have gone to another world. I am no longer able to find you, talk to you, or explain how I fought – oh, how I fought – to keep you as mine. It tears me apart to think that you might believe you were not wanted. That is so far from the truth that it makes me want to scream out to the heavens above.*

Christie stopped and looked up, tears rolling down her face and her shoulders shaking with silent sobs. A passing dog walker stopped and asked her if she was all right. She shook her head but then smiled, embarrassed, and said, 'Yes, yes, sorry, yes, I'm fine. I've just read something sad, that's all.'

The dog walker smiled, nodded and continued on his way, while Christie closed the lid of her laptop and allowed her gaze to fix on the other side of the harbour. She could see that outside the tackle shop a line of tourists were waiting to book their fishing trips; the restaurant next to it had flung open its doors and someone was sweeping the veranda which bordered two sides of the building. Christie watched, slightly mesmerised by the busyness of others. But then she sat up straight with small gasp as she caught sight of someone familiar, walking along the road above that led out of the town. He walked past a parked van and Christie craned her neck, trying to keep him in view until he emerged on the other side of the van. She could not breathe as the owner of the brown eyes shuffled up the hill, still wearing, it seemed, the clothes she had seen on him the previous evening. As she watched him, he stopped, and for no apparent reason turned his gaze. Her hand went to her mouth as she realised that he was, once more, looking directly at her

Chapter 4

James' first day in Porthtreval would have been spent with him locked away in his bedroom, if, firstly, he had been able to access the internet, and secondly, his mother had not had other ideas. With a ten pound note to sweeten the pill, she had hustled him out of the house with the command to 'go explore'.

'I don't know why you keep pushing him, Di,' said Pete as he watched his dejected son walk away out of the backyard.

'I wish I didn't have to, Pete!' she said indignantly. 'But you know what he's like: left to himself, he'll just sit around and mope. This way, he'll hopefully catch up with Christie, wherever she is.'

As if on cue, the back door opened with a hefty kick from the other side and their daughter came in, flushed and bright eyed.

'Where have you been?' her parents chorused.

'Just up the top of the steps at the end of this road that lead down to the town,' she said, pointing behind her. She had decided not to say anything about 'brown eyes' to her parents as they would probably get alarmed and worry that she had a stalker. Christie herself did not feel in the least intimidated by him; she did, however, feel intensely curious. 'This place is magical, Mum,' she grinned at Diane who gratefully returned her cheeriness with a matching smile.

'I know exactly what you mean, sweetheart. Dad's not so convinced, though, are you pet?'

Pete grimaced. 'Who knows?' he shrugged. 'I'm just made differently to you two romantics, I guess,' he added, leaning over and kissing his wife's cheek before going back out to the workshop.

Diane turned to Christie. 'Cup of tea, love?'

'Yes please, Mum.'

'So, tell me: what's happening?'

'What do you mean?' asked Christie, leaning against the counter top.

'Honey, I know you better than you know yourself. You're excited about something. Have you met someone interesting?'

Christie laughed nervously. 'Only a tramp in the launderette last night. Apart from that, no one of note.' She was not telling her mother the whole truth but she felt justified in keeping that to herself: she wasn't ready to share her impression of 'brown eyes', or the emotional outpouring of words that her fingers had just tapped out on her laptop. It was all too raw and unnerving. 'I'll just run upstairs and plug my laptop in to recharge,' she said, by way of a diversion.

Diane looked at her quizzically but decided not to press the issue. 'Do that, and then shall we have our tea down on the corner, looking at the sea?'

'Sounds good, Mum!'

The two women each took a steaming mug and a cushion down to a square of concrete just above the beach, where the view along the Cornish coastline was just about as good as it could get. They chatted about the two men in the family and worked on plans to help cheer them both up.

Unaware that his mother and sister were hatching plots to improve his welfare, James absentmindedly walked around the town. As the sun ascended higher, he was too hot in his sweatshirt and jeans, and took off his top layer before sitting on one of the huge blocks of granite that bordered the harbour wall – a good vantage point for viewing the whole harbour and its mouth, opening out into the ocean beyond. It was hard to imagine that on the other side of that vast expanse of water was the huge American continent – somewhere he would love to go to. Many of his friends had been to the States more than once, visiting Disneyland or shopping in New York. He knew that his Dad had cousins in Canada, but they had never had the money to go to places like that. They definitely wouldn't be able to now.

James contemplated his future, bleak as it seemed in that moment, but gradually the bright sun reached into his heart and he began to feel more at ease with his surroundings. Forgetting the big life questions, he turned his attention to two girls of about his age, who were walking around the quayside, dressed almost identically in shorts and skimpy T-shirts. They were both looking at him and as they came nearer, he had the feeling they were going to come and speak to him. He averted his eyes, feeling self-conscious and not wanting to encourage unwelcome conversation.

'Hello there! Are you on holiday?'

'I wish!' he found himself saying. 'No, I just moved here yesterday.'

'Oh!' one of the girls said in surprise. 'Where to?'

James pointed behind him. 'Up at the top of the hill.'

'What's your name?' the second girl asked, coming to sit beside him.

'James.'

'That's posh! Where have you moved from? Your accent is really funny. Do you come from up north?'

In spite of himself, James smiled at her inquisitive face. 'Sort of – just south of Manchester.'

'Oh,' she said, apparently not knowing where that was and not really caring. 'I'm Becky and this is Chantelle,' she said.

James nodded. 'You live here, then?'

'Yes, always have. It's a dump really – nothing to do,' sighed Becky.

Chantelle nudged her in disagreement, 'Shut Up! You don't say that when we're on the beach watching "surfs up"!'

James' brow furrowed. 'What's that?'

'This town is all about surfing,' Chantelle replied, seductively crossing her long, tanned legs now that James' gaze had moved to her. 'Haven't you seen the shops – all surfing and beach gear? The boys here are all surfers. They come from miles around. See the headland there?' she pointed a delicate finger towards the rocky coastline. 'It's really fab for the big rides – waves that is.'

James nodded, looking in the direction she had pointed. Sure enough, he could see little black dots in the water which he had not noticed earlier. As he watched, three of the dots grew into shapes on surf boards riding the waves, and one of them rode all the way towards the rocks until he disappeared out of sight. 'He did well,' James muttered.

'That'll be Ollie,' Becky informed him. She was pale and freckled with long auburn hair held back, with some sophistication, by a pair of sunglasses on the top of head. 'He's the best surfer,' she asserted.

'And an absolute babe!' added Chantelle, grinning and nudging her friend. 'You forgot to mention that!'

Both girls gazed into the distance and swung their legs in unison as they contemplated the dreaminess of the celebrated Ollie.

James had never surfed before, but he was a good swimmer and quite fancied the challenge.

'How do you get into surfing, then?' he asked tentatively.

Chantelle looked at him. 'You interested?'

'I might be.'

She laughed. 'You'll need to get yourself a tan first. You're a bit pasty.'

'Chantelle!' Becky gasped. 'You're so bloody rude sometimes!'

'Well he is pasty, aren't you, James?'

James nodded, looking resigned. 'No getting away from it, I suppose,' he said, holding out his pale arms and laughing.

'Your face completely changes when you smile, James,' commented Becky. 'You look really different.'

'Yeah,' Chantelle agreed, 'you looked proper miserable just now. You should smile more. It's nice.'

James was rewarded with two pretty faces smiling at him; he just had to smile back.

Becky's phone beeped a text alert, breaking the moment. She read it and leapt up. 'Oh god! Gotta go!' she squealed. 'I'm supposed to be picking up my little sister from her friend's house. See you later, James. Come down this afternoon and we'll introduce you to the boys.'

'See ya!' said Chantelle, joining Becky in a half run towards the town and leaving James to his thoughts.

He liked them, and they were both very pretty – popular with the boys, he imagined, wondering who the boys were and if they were his age, as the girls seemed to be. That would be good. But then how would they feel about a new recruit with pale skin and a funny accent? he wondered, aware of his lack of courage when it came to making new friends. There was something about this place, though, that made him feel it would all be all right and he would be welcome. In fact, the whole place seemed far more welcoming than anywhere he was used to. He hopped down off his perch, suddenly feeling more confident, and the warm breeze blew back his untidy hair as he tipped his face up to the obliging sun. With a lighter step, he made his way back towards the town to find a shop where he could buy something to eat; he was starving.

Christie had enjoyed sitting and chatting with her mum, although it was difficult to ignore her own unspoken preoccupation with her recent, inexplicable experiences. Back in her tiny room, as she replayed events in her mind, she sat on the bed and absentmindedly stared out of the window at the expansive balcony of the property opposite. French windows had been installed to open up onto the flat roof of an extension, which was fenced off for safety with wooden slatted railings and bordered with tubs of green and white plants, which appeared to be growing and thriving in the salty air.

As she sat there, she once again felt the presence of someone else in close proximity. This time, she also noticed a pale face looking directly at her from behind the French windows opposite. In the normal course of events she would have looked away for fear of being thought nosey, but this time she could not tear her gaze away. The face was surrounded by a cloud of white or very fair hair – difficult to tell which – and she sensed more than saw that the person was an elderly woman. As she stared, transfixed, the face softened into a smile and a nod in acknowledgment. Christie nodded back and lifted her hand in a tiny wave. In that instant, the vision was gone and she was once again looking at a set of ordinary French windows. She wondered who lived in the house and even as the thought crossed her mind, an answer came to her.

Picking up her now fully-charged laptop, she went out again into the bright day, learning to follow her instincts, which were saying that a place in the shade by the quayside might be a good spot to sit and write. Once down in the town, Christie walked round to the opposite side of the harbour, her destination being a pub that was on a corner where the outer harbour met the ocean. It had some inviting looking picnic tables in the sloping garden, she remembered, and with her laptop now in her back pack she was able to walk fast: she felt a sense of urgency to get there and continue writing.

'What can I get you, my lovely?' A tan-faced barman smiled at Christie as she walked up to the bar.

'Orange juice topped up with lemonade, please.'

'Coming right up! So, you on your holidays, then?'

'No, we've just moved in on the other side of town, actually.'

'Really! You don't come from round here, though, do you? If I'm not mistaken that's a northern accent you have there.'

'Manchester,' Christie replied. 'Have you always lived here?' She wondered if this friendly bar tender would be able to answer some questions for her.

'I have indeed, man and boy. I've been running this place for ten years now.'

'Well, it certainly is a lovely place and I suppose you know most of the residents.'

'I'd say so.'

'I was at the launderette yesterday and there was a man there who was odd and looked a bit of a misfit – dark hair, untidy – well, dirty, to be honest.'

'Ah! Don't tell me: about six foot tall, beard and wearing a smelly old parker.'

'That's him!' Christie said, a mite too enthusiastically.

'Haydon,' the barman nodded knowingly as he put Christie's drink down in front of her. 'Harmless, but I suppose he could be pretty scary to someone who doesn't know him.'

'Is he homeless?'

The bartender laughed. 'You wouldn't be the first to think he's a bit of a tramp; but no, he has a tiny cottage in the middle of the town. Not sure he will for much longer though. There's no power to the house any more. Suppose he didn't pay the bills. You can see flickering candle light at night. Fire hazard. The neighbours have been complaining about him for years. They say his brain is a bit addled, just like his mother's.'

'His mother? Does he live with her?'

'No, she went years ago, when he was still just a boy really. No one knows where she went, and it was then that Haydon started to act strange.' The barman looked thoughtful for a moment. 'That must have been ten, fifteen years ago, now I come to think of it.'

'So who looked after him then?'

'Well, no one really. Neighbours tried to get involved and invited him round but he never would go: he just became a recluse. You see him round the town, just sitting, watching. He's always watching. '

'Well that explains him staring at me in the launderette last night. It unnerved me a bit, but mostly I felt he was very sad.'

'Oh, he's that all right! Very sad. That's one ninety-five please.'

Christie paid and took her drink out to the highest picnic table she could find in the garden. So he was called Haydon – an unusual but strong name, she thought as she sat down. And if he had been left as a boy only fifteen years ago, then he could not be much more than thirty.

The scene below her was nothing short of idyllic and reminded her of the busy pictures in her childhood story books, where she had to point out all of the different people and vehicles. In this picture there were boats bobbing about in the harbour – it was high tide; holiday makers filling all the available tables outside the coffee shop; occasional cars creeping along the cobbled road, taking care to avoid pedestrians as well as the sheer drop into the water. At eye level, directly opposite her, was a row of majestic looking town houses, their pointed gable ends painted predominantly in the colours of the sea and sun: blues, aqua greens and yellows. Along the end of their pathways ran a footpath linking them all together, twenty feet up from ground level. She could see people walking along with bags of shopping or polystyrene body boards recently purchased from the town shops. Then she saw him again, at ground level and just below the town houses, he was sitting beside a huge anchor that was displayed with the customary tourist plaque, and, true to form, he was simply watching the passers-by. Once again, an overwhelming sensation of sadness come over her – his sadness – and it ground into her heart; for a second she wanted to go to him and simply hold his hand. Instead, she pulled her laptop out of her backpack and opened it up ready for use. When she glanced back to where Haydon had been sitting, she was not surprised to see that he had disappeared.

The blank screen stared up at her and a current of energy ran through her. She did not hesitate: her fingers danced across the keys.

So, my darling, now you know that you were always wanted and hold a precious and exquisite place in my heart. I, however, carry a huge sadness in that I am unable to give you what is desperately lacking in your life: the yearning that a mother feels for her child; the bond that nothing should ever come between.

How can I bring you to the point of consciousness to make you aware? What actions can I, such as I am, take to make sure that you do not suffer the long-lasting regret and emptiness of an unfulfilled love. Because just as you are part of me wherever you are, my darling, there is someone who is a part of you and he suffers the need of a warm embrace. I know this because that part of you is in my sights and I look on him daily. I watch his demise as he shrivels from loss and rejection, feeling your pain as well as his own. I watch as the years tick by, never to be regained. No one of human flesh should be so tortured, and I know that if you fully understood you would come back to redress the harm unwittingly done.

Our town is still a beautiful place. It sits battling the elements bravely like a soldier on guard, protecting our glorious coastline. The memories that you have of this place have faded to sepia now, my darling – forgotten by all but you. It is time for you to return to your home and claim what is yours; to reignite an enduring love that is struggling to survive on the embers of what once was.

Please come home, my darling. Come home.

Christie was shaking. How was this happening to her? Her head felt fuzzy and she had to close her eyes to compose herself.

Someone was speaking through her, of that she was sure, because she had no idea where the words were coming from, only that they were not *her* words. She was surprised that she didn't feel scared; in fact, she felt sort of privileged that it was she who was bringing this message into the physical world. Not that she knew what to do with it.

For a few minutes, she focused her mind on the normality of the busy scene below her, needing to feel fully part of her own everyday reality. Then she looked back over what she had written, hardly believing that it had been her fingers that had done it. An overwhelming thirst suddenly enveloped her and she picked up her glass and drained it. As she put the glass back down on the table, she saw him walking up towards her, his stare once more fixed on her. She looked back at her screen, trying to pretend she hadn't seen him, even though it was obvious that she had. He walked past her and swung his leg over to sit down on the bench of the table just to her left, unnervingly choosing to face away from the marvellous view. The only thing in his line of sight was her. She could feel his stare and with it came the internal heat that started at her feet and travelled up her body. This time it was so powerful that it made her gasp, and she immediately looked up to see if he had heard. The brown-eyes burned into her, causing her heartbeat to increase and a light sweat to break out across her forehead.

As quickly as it had started, the heat began to abate and she decided that it was time to put an end to the mystery of this person. 'I know you're called Haydon,' she said. He simply nodded. His eyes still burned into her, but the opening of communication between them had relaxed her enough for her to continue. 'The barman in the pub told me about you.'

It was Haydon's turn to look away, turning his head to gaze out across the harbour, as if in thought. It gave Christie a chance to get a really good look at him in profile; she noted a small, straight nose, a tanned cheek and a remarkably tidy eyebrow above noticeable eye lashes. The sound of his voice startled her, although it was hardly more than a whisper. 'What did he say?'

'Why do you want to know? I get the impression that you don't really care what people think.'

At this he shrugged and turned to swing his leg over so that he was straddling the bench. He looked out towards the ocean and as the wind blew the hair from his face, Christie could see that he was not nearly as old as he had first appeared – probably about thirty, as she'd estimated from what the barman had said. His face became a definite shape rather than just a mass of hair and she could see a dark line around his neck from many days without the use of water. She wanted to hear him speak again, so she continued. 'He said you've always lived here and your mother left you when you were quite young.'

At this disclosure Haydon dropped his head and looked down at the bench, tracing a knot in the wood with a blackened fingernail. When he looked up at Christie again she was shocked at the difference in his expression. The look in his eyes made her pulse quicken; it was full of sincerity and affection, as though he knew her, or she knew him. Either way, in that moment, she knew for certain that there was some kind of connection between them and they were supposed to meet. Since he made no attempt to speak again but continued to look straight at her, she thought that if she talked it might encourage him.

'We've just moved from Manchester to a house on Mount Road, and I've just finished university.' In offering him personal information, she hoped he might start to trust her.

'I know,' he nodded.

'You do?' she said in surprise. 'How?'

He thought about this and after a few moments answered. 'I knew you were coming.'

Now she was completely flabbergasted. 'How could you? We've never met before. Haydon, that sounds creepy and slightly mad, and I don't understand why you're saying it.' She was trying to keep the emotion out of her voice, but it was tricky.

'I just know. Some things are too big to explain – too difficult. The brain can't take it in,' he said, as though it was the most obvious thing in the world.

Christie was now at a complete loss. This was all crazy: here she was in a strange town that she'd never been to before and within twenty four hours, God knows who had been writing through her, and someone she'd never met before was insisting he knew she was coming to live there. Yet despite all this, her instincts were telling her that this man was not a lunatic, talking fanciful rubbish, or an alcoholic with an addled brain; although she could certainly see why people would have thought him crazy, if he regularly came out with such comments.

Without preamble he stood up and walked away, nodding to her as he went. She watched him go, wondering: was it her imagination or was he actually shuffling less and walking straighter?

Chapter 5

Early on Monday morning, Diane was up and ready to leave for her interview with her contact in the local paper. It wasn't really an interview, she had told herself – more of a meeting with the chief editor. At the same time, she was trying to forget that there was a certain amount of history between them that she was not proud of, and if it had not been a case of 'needs must' Brian Bucannan would have been the last person she would have approached for a way into West Country journalism.

She had met him four years before in Brighton, during the week of a party conference, when she had been covering a piece on local tourism and was staying at the same hotel as Brian, who was a senior journalist for one of the nationals, at the time, and had been working at the party conference itself. The week had been exhausting for all the Press as they jostled to get the best interview or story, and on the last evening a few of the journalists had decided to get together for a curry and some downtime in a local club. Since Diane had been socialising with them throughout the week, they had asked her along and she had happily accepted.

It had all started in extremely jovial fashion with the week's work mostly behind them and just a press conference to attend the next day, so after the meal they all decided to go clubbing. Diane wasn't in the mood for that so she had bid her fellow journalists a goodnight and was walking the short distance to the taxi rank when she became aware of someone beside her. To her surprise, she had turned to see Brian's smiling face.

'Mind if I join you?'

It had been more statement than request as they both knew they were headed for the same hotel. She'd felt a bit awkward, but had nodded and smiled meekly. Brian was a good looking man with an even-toned, swarthy complexion and thick, grey-flecked, black hair that was swept back apart from a casual lock that hung seductively over part of his forehead. He had developed a disconcerting gaze from dark eyes that could be unnerving; he was certainly in the right profession. To most women, he was sexy, but Diane found him a little too 'obvious'. She had not been on the lookout for a man, but even if she had, she would undoubtedly have avoided him as she preferred more subtle looks than Brian possessed.

'Not your scene either then?' she had asked, making conversation.

'No, I'm a bit old for all that; and besides, I'd rather spend time with you, if that's not being too forward.'

'Not at all,' Diane had replied to be polite, 'we can share a taxi.'

In the cab, Brian had put his arm along the back of the seat, sitting so close to her that she had felt quite overwhelmed, although not unpleasantly so, by his expensive and sensual aftershave. On arriving at the hotel, he had persuaded her to have a night cap in the bar. Three gin and tonics later she had found herself sitting in a secluded corner, laughing with this man she hardly knew as if they had always been friends. She had then attempted to extricate herself from his insistent company, but he would not hear of her walking to her door alone. Even in her tipsy state, her hackles had risen and she had hoped there would be no awkward moments. 'Well, goodnight Brian. See you at breakfast,' she had said, turning to put her key in the lock.

Before she realised what was happening, he had pulled her firmly to him and was kissing her passionately. His hot, male form had moulded to her shape and he had brought his hand up to cup the side of her head as his tongue played at the entrance to her mouth. Almost without thinking, she had closed her eyes and kissed him back, allowing his tongue to enter her mouth.

Suddenly, she had seen Pete's face in her mind and with it, the implications of what she was doing; immediately, she had placed her hands on his chest and pushed him away. 'No, I'm sorry, Brian, this isn't going to happen,' she'd said, opening her door and shutting it between them before he could object, persuade or otherwise endeavour to gain entrance to her room. Holding her breath, she had leaned against the door, listening intently until she heard the sound of the lift opening and then closing as he left her floor. Her breath had come out in a rush of relief. *Oh my god what was I thinking!* she'd silently berated herself. *I could have made such a bad mistake with a man I don't even much like!*

At breakfast the next morning she had been helping herself to some cereal and fruit when he had moved in directly behind her and whispered a hot, husky 'good morning' into her ear, as though they had spent the night soiling the hotel sheets with their frenetic love making. She had ignored him and moved away, conscious of a few raised eyebrows around the room, and she had not spoken to him before leaving Brighton to return to Manchester.

It had been against her better judgment to make contact with him again; after all, she had rejected him and here she was asking him to offer her work. Nevertheless, he had seemed pleased to hear from her. *Fingers crossed, he's moved on too,* she thought, as she checked the mirror for the umpteenth time before going down to the kitchen where Pete was buttering toast.

'Want some?'

'No thanks. Too nervous.'

'You? Nervous? Never! You'll walk it.'

She gave him a grateful smile, kissed him on the cheek and opened the back door with pleasing ease. Pete had dealt with it the previous day.

'Good luck, darling!' he called after her as a bit of an afterthought, as she walked up the little hill to where the car was parked.

He was planning to start work on the outside of the cottage while the weather was good. The house looked so neglected with its peeling paint and rust stained walls that he had made it a priority. Setting out his paint and brushes on the garden table, he was about to go to the workshop to find a screwdriver when he heard the handle of the connecting door to the property next door start to rattle. It was an odd arrangement: the access to the next door yard was through theirs.

He could see that whoever was on the other side was having an issue separating the door from its frame, so he assisted and was soon standing looking at the bronze face of a woman of about his age, who was holding a bulging black bin bag in her hands.

'Oh, hello! I didn't mean to intrude. I just need to get this out to the bins. Have you moved in or are you the decorator?'

Pete laughed. 'Right first time. We moved in on Friday but I think I'm going to be doubling up as decorator for a while yet. It's a bit of a mess, isn't it?'

'Certainly is, my lovely! Can't say I'm sorry you're going to be making the place look better. It's an eyesore for us to look out on to.'

Pete looked puzzled.

'Oh, I don't live next door,' she laughed. 'I live opposite – the house with the wiggly roof. Next door is a holiday home and I'm cleaning it, ready for people coming in next Saturday.'

Pete was trying not to look at the neighbour's cleavage, although it was certainly on show for all to see, and he could not help but notice her sheer earthiness. Devoid of make-up, she had the natural glow of a woman approaching middle-age who had the confidence of the years she had lived through and no longer sought to impress. And her infectious laugh was as fresh as rain on a scorched day. Pete was instantly drawn to her.

'Wiggly roof?' he asked, gathering his thoughts and focusing on her eyes so as not to look down.

'Oh, yes! I know you can see it, 'cos I can when I'm doing me bits upstairs here,' she pointed to the cottage next door. 'It's wiggly in the middle so as to fit while making the most of the space. Drives my Stevie mad when he's trying to fix the gutters.' She laughed and Pete found himself laughing with her.

'That sounds like common sense to me,' he chuckled, realising he hadn't laughed much in a long time, and shocked that he was giggling like a teenager with someone he had only just met.

'It certainly is, my lovely! We don't do posh and pretty here, just practical. Anyway, I must get on. See you later.' She bustled through the gate and into the road to dispose of the bag of rubbish in the bins in the tiny pub car park. He was not sure the publican would have agreed to that, but then, in this place, he would not be surprised if it were the norm. Smiling to himself he went about his day and had to admit to himself that he felt a bit happier. The sound of a particular laugh and a buxom lady with a Cornish tan had made his day feel that much brighter.

The coffee shop was crowded with people dressed in shorts and T-shirts enjoying the holiday weather. As she walked in Diane craned her neck to see if Brian had already arrived and smiled as he rose to greet her.

'Settled in all right then?' he asked as she sat down and ordered a latte from the swiftly attendant waiter.

'Oh, yes, just about. It's all a bit rough and ready but Pete will soon knock it into shape.'

'How is he?' Brian's furrowed brow depicted concern but Diane couldn't help wondering if it was sincere.

'He's fine. He's made of strong stuff.' She realised she sounded a little abrupt but she was not about to start discussing her husband with Brian Buccannan of all people.

'Good. So, you're ready to get amongst it then?'

'Sure,' she said with a weak smile. Her heart felt heavy and she really did not want to be there, but she just reminded herself that she needed the work and the money that came with it.

Brian had gained a little weight, she noticed, although it looked quite good on him and he carried it well. She began to relax. Sitting and drinking coffee in the bright painted café, there was no awkwardness between them and she assumed that all had been forgotten. Relief flooded through her as they chatted about the type of work that he thought would be right up her street.

Pete had been busy painting the outside of the house, which seemed to be smiling with the onset of its new coat. 'I met one of our neighbours today,' he volunteered.

'Oh yes? Nice?' Diane asked, pouring tea into mugs from the ancient teapot they had possessed all their married life. It had a non-matching lid but Diane had never been able to bring herself to throw it away.

'Yes, she seems to be. She lives opposite and cleans next door, which is a holiday cottage apparently.'

Diane noted that he was looking intently at his tea. She knew he was always nervous about mentioning encounters with women. He had been indiscreet once, in the early years of their marriage, and it had been a big challenge to get their marriage back on track. Despite the fact that they'd got over it and she had long forgiven him, he had never succeeded in fully regaining her trust. She looked at him, waiting to catch his eye. He didn't look up. 'What's her name?' she asked.

'Oh, I don't know,' he said, finally looking up and giving her a frank, grey-eyed stare. 'She's married to someone called Stevie, though; she told me that. How was your meeting with the good looking Brian?'

Now it was Diane's turn to feel a shade uncomfortable. 'OK, I suppose. I'd rather not be having anything to do with him, if we didn't need the money.' She regretted the words the second they were out of her mouth as she looked at her husband's crestfallen face. He wore his guilt like a massive Stetson on his head – there was no missing it. She put her hand over his. 'It's no big deal, Pete. I'll soon get more contacts and sort something else out.'

They were interrupted by the door crashing open. Christie and James fell into the kitchen, laughing helplessly. Diane and Pete looked up at them and smiled. It had been a while since they had heard such happy noise from their children.

Chapter 6

Christie was up early the next morning and she strode off purposefully through the waking town to buy the local paper – she wanted to look for jobs – as well as to pick up some fresh bread, milk and butter for breakfast. Even though it felt as though she was on holiday, the truth of the matter was that she needed a job. She had had some opportunities lined up in Manchester but that was in the past now. She wasn't sure what she wanted to do but she had a feeling that this place would show her the way, and since she was happy to try her hand at anything for the time being, she decided to ask around the town as well as check the paper.

The newsagent's opposite the harbour was tiny and crammed to the rafters with just about anything anyone might need. It also had a huge ginger cat, whose name she learned later was Puddles, sitting quite comfortably on top of the ice cream freezer. As she walked in the door, the cat gave her the look of utter contempt that only cats can. She was nevertheless found acceptable, however, when she stroked his big, furry head until he couldn't help but purr.

'Oh, he'll put up with that all day if you have the time.' The lady with curly ginger hair almost the exact same colour as Puddles' stood behind the counter sorting the newspapers ready for the paperboys and girls to pick up.

Christie grinned at the friendly comment. 'Is he yours?'

'Not really sure. I think he has a few homes, like most cats. It's probably why he's so flippin' fat!' she laughed and looked down at her work.' Anything I can help you with, my lovely?'

'Well, yes. We've just moved into a cottage at the top of the hill and I need to find work. I don't really mind what I do; I just need to earn some money to help my parents out with some rent.'

'Ah… I just thought you must be on holiday. Moved in, eh? Where, exactly?'

'On the corner of Mount Road, just down from the pub that looks out across the sea.'

'Ah yes, I know where you mean. It's been empty for a while, hasn't it? I'm surprised they didn't turn it into yet another holiday cottage. It's nice to know there will be someone there all year round. You'll find it quiet during the winter, though, my love.'

'Not if the seagulls have anything to do with it!' Christie responded, rolling her eyes.

The shopkeeper laughed and nodded knowingly. 'You'll get used to it. I'll keep my ear to the ground for any work going. You seem like a nice bright girl.'

Christie nodded appreciatively and began to look round the shop. Her attention was drawn to some bright picture postcards on a rack near the open door, and, as she was browsing through them, there came the now familiar feeling that someone was looking at her. Sure enough, when she looked out of the door and over to the grassy area at the head of the harbour, she could see him standing there leaning on the railings. Her breath caught in her throat and she found herself meeting his gaze. He nodded and then walked away towards the bottom of the high street. 'I'll pop back in a little while and pick up the paper and some milk,' she told the newsagent, giving Puddles a final tickle before stepping outside to follow her mystery man. Christie was shocked to feel the heat start to rise in her body again, starting at her feet as though she had stepped into a hot bath. With it came the compulsion to follow this man to wherever he was going, whether he had intended her to or not. Just yards from the launderette he turned right and was out of sight. She laughed to herself, thinking back to the first night she had seen him in the launderette and how she had thought he was some kind of spectre when he had just vanished – not so mysterious after all.

Turning the corner herself, she cried out with fright as she was brought up short by his real and human presence right in front of her. There was that smell: damp clothes that had not been dried properly, and the sea, like driftwood.

'You're following me.'

Christie had to admit to herself that she was, in fact, slightly fixated on this strange, grubby man with his odd ways, so she thought she might as well admit it to him, too. 'Yes,' she said, waiting for his reaction.

'Do you know why you're following me?'

She didn't, but she had the feeling he did. She found the moment so surreal that she stepped back, suddenly afraid, as she realised that there was no one else around and that he could grab her, stab her, hit her – anything could happen. But then looking into his deep brown eyes, all fear evaporated and she stood her ground. She was so close she could see the ingrained dirt in the pores of his face – at least in the parts where facial hair wasn't growing. The huge sadness came over her again and she could feel years of hurt rising in her chest: love not returned, abandonment, loneliness and desperation. She felt a lifetime of unhappiness move through her and tears welled in her eyes. *His eyes immediately softened and he brought a dirty hand up to her shoulder and simply laid it there, gently. Her tears spilled over and rolled unchecked down her cheeks; at the same time, the heat in her body was building, consuming her. In the seconds before she lost consciousness, she saw his arms come out to catch her as she crumpled and fell.

'Where on earth has she got to?' Diane was at the back gate, anxiously looking up the hill to see if she could see her daughter coming back with the much needed breakfast provisions. Apart from some stale cornflakes and a few tins of baked beans, the proverbial larder was empty.

'I'll go and meet her,' said James, retrieving his baseball cap from its resting place on top of the boiler and ramming it on his head.

Diane was surprised that he was so keen to go out. He was certainly settling in a lot more easily than she could have hoped, and he and Christie were getting on so much better, as well. Strange boy, she thought. Maybe he was coming out of the teen years, which would certainly be a relief.

His mother would have been more surprised had she known the ulterior motive behind James' enthusiasm for going out to find his sister. Becky and Chantelle had introduced him to the surfer boys, five of whom surfed most days, depending on tides and weather. They were all friendly enough, but James' favoured the ring leader, Ollie. He was everything James would like to be: tanned and well-built with a flashing smile. He was an obvious hit with the girls but apart from chatting to them, his interest was more with his friends in wet suits. As James made his way along the top road, he had a perfect view of the headland where all the surfing took place. The best view was from a funny looking pier that jutted out rather uselessly into the water just below the crooked clock tower. He had taken to sitting there, watching them surf and picking up as many tips as he could.

The first day James had met the gang, Ollie had invited him to give it a go. He even had a spare wetsuit that James could borrow if he wanted to. James had readily accepted and was looking for an opportunity to talk again and make arrangements. He was a reasonably good swimmer, as was Christie; they had swum at the local leisure club from the time they were small. Then, when he was fourteen, James had contracted glandular fever and was off school and away from swimming for almost a year, after which, he had lost interest and never gone back to it.

He regretted that, now, as his body had grown slack after three years of virtually no rigorous exercise, and he hoped that maybe he could build a physique like Ollie's, if he really tried. His pace quickened as he reached the viewpoint at the top of the hill and strained his eyes, looking for any familiar little black dots near the headland. He was disappointed when there were none, and walked down the pathway that led to the harbour side and the start of the pier. When he looked over the railings, however, his spirits rose because he saw Ollie down on the cobbled road below. The morning was hot; Ollie was dressed only in shorts, and James stopped behind an obliging shrub and just watched him for a while, hidden from view. He felt wrong doing it, but couldn't resist. Ollie was now doing something with his surfboard, leaning over and apparently polishing it. The muscles in his shoulders flexed as he worked and the sun glinted on his taut arms and back. James watched him look along the road, a smile breaking out over his handsome face as he waved to someone and called out a greeting. That brought James out of his reverie and he continued his descent, making his way over to the pair of friends, who looked up as he approached. Ollie smiled warmly while Bruce, his friend, just looked at James indifferently and then looked away. James simply focused his attention on Ollie and returned his smile.

'Hi! How are you doing? Settled in?' Ollie put his hand out to shake James'.

It was a mature gesture that surprised James and he shook hands firmly, returning Ollie's gaze for a second, which made him feel good. 'Getting there.' he replied. 'It's a bit rough and ready, though. No broadband!'

The expression on Ollie's face changed to one of mock horror. 'Hey, why would you want to spend your time in front of a computer when you've got all this?' he said, spreading his arm wide to indicate the vast ocean.

James laughed. 'Yep! I see what you mean.'

'Come on, Ollie! Let's get going, mate.' Bruce was clearly ignoring James and impatient to start the day's surfing.

Ollie grinned at James and shrugged apologetically before slipping off his shorts to reveal brief, bright red swimming trunks. James looked away across the harbour, slightly uncomfortable and not wanting to be caught staring at Ollie, although the situation was quickly resolved when Ollie stepped into his wet suit and his bronzed body disappeared from view as he grasped the long tab on the zipper at the back and pulled it up in a practised movement.

'See you later, mate,' he nodded, picking up his board and trotting after Bruce who was already making his way down to the beach. 'Come down tomorrow morning at ten,' called Ollie, turning to face James and jogging backwards. 'Wear your trunks and I'll bring an extra board and a suit. Yeah?'

'Great! I'll be here!' James called back.

With a wave Ollie disappeared from view and James stood watching as two black shapes appeared around the edge of the pier head, paddling their way out to the headland to catch the good waves. He felt light and spacious inside, his stomach churned with excitement and his face felt hot. Tomorrow he would lose his surfing virginity and start to get a tan!

It was the smell that Christie was first aware of as she began to regain consciousness. Although there was not much light in the place, she quickly realised that she was in some kind of cottage and the smell matched that of her sad, brown-eyed friend. There he was, crouching down in front of her, holding out a mug.

'Drink this. It's just water.'

Christie took the chipped yellow mug and sipped the cool water gratefully. She felt dizzy, slightly nauseous and generally discombobulated. He remained crouched in front of her; she was sitting in a small armchair, the only piece of furniture in the room apart from a table and a wooden chair that stood over by the one window. As her eyes became accustomed to the dimness, she could see that the floor was bare floorboards with no rugs to relieve the coldness. There were no curtains, no pictures, no lamps, and a single light fitting hung desolately from the centre of the ceiling – without a bulb.

'How did I get in here?' she asked, putting her hand to her hot forehead.

'I carried you. You passed out.'

Despite being intensely aware of his presence and his close proximity to her, she still did not feel remotely threatened by this strange man. 'Like some knight in shining armour!' she said.

When he smiled, her breath caught in her throat at the change in his face. Brown eyes shone back at her, and a set of surprisingly white, straight teeth emerged from the facial hair that dominated his face. When she returned his smile, it was as if he'd been caught out and he immediately resumed his sullen expression, stood up and moved to the chair by the table. Pulling it out and turning it to face her, he sat down and once again silently stared at her.

'Now, you're staring at me again,' she said in frustration. 'Haydon! It's rude!'

He just shrugged, as though good manners were not something that featured in his life. 'Why were you following me?' he asked.

It was a simple question but not one that Christie could answer. 'I don't know,' she said. 'I just felt I had to.'

He nodded. 'Do you feel it too?'

All of the hairs stood to attention on the back of her neck as comprehension dawned and she knew exactly what he was talking about. 'Yes. What's happening? Do you know?'

He shook his head.

He's not overly chatty, thought Christie with growing impatience. 'Haydon, when I saw you at the pub the other day, you said you knew I was coming. How did you know and what did you mean?'

Haydon looked out of the window, stroking his beard, and then he looked back at her, shifted in the chair, leaned forward and, taking a deep breath, spoke for longer than he had so far. 'Some things in life you just know. You know what I mean?'

She nodded, willing him to continue.

'Well, in here, I just knew.' He tapped his chest. 'I knew you were coming and all that. I just knew – like I was supposed to know, sort of. Like I said, some things are just too big to understand.'

Christie nodded again. It was the same for her when she felt compelled to write. It wasn't a choice: it felt like an obligation. 'Don't you wonder why you felt that way?' she asked, hoping he might come up with the answer.

He looked down at his dirty hands and thoughtfully rubbed them together. She had no idea what might be going on inside his head. He was such an unknown to her, and her inquisitive brain was fascinated.

'I don't think I have any choice,' he said simply, resuming his gaze.

Christie sighed and continued to return his stare. They seemed to do a lot of that – staring. She took her phone from her pocket and checked the time. Leaping up, she realised she had been out for over an hour and her parents were waiting for breakfast. They would probably be quite worried by now. 'God, look at the time! Is there a phone signal anywhere in this place?'

Haydon looked at her blankly. What would he know about phone signals? she tutted to herself. She still felt slightly dizzy and the room was beginning to close in on her; she needed to get out into fresh air and sunlight. The sensation of heat was also starting up in her again; she now recognised that it seemed to precipitate the compulsion to write.

'I have to go. Can we talk again?' She saw fearful uncertainty return to his eyes and she understood that he was fragile and needed careful handling. He didn't answer, but she was sure their paths would cross soon, especially since she now knew where he lived and could always come and find him. She was not remotely worried about her own safety with him, she was more concerned about his ability to cope with what she felt may have to happen; it could make or break him. One thing was certain, though: whoever or whatever was trying to communicate with or through both of them, things would never be the same again, for either of them.

As she walked out into the street, she took a deep breath, feeling, with relief, the sun on her face. She glanced back at the cottage as she walked away. There was no sign of Haydon, but she was pretty sure he would be watching her through one of the grubby windows.

'Chris! Chris!' James was running towards her. 'Bloody hell, Chris! I've been looking for you everywhere!' He was out of breath and quite taken aback when his sister flung herself into his arms and held him tight. 'Blimey sis, you okay?' He patted her back as she seemed unprepared to let him go.

'Yes, I'm fine, thanks, Jay.'

James looked doubtful. 'What were you doing in that house? Whose is it? It looks derelict.'

Christie decided to be as honest as possible without saying too much. 'It belongs to a guy who has a few issues and seems to have become a bit of a dropout. He's odd, but I'm writing about him so I was just asking him a few questions.'

'Hmmm!' said James, certain she wasn't telling him everything but respecting her privacy. After all, he didn't tell her everything about his life either. 'Come on, we'd better get back. Mum was wondering where you were. I came out to look for you and then got caught up with the surfers, so she'll be beside herself by now!'

Following a quick trip into the supermarket for provisions and a return visit to Puddles and his ginger-haired owner to buy the paper, they hurried up the hill to the cottage and a pair of hungry, concerned parents.

Over breakfast, Christie was unusually quiet and dodged her mother's questions. James could see she didn't want to discuss her latest project with their mother, so he kept his own counsel and said nothing. His mind was on other things, anyway, as the image of a bronzed body and laughing eyes played across his inner vision.

Chapter 7

Christie lay on her bed and stared at the ceiling. Was she being possessed by someone no longer in this life? If so, why? And why her? And what was the connection to Haydon? It must all be linked somehow, although, as yet, she could not make the connection.

She drifted into a light doze, vaguely aware of street noises dancing around her head, a gate being opened and noisily closed, a dog barking. It was the heat starting again that brought her back to wakefulness. It was not unpleasant: it ran like a current of energy, imbued with affection, running through her: she felt love, but it had an impersonal quality, as if it was coming to her but was meant for someone else – or maybe coming *through* her *to* someone else. She lay still in its unquestionable warmth and allowed herself to be consumed. Was it minutes or seconds later that she heard a scuffling sound, followed by the soft mew of a kitten? At first, she thought it was coming from outside, but then she heard the scuffle again, followed by the sound of a cat purring. It was in her room, and seemed to be coming from the corner at the foot of her bed; she leaned over to look. There was nothing there except her previously discarded trainers. She leaned right over and looked all around, finally sliding down onto the carpet and peering underneath the bed. There was nothing, yet she could still hear the contented purr of a cat. She sat on the edge of the bed, every sense on high alert, trying to make sense of it. Then the purring stopped. There was another kitten-like mew, and then silence.

She was utterly perplexed: there was no rational explanation for any of it. She went to the window, her logical mind insisting that there must be a cat outside, but her eyes were immediately drawn to the French windows opposite, where she was once more looking at a shadowy face shrouded by white hair. She stared hard as the figure moved closer to the window and part of the body became visible. Now she could see that it was definitely an old woman, her hair slightly luminous against the gloom of the room behind her. She was smiling at Christie and carrying something in her arms. With a sharp intake of breath, Christie saw that it was a little cat, which the old woman was stroking. No sooner had Christie realised this, than the shape of the woman faded and was gone.

This was too surreal. Christie searched her room again, for the cat she had clearly heard. She looked in James' room and her parents' room, all to no avail. Returning to her own room, she was struck by the warmth of it as she went to the window and looked over at the French windows. The windows just stared blankly out onto the world. Turning to her laptop, Christie switched it on and waited impatiently for it to boot up. Going straight into a blank document she started to write.

I love this time of year in Porthtreval. It is so busy with people enjoying the sun and the soft sea breezes that buffet the coastline. My favourite time of day is early morning, before most people are up and when all is so very new, so perfect and unspoiled by the heat of the day and those who will wander in from near and far. At that time, my darling, Porthtreval, I feel, belongs to me.

I hope you will be able to enjoy it as I do one of these days. Your self-imposed banishment is currently preventing this but I am hopeful that soon you will return to hear the sounds of the sea and know that you are truly home, once more.

I sit now, looking across the pier to the headland beyond, and I think of you. I picture how you might look as you return: joy filling your eyes when you realise how much you are loved. There is so much love just waiting to flow like precious gold into your veins. It's a perfect love that is just for you and has always been there for you. It is time now, my darling, for you to return to the place that is calling you and to the one who waits patiently for you to share that bounteous love with him. He is in need of its healing power, but you, my darling, are the healer that needs to administer it.

We all wait for you, my darling, we all wait ...

Christie stopped writing, feeling perspiration running down her back. Putting her laptop aside, she went and opened the window, breathing in the fresh air as questions lay scattered in her mind: What was this all about? Why was she being spoken through? Was Haydon the male person mentioned in her writing? She felt so alone but realised that there was no one she could speak to about it. Besides which, she was afraid that if she were to share her experiences, they would not come to her anymore; in the sharing she would somehow be sullied and no longer a useable channel for this ethereal being. A cup of tea and an everyday chat with her mum would be good, though, she decided, closing her laptop.

Pete was looking in the window of the hardware store. He loved this kind of place and found it sad that so many were shutting down, unable to compete with the large, impersonal DIY superstores. He loved the smells in these dusty stores – hessian and creosote being the predominant ones that would meet his nostrils the minute he walked in, he was sure.

'Hello again, how are things going?'

He recognised the voice of the neighbour with the cleavage and turned round, instantly noticing that her low cut top did not disappoint.

'Hello. You've caught me looking in my favourite shop. I could spend all day in there.'

She laughed and he was once more enveloped in the magic of her sound. He smiled at her and their eyes locked, fleetingly sharing something forbidden, which passed as soon as it came.

'Well, if Tom in there can't help you with whatever you're needing, pet, no one can.'

Making conversation, he pointed to her wicker basket. 'So what have you been buying?'

'Just a few cakes from the market stall; they do a lovely coffee and walnut – my favourite.'

'Mine too!' said Pete, perhaps a little too enthusiastically.

'Tell you what, then, if I see you out working later on, I'll give you a shout when I've got the kettle on. Fancy that?' Her eyes were speaking to him, but Pete was not quite getting the message.

'Okay, why not?' he shrugged.

'I'm Rosie,' she introduced herself.

'Pete,' he replied, offering her his hand.

She took it, noticing it was warm and dry and strong. She had watched him working on the house over the past few days. He was certainly a grafter. Once the scaffolding had been put up, he had wasted no time in making the most of the good weather and had been up there working most of the day. She had been admiring his strong arms as he rubbed down and then started to whitewash the walls.

Rosie Brown was a warm, loving woman who was well known in the town for always making time for people. Her Stevie, as she called him, had worked at the harbour, maintaining the boats that berthed there, since he was sixteen. Now in his forties, he worked on all types of boats from little wooden dinghies right up to yachts worth in excess of five million pounds. Their son, Archie, lived with his girlfriend in Penzance and rarely came back home, which saddened Rosie as she often felt lonely. Steve worked long hours and then spent time at the pub at the top of the hill or watched football in the big inn at the harbour mouth. She had lots of friends, but little real love from her inattentive husband and absent son, and being someone who had a lot of love to give, she was dissatisfied with her lot, feeling her life was becoming meaningless.

Inevitably, her interest was piqued by her new neighbour. Was she imagining it or had she seen interest in his eyes? She liked his solid, square build and his cropped hair, flecked with grey, which suited his tanned complexion so well. She had seen that there was a wife and two children, so she would just be looking, and chatting of course. That would be all, though, she decided.

Diane had been in the office since eight that morning. The editors' meeting lasted about an hour and everyone had something to bring to the table, except her; as it was her first week, however, no one was expecting anything, anyway. Brian, editor in chief, sat at the head of the table and Diane felt relieved that she'd resisted him four years earlier: there was no denying his good looks and she did not fancy being one of his conquests, of which she presumed there were many.

After the meeting, he called her into his office, smiling and indicating for her to sit down as he took his seat behind his desk and looked at his computer. 'I have a nice little job here for you, Di,' he said, putting on a pair of reading glasses as he peered at the screen. 'How would you like to cover a story of a rat infestation in your very own home town of Porthtreval?'

Diane raised her eyebrows. 'Really? Sounds fascinating,' she said with heavy irony.

'That's what I thought you'd say,' he said with a smirk, as the printer kicked in and made a copy of the email from the source of the tip off.

Taking the copy from his outstretched hand, Diane noticed that it had been sent anonymously, which always put her off and she would not usually take seriously something that did not have a name attached to it. However, this was her first assignment in her new position, so she decided to show she was a professional and could produce a story from just about anything.

Casting her eyes over the email, she saw that it alleged that huge rats had been spotted coming from the recluse's cottage in The Nip, a group of fisherman's cottages just off the high street. It concluded by saying that he was 'a dirty tramp who never kept things clean'. 'Well, I'll interview initially this recluse fellow,' said Diane. 'Do we have any information on him?'

Brian checked the newspaper's files. 'His name if Haydon Rouse,' he said. 'There was a bit about him a few years ago which came from the police: he'd been badly beaten by a group of local louts who then broke into his house and trashed it. Nice people!' He read on. 'Oh, and last year his neighbours were concerned that his house was a fire risk because he doesn't have electricity and uses candles. Nothing else apart from that.'

'Right, I'll see what I can find out from the locals before I go banging on his door. He doesn't appear to be dangerous, then?' she asked.

'Not as far as history shows. Be careful though, Di.'

She nodded and smiled, thinking Brian seemed to have mellowed with the years.

Back in Porthtreval, her first port of call was the newsagents. It was not a huge story, but it would be interesting in that she would enjoy the information gathering process and chatting to a few of the people she had started to get to know.

'I've just brewed the tea if you fancy a cuppa.'

The voice came from below and Pete looked over the scaffold bar to see Rosie's face beaming up at him. 'Okay, I'll be right there. Thanks.' Climbing down the ladder, he could not ignore the excitement bubbling inside him, despite telling himself he was doing nothing more than having a cup of tea with a neighbour. She was standing in her kitchen cutting large slices of coffee and walnut cake when he reached the open stable-style door.

'Come on in and take the weight off your feet for a minute,' she said, looking at him with laughing eyes as she passed him his mug. 'Sugar?' she asked.

He shook his head and they both sat at the breakfast bar. As she chatted, he relaxed, feeling normal, happy and at ease for the first time in a long time. He didn't feel good about the fact that he was feeling this way with a virtual stranger, but whenever he looked at his wife he felt excruciating guilt at his own failure. To the woman sitting across from him, he was just the man over the road – no history, no failure.

Chapter 8

Diane was becoming a little concerned about her daughter: open, happy, cheerful Christie was becoming fractious and withdrawn. She had mentioned it on several occasions but Christie had just clammed up and said everything was fine. 'Something is going on with Christie,' she remarked to Pete as they lay in bed early on a Saturday morning, sipping tea and listening to the radio. 'She's not herself.'

The weather forecast was promising another hot and sunny day, so Pete was planning to finish off painting the front wall of the house and wondering whether he had enough paint for the job. All the houses in this part of the country were either whitewashed or the natural grey stone, and although it would be hard work keeping the house brilliant white, he preferred that look to the rather sad, dull look of the stone. When Diane alerted him to the disposition of their daughter, he was ashamed to realise that he hadn't really noticed and that his attention had, at times, been playing away from home. He had to get a grip and not let that laugh and those warm eyes invade his mind and act as a wedge between him and his family. The warning signs were there, but the excitement of it made him feel alive: there was definite chemistry there.

'I suppose she has been a bit quiet,' he said, bringing his attention back to his wife. 'She'll be all right when she finds a job.'

'I hope you're right.' Diane picked up the *Times* and scanned the headlines, reading glasses perched.

Pete lay looking at her. She was an attractive woman with her dark, shoulder length hair, which, disappointingly from his point of view, was rarely allowed to flow free. At the moment, it was confined in a plait which was how she wore it overnight and which he enjoyed undoing whenever they made love. There was no finer sight than his wife in her place of passion with her eyes closed, a faint smile on her lips and her face surrounded by those dark tresses. But none of that had been happening since they had moved into the cottage, the close proximity of their children's bedrooms being a constant deterrent.

Reaching under the quilt, Pete started to rub her thigh in slow sensual movements. She immediately responded with a glance and a smile, flinging the paper onto the floor and snuggling down into his strong arms. Their lips met and the familiar stirring immediately began as he gently pushed his tongue into her mouth and very quietly made love to her. They reached their climax together with tight, stifled moans and muscles clenched. Giggling like naughty teenagers afterwards, Pete felt himself beginning to return to the man he once was and the man she wanted him to be.

Christie had slept for at least ten hours, but still she felt washed out and exhausted as she lay listening to the holiday makers begin their day with jovial greetings as they passed each other on the hill outside. Swinging her legs out of bed, she sat and thought about her current situation: at twenty one years old she had no job, no boyfriend, no friends nearby (apart from a suspicious hermit who seemed to be strangely connected to her) and to top it all, she seemed to be a channel for a dead person. Could life be any more surreal?

She stood up and shuffled through to the bathroom, ignoring the odd giggles coming from her parents' room. Switching on the shower, she let hot water cascade over her tired body and took the time to think. There being no distractions, her thoughts inevitably turned to Haydon, her strange new acquaintance. Unable to get the vision of his smile out of her mind, she acknowledged that although he was the oddest person she'd ever met, he was also the most interesting: his gentleness astonished her; his past fascinated her, and the questions surrounding his future absorbed her. Why did she feel responsible for him? Why had she passed out as soon as they had any contact? How could she get to know more about him? It was all surrounded in mystery.

Feeling better after a breakfast of toast and coffee, she pulled on her trainers, picked up the local paper and went out into the sunshine, heading for her favourite spot: the little slab of concrete down on the corner just to the side of the roadway, where she could sit with a view of the beach before her and the pier jutting bravely out into the ocean; beyond that the headland stretched away into the distance. The idea was to check for available jobs in the paper, but a warm Atlantic breeze caressed her face as she settled down, and she closed her eyes, letting her mind go still, aware of the gulls flying above her, argumentative as ever, the occasional passing car, and voices in the cottage gardens behind her. The sounds gradually blended and became indistinct as she slipped into a warm reverie, the newspaper lying unread by her side.

The feeling that she was not alone swept through her, familiar now, so she remained relaxed and did not open her eyes. She felt loved and supported, calm and resigned, and then came the sensation that someone was holding her hand, causing tears to well under her eyelids and slide down her cheeks unhindered. Still she remained motionless in a serenely beautiful trance-like state. A voice as soft as the breeze spoke in her ear; whether male or female she could not tell, but she knew that was irrelevant. 'Save him!' it said, and then again, 'Save him!' The feeling of warmth inside her intensified and she smiled: someone was watching over her in her strange, new experiences and she now had an inkling that there was a purpose to them. With renewed vigour, she opened her eyes, dashed the tears from her cheeks and strode purposefully down the hill to go in search of Haydon.

Pete could hear them shouting from the bedroom as he got dressed. Recognising Rosie's voice, he stopped and unashamedly eavesdropped. He couldn't hear what was being said, but he could tell there was a vicious argument underway and his stomach clenched with fear as two questions sprang to mind: was it because of her attention to him, and was she about to be physically hurt?

All went suddenly quiet, only to be followed by a crash and a scream. Rushing to the window, no longer caring if he was going to be seen, he peered over to the house opposite and saw Rosie's husband banging the gate behind him as he stomped up the hill with a look of pure venom on his stubble covered face. Unable to see Rosie in her kitchen, he pulled on his T-shirt and dashed down the stairs, out of the rarely used front door and straight across the road. He jumped the gate leading to Rosie's back door and peered in through the top half of the stable door. 'Rosie! Rosie!' he called, still unable to see her. There was no answer, but he thought he could hear muffled sobs from within the house. He went in and ran up the stairs, following the sound. She was curled up on the bed, her face buried in the pillow she was hugging as sobs racked her body. He went to her, speaking her name so as not to startle her, and gently pulled her shoulder round to bring her into his embrace. She pressed into the comfort of him until her sobs began to subside and he was able to tip her face up towards him. Under her streaked make-up there was a reddened area on her right cheek.

Pete was enraged. 'Has he done this? Has he punched you?'

She nodded and nestled once more against his chest. Gently, he pulled away, remembering that just an hour ago he had made love to his wife and realising how this would look to her. 'Does this often happen?' he asked as Rosie sat up.

She shrugged. 'Only when I do something wrong.' She blew her nose on a tissue and looked into the dressing table mirror. 'God! I look a mess! That's going to be some bruise!'

Pete was appalled: as far as he was concerned, a man never hit a woman, whatever the provocation. 'What are you going to do about it? How long has it been going on?'

'Oh, I don't know ... since before we got married.'

He looked at her in astonishment. 'And you still married him!'

'I loved him, Pete! I still do, in a way. I just do things wrong and he gets angry with me. It's my own fault.'

Pete couldn't believe what he was hearing. 'Rosie, no one has the right to hit you. No one!' he emphasized, looking directly into her sad eyes. 'If I were ever to hit Diane she would be out of the door before you could say "I'll have a pasty" – never to be seen again!'

His turn of phrase made her smile and Pete joined in as he realised how ridiculous he sounded.

She stroked his tanned cheek. 'You're a lovely man, Pete. I hope Diane realises what a lucky woman she is.'

For a few seconds their eyes locked and if anything was going to happen, that was the moment. Desire rose in Pete as his senses took in the voluptuous woman beside him. His body and his heart were urging him to take her in his arms and kiss her, but his mind was screaming at him to leave. He took heed, let the moment pass, and stood up to leave.

'Thanks, Pete,' she said as he reached the bedroom door. 'I appreciate you caring.'

He turned to say something, wanting to help her but feeling inadequate because he knew that this was not something he could simply solve. Other people's lives were just that: other people's. His intervention may have helped Rosie feel better in that instant, but she was vulnerable and his long term involvement was not the answer.

As he closed the gate behind him, he walked thoughtfully across the narrow road and back to his family, feeling grateful and relieved that he had made the right decision. If Rosie asked for help he would point her in the right direction, but that was all he could or should do.

Diane was busy washing up in the kitchen on his return. She looked at him expectantly as he walked through the back door. 'Where did you go?'

He realised that this was the moment that he either told the truth and took the consequences or he fabricated a tale and risked her finding out. Many years had gone by since his dalliance with a client, but Diane still smarted from it, so he knew this situation needed careful handling. Above all, he had to be truthful. 'I heard people arguing over the road, then a scream and a crash. Right after that I saw that guy, Steve, storming up the road, so I just went over to make sure Rosie was all right. She was, but he had hit her.'

Diane looked up at him with a gasp of obvious shock. 'He hit her? Is she just going to let that happen? That's terrible!'

Pete nodded, relieved that the focus of the conversation had not centred on the fact that he had gone straight over there. Diane did not, however, let it pass. She grabbed his wrist with a soapy hand as he passed her on his way out of the kitchen.

'Be careful, Pete. It's none of your business … and you know what I'm saying, don't you?'

'I know,' he said, annoyed that she felt she had to refer to the past but hoping it didn't show on his face.

Gathered around a Volkswagon Camper close to the pier, the surfers were getting ready to ride the waves: bronzed bodies were being squeezed into black wetsuits, worn even when the sun was high in the sky, and James was being zipped into one by Ollie, who was bare-chested and clad in Bermuda shorts that hung on his hips below a firm, tanned abdomen.

'James!'

He looked up to see Christie coming down the hilly footpath towards them.

'Who's this then?' asked Ollie as she reached the group.

'Are you going surfing, James?' Christie asked, glancing at Ollie and smiling.

James was not pleased to see her and hoped she would get the message and keep walking when, after a brief acknowledgement, he turned to pick up one of the surfboards.

'Are you going surfing?' she asked again. 'Do you know how?'

'No, not yet,' he said, looking back at her. 'First lesson about to commence.'

'Aren't you going to introduce us?' asked Ollie.

'My sister, Christie.'

Ollie stepped forward to shake her hand. 'Ollie. Nice to meet you, Christie.'

She smiled and was rewarded with a breathtaking grin in return. 'You giving James a lesson in surfing, then?'

'Yep. Can't do much about all that white skin, though; he'll have to tackle that one himself.'

Both of them laughed, but stopped abruptly at the thunderous look on James' face.

'Sorry James,' said Christie. 'I'm just off into the town. Have a good day. Hope the water's not too cold.' And with a wave she turned and made her way along the harbour side.

Ollie's eyes followed her and James was livid that she had encroached on his territory – a 'no go' area for sisters – and diverted Ollie's attention away from him. Why did she have to be so likeable, so easy going and popular with everybody? He always felt like a grey shadow beside her. And now she had just ruined a great moment: it had been wonderful being so close to Ollie, feeling his breath against his skin, watching his tanned fingers working on the wetsuit and imagining running his own fingers over Ollie's taut, muscular chest, tracing the shape of the tribal tattoo on Ollie's left upper arm and then running his tongue along it. The last thing he wanted was Princess Tippytoes coming along to dash his fantasy right into the dark water of the harbour, especially since Ollie obviously fancied her.

'She's nice, Jay. How old is she?' he asked as he slipped effortlessly into his wetsuit.

'Twenty four,' lied James, knowing Ollie was nineteen and not wanting him to think he would have a chance with Christie, 'and she has a boyfriend,' he added a little too quickly.

'Okay, I get the message!' retorted Ollie. 'No need to be so protective, mate. Anyway, come on, let's get going.' Ollie picked up his board and walked off towards the rocky beach. James followed, smarting from the rebuff.

Surfing was not nearly as easy as it looked and James spent very little of his first outing on the board; most of the time he found himself plummeting into the swelling sea, gasping and swallowing copious amounts of brine. Despite aching limbs and numerous bruises, however, he thoroughly enjoyed himself. He watched in awe as Ollie chose the right wave to ride and then nimbly and seemingly effortlessly mounted his board, knees bent, arms outstretched and disappeared towards the coastline.

Hours later the group was gathered around the back of Ollie's car, drinking Coke and laughing about James' lack of surfing skill. They had been joined by three others: Sam, Jack and Andy, who had been body boarding on shorter boards and James was seriously considering whether that might have been a better option, not that he cared. The main thing was that he was spending time with Ollie, who was now laughing with the others. A natural leader, his dark eyes and flashing smile were captivating, and James was simply enjoying seeing his facial expressions and focusing on his strong hands as they busied themselves with wetsuits, towels and the variety of accessories that surfing required. He was pretty sure Ollie would not be returning his affections in the way he would have liked, but he didn't mind. These feelings of attraction were new to him and he was enjoying the closeness and intimacy – for the time being anyway.

'So James, do you think your sister would like to take up surfing? I wouldn't mind giving her some tuition.' James turned to find Bruce standing at the edge of the group.

'I've no idea, Bruce, why don't you ask her?' he said, not liking what Bruce's tone implied.

'I'll do that. She's a bit of all right, that's for sure.'

James turned away, his blood boiling; not only with the comments from Bruce but because Ollie seemed to be affected by what Bruce was saying. He just wanted his sister out of the picture. It was a complication he did not want to have to deal with.

'It's okay, mate, I'm only gonna shag her!' sneered Bruce.

'Cut it out, you twat!' stormed Ollie, stepping in before James got embroiled in a fight. When trouble was brewing, it was always Bruce who had started it and though everyone else was used to his antisocial behaviour, James was not yet accustomed to it. Ollie gave him a sympathetic look as Bruce shrugged indifferently and turned to talk to a group of girls who had just arrived on the scene.

Ollie came and stood beside James. 'Ignore him,' he advised. 'He's all mouth. He pisses me off at times; he can be such an idiot.' Ollie shut the boot of the car with a resounding bang. 'Tell you what though,' he nodded towards Bruce's back, 'he's the one you want behind you if you ever get in trouble out there.'

'No kidding?' said James.

'Surprising, I know, but he's saved my back a few times. He's one of the strongest men I know in the water,' said Ollie as he got into the driving seat. 'See ya, Jay,' he waved as he drove off.

That night James lay in bed with his arm behind his head and his eyes fixed on the ceiling. Sleep was eluding him; his mind was full of Ollie, who was obviously into girls. The look on his face when Bruce had made remarks about Christie said it all, or so James thought.

He had understood that he was gay for some months now, ever since the night with Vince, who had left for Australia the following day, but not before giving James the courage and the acceptance to acknowledge who he truly was. Looking back, he still felt a fool for not having realised what was happening between himself and Vince. Their friendship had always been so easy, Vince being the one person who seemed to *get* him. That night as they had sat together on the little sofa in Vince's flat, he had told James that he was moving away so as to distance himself from him. James had been horrified and had totally misunderstood; his first impulse had been to verbally lash out, but the look on Vince's face had stopped him. They had gazed into each other's eyes for what seemed like an eternity that made sense of all that had gone before. Vince had then gently and lovingly leaned over and kissed James softly on the lips, bringing his hand up to the back of James' head and cradling him while continuing to kiss him ever more deep and passionately.

James had kissed girls before, although he didn't relish it. In his early teens it had just been what he and his mates did on Sunday afternoons with the local girls. For James it had been a meaningless laugh and he hadn't felt the need to 'cop a grope', which was what his friends were always boasting about. In fact, as time passed, he had hung out less and less with those friends, and once he had met Vince, he drifted away from them altogether; they had seemed so juvenile. His minimal interest in girls had also subsequently flatlined, and that night he had finally understood why. Vince had led him into his first love-making experience, and he had put his trust in Vince, who had been gentle and taught him lessons that he could never have imagined. Afterwards, they had lain in bed talking until the early hours, by which time Vince had to pack his last few things away, ready for the taxi that was booked to take him to the airport. James had then walked home, his head spinning with this new understanding and how it would shape his future. Vince had asked him to promise to be true to himself and do what felt right, and James had given that promise. But without Vince by his side it had all seemed hostile and terrifying.

      Thinking about Vince now, James had to admit that he had not been so fiercely attracted to him as he was to Ollie. Then again, he reminded himself, he had only had a few hours of Vince the lover as opposed to Vince the best friend. Maybe he ought to try to get in touch with him, he concluded as he finally drifted off to sleep.

Chapter 9

She could see him as she approached the rickety gate that opened onto the scrubby path leading up to the cottage: Haydon was sitting on an upturned barrel to the side of the front door. The heat of the morning had not encouraged him to take off his grubby coat and Christie paused at the gate to observe him for a few seconds as he sat reading something – a letter, or was it a photograph? At his feet was a small, wooden box, which looked like the type in which expensive cigars were packed. As he carefully and almost reverently replaced whatever it was in the box at his feet, she waited, knowing he would look up and see her. He raised his head and his dark gaze fell on her, making her pulse quicken. His deep eyes held hers blankly, devoid of expression, interest or recognition. Feeling awkward, Christie smiled and gave a tiny wave, in response to which Haydon almost imperceptibly nodded before reaching down to pick up the box and then turning to the front door of his ramshackle cottage. Unsure whether or not to follow him, she remained where she was until he turned, and with a slight incline of his head, beckoned her into the gloom beyond the opened door.

    The gate emitted a mournful creak as she opened it and made her way up the path feeling carried onward as though in a dream – drawn in by a force she could not have explained and filled with an emotion that she could not pinpoint. Once inside the dim little sitting room, she gave a slight start at the sight of him standing facing her, motionless, in the doorway of another room at the rear of the house, the light from which silhouetted his shape but left his face in shadow.

'Oh! You made me jump!' she exclaimed, bringing her hand to her chest.

Without responding, he turned and walked into the back room, so Christie decided to follow without waiting to be asked; good manners were obviously not on the agenda. She found that this was the kitchen and a complete contrast to the dark sitting room: light poured in through a partly glazed roof which sloped towards a small garden; cupboards along one side were painted yellow and added to the overall sunny effect; a small pine table stood in the middle of the room with just two chairs, and a pine dresser sported a variety of coloured mugs and plates stacked neatly in a row. There was no sign of a fridge or washing machine; a copper kettle stood on a little three ring gas stove which had an overhead grill, and a stand-alone Butler sink with wooden drainer completed the utilities in the room. Christie was taken aback. It was bright, airy and surprisingly clean. Haydon, she noticed, was looking nervous and unsure – a side of him she hadn't seen before.

'What am I doing here, Haydon?'

The question sounded odd but was somehow necessary and though Haydon seemed to understand, he simply shrugged, leaned against the sink and looked down at the draining board, running a dirty fingernail along one of the grooves. 'I knew you'd come,' he said.

'How?' Christie burst out, jumping at the chance of some interaction with him. 'How did you know?'

'You just had to,' he shrugged. 'I don't know why.' Once again, he fixed his eyes on her and she held his gaze, finding those eyes captivating. Whether it was because they shone so clearly through the mass of facial hair, she was not sure, but looking into them was as pleasant as walking out of the gloom into the sunny kitchen, the juxtaposition making the contrast that much more acute.

For some moments their eyes searched into each other, both knowing that they were powerless to stop whatever it was that was happening. It was as though their story had already been written and they were living out the script like actors in a play, yet there was a wall between them that prevented normal communication. It was not of Christie's making but she could feel it and wondered how she could push through it to get this strange character to open up to her.

'Sit with me and talk, Haydon,' she said, sitting down at the table and leaning forward, clasping her hands together in front of her.

He dragged the other chair out across the cold, tiled floor and sat opposite her, eyes downcast like a compliant pupil in a head teacher's office.

'Can I ask you some questions?' she asked, watching his face for a change in expression. There was nothing, just the usual shrug. 'How old are you?'

Haydon was looking down at his grimy hands. 'Almost twenty nine.'

'How long have you been living alone?'

'Since she left.'

'Who, your mother?'

He nodded, still looking down.

'Haydon, how old were you when she left?' Christie asked gently.

'Sixteen. I was going to school, still.'

'So, you've been on your own for nearly foureen years. Why didn't someone help you? Why did she go? How did you manage all on your own?' As soon as the questions were out and Haydon looked at her like a bewildered child, she realised that more than one question at a time was too much for him and changed tack. 'It must have been difficult for you and frightening,' she said, and waited. All she got was the inevitable shrug. 'Has she been back since?'

He shook his head.

'Do you know where she is now?'

At this Haydon's eyes blazed and words came out in a rush. 'I don't know! I don't know where she went! And I don't know why she left me! She was my mum ... she *is* my mum!' He shook his head, still sad and confused after so many years, and lowered his eyes again, overwhelmed by his own emotion.

'Is that why you've ... well ... sort of "dropped out"?' She waited to see if he might find this question offensive. When he reverted once more to a shrug, she sat back and folded her arms, contemplating the situation: here was a man who had been abandoned when he was a teenager and left to fend for himself, an experience that had obviously traumatised him so much that he had shut himself off from the world. The whispers from the breeze reverberated in her mind: 'Save him.' But how? And who was it pouring out heartfelt messages through her writing? None of it was making sense and Christie began to question whether, in fact, it was all connected. She was getting more than a little frustrated as the words 'save him' continued to repeat in her head. Taking a deep breath, she sat forward and resumed her attempt to at least gain some clarity about the sad figure sitting across from her.

'What were you like when you were sixteen, Haydon?'

He looked up and offered her a tight-lipped half smile. 'Just normal. I was shy.'

'So what happened when your mother left? What did your teachers say?'

'They didn't know.' Haydon averted his gaze and looked towards the window. 'No one knew.'

'Why didn't you tell anyone? You must have been frightened, being on your own.'

'I thought they would have put me in care, so I didn't say anything – tried to be invisible.'

'But how did you manage for money?'

'Mum had left some for me – a lot actually. She had put it in my post office account; she still puts money in there every now and again, but I've never known how long she was going to be away so I didn't spend any. I learned how to live cheap and get by.'

He nodded towards the garden so Christie got up and went to look out of the window above the sink. There were three earth-filled troughs made from old pallets, all of them overflowing with a variety of vegetables: she could see lettuce, onions, radishes, carrot tops amongst other sprouting plants she couldn't immediately identify. 'That's fantastic, Haydon!' she said, turning and beaming at him. 'All those vegetables in such a tiny yard! Brilliant!' She laughed with delight and was rewarded with flash of white teeth from Haydon's furry face. It was momentary, gone as quickly as it came, but it had been like a stream of sunlight splitting the clouds on a rainy day. He quickly looked down again, as if smiling was just one step too far.

The mood seemed to be a lot lighter for all four of the Styles family that evening as they had tea together. Christie noticed a spark between her parents that had been missing over the past few months, and even James was smiling and chatting. As for herself: although her talk with Haydon, earlier in the day, had been stilted, she thought she was getting somewhere with him. Where that somewhere was, she was not entirely sure and she was a little concerned by a desire to help him that was bordering on obsessive. Nevertheless, she felt sure there was a reason behind all the mystery. She looked at her mother and tried to imagine her walking out and abandoning her teenage child without rhyme or reason. Diane would no more do that than fly to the moon, unless of course she was forced to for some reason. What could have made Haydon's mother just suddenly up-sticks and leave him to fend for himself? Haydon obviously didn't know. Why was he not angry with her for leaving him? So many unanswered questions.

Diane interrupted her thoughts. 'I've got my first story to cover for the paper,' she announced.

All eyes turned to her, waiting expectantly.

'Guess what it's about,' she said with a grin.

Three blank faces looked back at her.

'Go on then, tell us!' Pete urged.

'Rats!'

'Rats?' echoed Pete. 'Whereabouts?'

'Here in the town – well, allegedly. They've been seen in the area of the fishermen's cottages just off the high street. Apparently, there's a chap there who's a bit odd and the source said they may be living in his shed. He has a load of rotting veg in his garden, apparently.'

Christie was staring at her mother with a piece of cake half way to her mouth, frozen in time by this piece of news.

'You okay, sweetheart? You look a bit shocked,' said Diane.

'I'm fine,' said Christie, giving herself a mental shake and recovering her composure. 'I can't stand rats! How gross! Who reported it and where, exactly, were they seen?'

'I don't know yet,' her mother replied. 'That's what I have to find out.'

'No big deal, is it?' said James. 'Rats are everywhere.'

'I think it's the sheer size and number of these,' Diane explained. 'Anyway, it's my first story so I'm going to get stuck in tomorrow.'

Christie opted to keep her mouth shut. It wasn't really any of her business, anyway, so she decided to keep it that way.

Chapter 10

As the summer weeks unfolded effortlessly in the pretty coastal fishing town, the friendship between Christie and Haydon continued to develop. A fortnight after the conversation in Haydon's kitchen, the two unlikely friends were sitting together looking over the lake that lay in the gardens of the majestic manor house on the outskirts of town. In contrast to the noise and energy of waves crashing onto the coastal rocks only a few hundred feet away, the lake was amazingly calm, still and quiet. They sat side by side on a bench high on a bank from which the stunning view of swans and sea birds through the trees epitomised nature at her very best.

Haydon sat on his hands and kicked the gravelly soil under his feet. Although his conversation was still sparse, Christie was never at a loss for something to say and she was also getting to know how to engage him with questions. He answered most of them with simple honesty and an abrupt clarity that sometimes shocked Christie, causing her to appreciate more deeply the sheltered upbringing she had enjoyed, during which she had been protected, cherished and encouraged; unlike Haydon, with his long absent mother and his permanently invisible father.

Since her friendship with him had got underway, there had been no more emotional visitations of a spiritual nature with their attendant compulsion to write. It was as though their absence was confirming that she was on the right track.

'You look different today, Haydon.'

He gave her a ghost of a smile in response and continued to disturb the dust beneath his feet while Christie looked at him.

'I know what it is: I can see more of your face. I like it!'

Haydon's colour heightened slightly as she noted his scrubbed face and clean hair, now smoothed back off his face. Crude attempt at improvement though it was, it was a sure sign of something in him changing. Christie squeezed his arm and smiled to herself, returning her gaze to the scene before them and thinking about how the rat infestation story had proved to be false. Her clever mother had, in fact, turned it round into a far more gentle story of a young man, obviously damaged by circumstances, who had managed to feed himself from his tiny garden and quietly live the lonely life of a hermit without intruding on others and without State benefits. Local people said they had become accustomed to his shabby presence around the town and were too busy to take much notice of him, so Haydon had become part of the colourful fabric of the place and, for the most part, was left alone to continue his strange existence.

Christie had said nothing to her mother about her friendship with him. James was aware, but he had secrets of his own and they had an unspoken agreement not to discuss their new friendships. She had, however, begun to suspect that her brother may well be enjoying a certain *kind* of friendship with other boys and had attempted to broach the subject with him the previous week. James had been engrossed in a magazine article about the latest complex advances in computer technology, as they sat together at the picnic table in their backyard, late one afternoon. Contemplating him as she sipped ice cold water, she had decided to jump right in.

'Have you heard from Vince at all?'

James' eyes had shot up to meet hers above his magazine. 'No, why?' His defensive tone spoke volumes.

'Oh, I just wondered. You were such good friends for years, and then, all of a sudden, he disappeared.'

'He didn't "disappear"! He emigrated. Loads of people do it and there's no rule to say they have to keep in touch, is there?'

She had shaken her head. 'Of course not, but maybe you should try and get back in contact. He was a good friend,' she had said, wanting to probe further but understanding that her thoughts had to be filed away until James was ready to talk openly. So she'd got up and left him to his magazine.

Sitting by the lake with Haydon, she was now realising that she was currently in limbo. Most of her friends had definite plans for the future, while she was more at sea about such questions than ever. Nevertheless, here beside Haydon, she felt serenely calm about it and, at that moment, was sure she was where she was supposed to be. Turning to him again, she asked, 'What do you want to do with your life? I'm just thinking that mine seems to be on hold at the moment.'

He sighed, a faraway look in his eyes. 'I don't know. Getting through the day is all I think about.'

Christie was taken aback. 'Don't you ever think there must be more to life than just existing? Don't you want to try new things?'

'Such as?' he asked, fixing her with a puzzled stare.

Had this man ever felt happiness, joy, desire? she wondered. Had he conditioned himself to a life of lack from all angles? The acute sadness she felt on his behalf washed over her again and she looked away, unable to speak for a minute. Involuntarily, under the spell-binding intensity of his gaze, her eyes returned to his face and her heart skipped a beat. 'Well, like having friends,' she said, 'travelling to see different places, going to a film, eating ice cream; it doesn't have to be complicated – just something that makes you feel good to be alive. Does that make sense?'

He tipped his head back and looked up through the trees, revealing a grey ring encircling his neck where his wash had not reached. Blowing air out in a long puff he pondered on her words while she remained quiet; she had learned that it was best to give him time to consider what he was going to say and formulate his answer.

'I do feel different to how I used to,' he finally said, glancing at her with a softness she had not seen before, 'because of you.'

'Because of me?' she repeated, pleasantly astonished and half smiling.

'Yes. You're the first friend I've ever had and I feel different when I'm with you.'

Christie lowered her eyes as her throat constricted with emotion. Crying was not on the agenda and she laughed to ease the tension rising in her chest. 'Thank you. That's a lovely thing to say.'

He shrugged and looked away, apparently not understanding how such a straight forward, honest statement could make anyone so emotional. Christie smiled at his predictable reaction, and then ventured onto a road she had not been down before.

'Haydon, how do you feel about getting some work to ease the money situation? Maybe it's time, given that you never know when or if you're going to get money from your mum.'

After a long pause, Haydon turned to her with something like fear in his eyes. 'I don't think I can,' he muttered.

'Why's that?' she asked gently, not wanting to push him too far, too quickly.

'I don't know how.'

Christie took a deep breath, not sure how he would react to her next question. 'Would you like some help?'

To her surprise, and for the first time, she saw hope on his face and could not help taking his hand in hers. 'It's what friends do – help each other,' she said quietly.

He nodded and looked away across the lake to where a dense wooded area stretched up towards the sky.

'But there are going to have to be some changes,' she added. 'Will you trust me to lead the way?'

She was rewarded with a rare and heart-wrenching smile as he nodded and squeezed her hand. And for the next ten minutes or so, they just sat, as they often did, in silence, enjoying each other's company while pondering their own thoughts.

'Dad, how are you getting on with the work around the house?' Christie asked, later that day, as they sat with their feet dangling over the cliff edge, looking down at the summer fun being had by groups of tourists on the beach.

'Not too bad, but there's a lot to do and I really want to get it finished before winter sets in. I've been reliably informed that the winter weather can be evil down here.'

'You may need some help, then?'

'Who from? You?' When Christie gave him one of her long suffering looks he tried again. 'Are you thinking of James? He's about as much use as a bent screwdriver!'

'No Dad. I have someone else in mind who might be interested and wouldn't need paying too much.'

'Who's that, then?' Her father looked at her with interest. Apart from the house, which he could certainly use some help with in the decorating department, he had been asked to do some small building jobs by a couple of people he'd met at the pub, where he was becoming quite a regular, and he was anxious to bring in the much needed cash.

'Just someone I met the other day in the pub,' Christie fabricated, not yet ready to reveal all. 'I'll talk to him about it.'

'Well, let me know. We might be able to do each other a favour.'

Christie tucked her arm in his and grinned up at him. 'Are you ready for ice cream yet? You promised, remember?'

Her father sighed playfully. 'And you never forget, do you? Come on, then!'

The next day she decided to take the bull by the horns. Although she knew Haydon needed gentle treatment, there were radical changes needed if he was to take the next necessary step in his life. On her way to his house she paid a visit to the barber's in the high street. It was run by a colourful character by the name of Jeremy Forsythe-Williams, whose acquaintance she had made one night in the *Inn by the Harbour* on the night of a major league football match. They had both been elbowing through the crowd to get to the bar and had shared some friendly banter about who was going to get served first. As the doorbell jangled and announced her arrival, that morning, she was pleased to see there were no customers as she wanted a private word with Jerry. After a brief conversation, she skipped across the road to get Haydon ready for a very new experience.

She could see him through the windows of the little cottage, pottering about in his garden. She knew how proud of his vegetables he was and on more than one occasion she had sat and gratefully crunched on a carrot that he pulled up and washed for her in his sunny kitchen. Calling his name, she opened the front door and made her way through to the back. He waved as she approached and greeted her with a small smile.

'I'm getting some onions together for your mother,' he said.

Christie's heart nearly burst. She hadn't told Haydon that her mother didn't know about their friendship, and she didn't want him to think she was ashamed of him so she graciously accepted. 'That's lovely, Haydon. She'll be delighted.'

Chapter 11

Diane was pleased with her first assignment for the local paper. Brian was also happy that instead of giving up when she had found the information to be false, she had used her initiative and developed another local interest story – one that was creating a lot of chatter on the regional papers Twitter Feed. Some comments had been cruel and heartless, others had been supportive; either way, Diane knew that Haydon was blissfully unaware of them as he had never heard of Twitter. She had found it strange to meet someone who lived in a technological age and remained totally oblivious to it. Haydon had fascinated her: even though the interview with him had been short and difficult; even though he looked and smelled like a tramp, there had been something undeniably endearing about him.

Since then she had been working full-time and thoroughly enjoying the challenge of digging out interesting stories from the locality. General news had not been her forte in the past as she had concentrated on tourism, so the variety was very satisfying. She had been surprised that Brian had been so amenable to her, in view of their fumble and her rejection of him, but he seemed to be over it and it was never mentioned. She had to admit, she did like being in his company and found his energy quite stimulating. Every now and again, as she watched him during briefings and editors' meetings, she remembered hot kisses and a passionate embrace. It wasn't that she was unhappy with Pete – far from it – but twenty five years was a long time to be with one person; she felt she deserved a little fantasising, as she was doing in the present meeting.

'We need to cover the redundancies at Felan's – George, you okay to take that one? And then there's the death of the guy on the train. Susie, that's yours. Di, I need you to take on a bit of a sensitive one. I've got the details in the office so we can go through them after the meeting; we may need to work together on how to approach this one.'

Diane felt her cheeks redden but she nodded and made pretend notes on her pad to avoid eye contact with him. Why was she behaving like this? she wondered. It was ridiculous. She felt like a teenager.

When she later made her way to his office, he gestured for her to sit down and kept his penetrating grey eyes on her as she did so.

'How are you settling in?' he asked, innocently enough.

'Fine, Brian, thanks.'

'That's good. Pete and the kids okay?'

'Well, it's been a big change for all of us, but they all seem to be happy enough doing their own thing. Why do you ask?'

'I'm interested. It's my job to make sure my staff is happy, in general anyway. Happy people make better employees, especially in this game.'

Diane nodded in agreement. Even though she had no idea if this was leading anywhere, her pulse was racing and she felt young and nervous – and not unpleasantly so.

'Right!' he said, turning to his computer screen. 'We have a bit of a sticky one to cover here. It's going to need careful handling, but if we get it right it could be a great story. We could be the first to report on it, too, which we get precious little opportunity to do these days with everything being digitally instant. Not like in the old days, eh?'

'Oh, I think we've moved with the times, Brian. We're not dead in the water yet.'

'No, of course not.' Brian took the rebuff on the chin and continued. 'Anyway, this job is a bit heavier than we're accustomed to, so I need someone a bit more mature – don't take offence – to cover it.'

Diane waited while he brought an email up on his screen, watching his handsome face as he opened and re-read it. Her mind took on a life of its own as she imagined walking over to him and turning his chair round, loosening his tie and slowly starting to unbutton his shirt while he took her by the hips and guided her into straddling him, slipping her hands inside his shirt, touching hot, male flesh ...

'Di! Diane! Are you okay? You look a bit flushed.'

'Oh! Sorry! Sorry, Brian. I'm fine. I'm ... er ... just tired – late night.'

'Oh yes?' he teased, causing her blush to deepen.

'Oh, stop it!' she laughed, more at herself than him. 'What were you saying?'

The conversation became more business-like as Brian briefed her on the imminent and unexpected merger of two large local companies. Brian had personal contacts who had promised him the story before it went national, hence his excitement, and Diane was pleased that he considered her the right person to cover it.

Christie was sitting on a bench at the harbour head, looking without seeing, listening without hearing the summer seaside life around her. She was a little anxious about how Haydon might be reacting to the transformation he was presently undergoing. It wasn't the haircut so much; it was his possible reaction to the close proximity of another human being carrying out so personal a service that concerned her. Taking a deep breath, she sipped the machine coffee she had bought from the supermarket and smiled to herself as she recalled Haydon's face when she had arrived at his house, that morning, and announced that he was going to have a hot bath. There was no running hot water, so she had instructed him to drag the old tin bath from the shed and put it by the back door – a better idea, she had thought, than lugging hot water upstairs to the unfortunate looking bathroom. Haydon had then looked on nervously as she heated pan after pan of water on the gas rings, using the first pan full to scrub the bath clean and engaging his help to tip the dirty water out onto the thirsty vegetable patch. Haydon had finally been presented with a soft, fluffy, red beach towel that she had brought with her, and a bottle of shower gel.

'I'll be back in twenty minutes,' she told him. 'Have a good scrub. Today is the first day of the rest of your life!' Looking at his worried face she had smiled gently. 'Trust me, Haydon?'

He had nodded mutely and she had left him to it.

Unsurprisingly, the finished effect had been quite startling: he had found some clean jeans and T-shirt, and although they still smelt damp, it was a definite improvement on the usual attire, which lay discarded on the kitchen floor; his hair had been damp and pulled back from his clean face, and his beard, though still bushy, was soft and fresh.

'Wow! You look so different!' Christie had exclaimed, feeling quite emotional. 'Are you ready to go?'

For a minute, Christie had thought he was going to back out: his hesitation was excruciating.

'Okay,' he had nodded with a deep breath.

That had been an hour ago and there was still no sign of him, but she comforted herself with the thought that she had left her mobile number with Jerry, so he would call if there was a problem. She stood up, stretched the stiffness out of her limbs and decided to go and see what the hold-up was. Throwing her empty cup into the bin, she turned towards the high street and stopped dead in her tracks. Heat was suddenly coursing through her body from her toes to her head; she felt faint and her knees were weak, as though they were about to buckle under her weight. She turned and grabbed the railing that lined the harbour edge. What was happening? Had she got up too fast? She closed her eyes and breathed slowly to gather herself. Then came the rushing sound in her ears that she had heard before; on the back of it was the voice, soft and loving. 'Love him,' it said, just once, very clearly. It seemed to be coming from behind her and when she looked round to see if anyone was there, her heart missed a beat. Haydon was standing on the opposite side of the road looking towards her. It was the slight stoop of the shoulders that she recognised first, and the faded green T-shirt that confirmed that it was Haydon. Apart from that, he was unrecognisable. She just stared at him, as a slow but sure smile spread over his face. Its warmth reached her where she stood and her heart sang. She let out a joyous laugh, causing a passer-by to give her a quizzical look, which she didn't notice. She was too busy looking at a stunning young man who knew why she was laughing and was now joining in. She checked for cars and then crossed the road to stand inches away from him. Although she could still smell damp clothes, her eyes were feasting on one of the most beautiful men she had ever seen. He looked down at her as she studied his close-cropped hair, the shape of his head, his small ears and his beard, now trimmed to stubble, framing sensual lips and strong white teeth.

'Haydon Rouse, you look fucking amazing!' she announced, taking one of his hands and standing back, open-mouthed in amazement. She then inspected his hand. 'You've even had a manicure!'

Haydon nodded, apparently already comfortable with his new look and enjoying her attention.

'How do you feel?' she asked, suddenly aware that she was getting a bit carried away.

'Different,' he grinned, 'but nice. I didn't think I'd like it, but I do.'

Christie stretched up and kissed him gently on the cheek, making him blush and look around. No one was taking any notice; there was nothing unusual about two young people sharing a kiss. In fact, as they stood there, Haydon's neighbour, who had lived next door to him for years, walked straight past them.

'Hello, Mr Critchley,' said Haydon.

Mr Critchley nodded, looking slightly confused, and walked on, obviously having no idea how the young man with the pretty young girl had known his name.

Christie and Haydon looked at each other and laughed, a sound that Christie had not heard before and something that Haydon had not done for a long time.

'Come on!' she said, grabbing his hand once more. 'Let's go and celebrate.'

Chapter 12

Pete had just finished replacing a rotten window sill at the front of the house when Christie came home for lunch. She smiled at him as he stepped down into the little kitchen and went to wash his hands at the sink.

'Want one?' she enquired, indicating the ham and cheese toasties she was preparing.

'You bet!'

'I thought as much so I'm already making you one.'

'Thanks, love,' he said, pulling his daughter to him for a bear hug cuddle. 'What have you been up to this morning?'

'Funny you should ask, because that's just what I want to talk to you about.'

Pete picked up the hot sandwich Christie had put on a plate for him, and tentatively nibbled around the edge, being too hungry to wait for it to cool down. 'Go on,' he said, leaning against the kitchen worktop and noticing that she seemed nervous.

'You remember the other day we were talking about you needing help with the work on the cottage?'

Her father nodded.

'Well, I've spoken to my friend and he would like to help out. He needs to earn a bit of money, but won't expect a king's ransom.'

'Okay.' Pete still couldn't see why his daughter was so apprehensive.

'Thing is, Dad, he's a bit unusual in that he's never had a job before; he's lived pretty much as a recluse and hasn't really interacted with people for years.'

Her father nodded. 'He sounds like that chap your mum interviewed for the rat story,' he said between mouthfuls.

The look on Christie's face said it all.

'Oh my god! It's him, isn't it?'

Christie nodded and waited for his reaction. This was a significant moment for her. Her friendship with Haydon hadn't been something she had wanted to share with her family, until now. But Haydon needed to start working and she could not think of anyone better than her father to bring her fragile charge into the job world.

'Sweetheart, I don't know about this. This is our home and I'm not sure I want someone like this fellow around my family. You're all very precious and he could be dangerous.'

Christie sighed fractiously. 'Dad! You're no better than all those nasty people who judge and bully Haydon. He's odd. I know it and *he* knows it, for god sake, but he deserves a chance. He's as soft as anything – an innocent, really – and he's never been given a chance by anyone. I know most of it is his own fault but he's had a pretty sad life. How brill would it be if we could help him?'

'But honey, you hardly know him!'

'Actually, we've been friends for a while. I met him the first day we moved here, when he was warming up in the launderette.'

'Ha! Not washing his clothes, though!' Pete retorted cruelly. 'Sorry, pet,' he backtracked, seeing the look on his daughter's face. 'You've always been a soft touch when it comes to the underdog or the runt of the litter, and I can't help worrying that you're being taken advantage of.'

'Maybe I should have told you that I've been spending time with him most days since we moved here. It's been quite strange …' Christie desperately tried to find the words to explain how she felt compelled to help him get back into the outside world. 'At first, I just felt he needed me, but as I've got to know him I've grown really fond of him. Not in that way!' she exclaimed as her father's face registered horror. 'We're friends – I'm probably the only one he's ever had.'

 Her father continued to look concerned but he was still listening and hadn't outright refused to hire Haydon, so Christie decided to explain more and try to allay his fears; she could see how he might be getting the wrong end of the stick. 'Dad, I have no romantic interest in him. Haydon is damaged goods, but I've seen something else in him: a sensitive, intelligent person who simply "checked out" of society when he was abandoned by his mother. Instead of dumping his problems and issues on someone else, or the State, he fended for himself the best way he could. Yes, he's fallen into bad habits and he needs to clean up his act, to say the least, especially if he wants to be accepted by others, but he's a really interesting person under all that hair. He really is!' Feeling a rise of emotion, which was becoming a common occurrence where Haydon was concerned, she stopped talking and waited, anxiously biting her lip.

 Her father smiled and put his arm round her. 'Let's give it a go, then, shall we?'

 Christie looked up and saw what she knew Haydon had never seen: a loving look from a caring father.

 That afternoon, after running virtually all the way down the hill into the town and along into The Nip, she dashed in through the gate which creaked its usual welcome. 'Haydon!' she called as she pushed open the front door. 'Haydon!'

 Silence greeted her. The front door had been left unlocked which usually meant that Haydon was in the house somewhere, pottering in his garden or sitting at the table reading one of the old books he kept in a kitchen cupboard. But not today. Christie went to the foot of the uncarpeted stairs and called up. Getting no answer, she gingerly began to climb them, her heart, for some reason, suddenly beating so hard it was almost audible. To an accompaniment of ominously creaking boards, she reached the landing and stopped, just listening. A mechanic was attempting to start a car in the garage opposite; someone was whistling in a nearby garden; all seemed calm and ordinary. So why was she terrified that something was wrong? The stillness and silence of the cottage stood around her like a presence and she felt rooted to the spot, until she heard the unexpected sound of a mewing kitten coming from one of the two bedrooms. Did Haydon have a kitten? No, she would have known if he had. Maybe it had got into the house by accident and was trapped.

The sound stopped when she slowly inched the door open. The room was tiny and dim, the bright daylight being blocked by a dark blue roller blind. In one corner of the room there was a single bed on which was an untidy array of dirty blankets, strewn over a filthy, bare mattress; pictures of trains decorated the blue headboard; in another corner lay a pile of clothes. It smelt stale and damp, like Haydon's clothes, and she could see a large patch of damp above the window.

As she took in the squalor, she felt the now familiar warmth race through her body from her feet upwards. At the same time, she heard a loud and distinctive purr, although there was no cat in the room. As the heat travelled through her, Christie held onto the doorframe and closed her eyes, breathing through the sensation until a normal temperature returned. When she opened her eyes, the room was as it had been and the purring had stopped, but every nerve in her body was on edge. Not only was Haydon mysteriously missing, but someone or something was trying to communicate with her again. It had been weeks since she had felt the compulsion to write, but here it was again, both exciting and frightening her: was she going to find out something about Haydon that she would rather not know? The urge was pressing, so she knew she would have to respond to it soon.

She would not normally pry, but without thinking she crossed the tiny landing and opened the other bedroom door, and gasped. Like the two rooms downstairs, the contrast between the bedrooms could not have been more vivid. Closed pink curtains matched the colour of the candlewick bedspread on the double bed, where lacy white cushions lay in a tidy arrangement. The thick, pink carpet looked as though it had been recently brushed, and a dark pink rug bordered the foot of the bed. A rose fragrance added to the femininity of the room, and the dressing table housed neatly placed bottles of perfume together with a series of silver framed photographs of a little, dark- haired boy. Christie stepped over to a large white wardrobe and opened the doors to reveal a full rack of women's clothes. She turned and opened the top draw of a pine dresser, finding it full of underwear and night dresses, and each drawer was the same – crammed with clothes.

She stood back and looked around with mounting fear: this room was not that of someone who had packed up and left; it looked as though the owner had left it that morning and would soon be returning. Her father's words replayed in her mind: *But honey, you hardly know him.* He was right. How could she have been so stupid as to take Haydon at face value? Even as she gave vent to her anxiety, the purring started again and with it, the heat in her body. She felt her head was going to explode and sank to her knees on the soft carpet until it passed, at which point it was as if someone cloaked her in a mantle of love. She felt safe and at peace, and knew that everything was all right.

A noise downstairs pulled her back into everyday reality. Haydon. Oh no! He would think she had been snooping! *Well, you have, haven't you?* she reproached herself. Quietly shutting the door behind her, she made her way downstairs.

'Oh! You made me jump!' he said. 'I didn't see you follow me in.'

She was surprised anew at the difference in him. He was wearing a different T-shirt – a bright red one with blue piping – and glowed with health. 'I didn't. I was upstairs. I got here a little while ago and was looking for you; I was worried about you.'

'Oh,' he said, apparently unconcerned that she might have been in the pink bedroom. 'I went to the charity shop at the top of the high street and bought this,' he informed her, proudly pointing to his T-shirt. 'What do you think?'

'It's great!' she laughed, relieved that he was all right and that normality seemed to have returned to her world.

'And these, too.' He upended a carrier bag over the table and two more T-shirts, a pair of jeans and a sweatshirt fell out.

Christie was pleasantly surprised by the new attitude emerging with his new persona. He bore little comparison to the strange, animal-like individual she had met in the launderette. Nevertheless, there was a huge cloud now hanging over their friendship, sullying her enjoyment of the moment, and she knew she would have to speak with him about it, but not right away. She did not want to spoil his excitement, plus she needed some time to get her thoughts together about the strange experiences she'd just had in the rooms upstairs. Added to that was the need to write, which was drawing her back home so that she could sit in the quiet of her own room and allow words to travel through her onto the page. She had no idea what these outpourings were all about but she had a strong feeling that all would become clear at some point. In the meantime, just as Haydon was trusting her, she was going to have to trust that whoever was speaking through her had good reason for doing so, and that she was doing the right thing by cooperating. She quickly told Haydon about working for her dad and said they could go and meet her family after six o'clock, when they would be home; she would come and get him. Haydon looked apprehensive, and at the sight of a shadow clouding his previously delighted face, Christie could not help but hug him. He didn't respond, and Christie wondered if he had forgotten how.

Leaving Haydon to the rest of his day, she was walking down the path when a tall, grey-haired man opened the gate and came into Haydon's garden, smiling sweetly at her.

'Hello there!' he said, a white dog collar marking him as a vicar. 'And who have we here, visiting our Haydon?'

'I'm Christie, a friend of his,' she smiled.

'Really? He hasn't mentioned a pretty friend like you.'

Christie was sure he meant well, despite the patronising tone, which she assumed probably went with the territory. 'He's at home. I think you may notice a bit of a change,' she said mischievously, giving the kindly vicar one of her most endearing smiles as she continued on her way.

Diane had come home early from work, having put in several twelve hour days working on the story Brian had given her. As it had gained momentum there had been copious research to do and many interviews, and now it would be breaking first thing on the Thursday morning, when the local paper was printed; it would no doubt be featured on the local evening news, as well.

Eyes closed, she was relaxing in the shade of the patio umbrella in their miniscule yard, her feet up on the chair opposite and her head against the whitewashed wall, as she let her mind wander where it would. She had enjoyed the work challenge and it had taken her mind off the girly crush she had on Brian. There were times when it seemed that he was attracted to her, but they were fleeting moments and she was aware that, in her present frame of mind, she could easily have imagined them. She did not want to make a fool of herself, so she was intent on keeping any romantic fantasy to herself.

She wondered about other women her age. Did they also have imaginary relationships with their bosses, a friend's husband or the gardener? Was it normal? Her marriage to Pete was comfortable and she would not swap it for the world, but she longed for a bit of excitement. She remembered back to the early days of past relationships: not being able to sleep for dreaming about the latest handsome face; not being able to eat and jumping every time the phone rang, hoping it would be him but not knowing what to say if it was. Now she was a mature, professional woman with two grown children and a solid, dependable husband. Fluttering, heart racing moments were just sweet memories – but how she craved them!

'You all right, love? You're home early.' Pete came in through the side gate and put a bag on the table. 'Some walnut cake from Rosie. She said we're welcome to it because there's always too much for the two of them.'

Even though he was shrouded by the bright sky behind him, Diane could see that he was pink faced and slightly flustered. 'I wondered where you were,' she said evenly, ignoring the cake. 'The house was all left open.'

'I know. I just popped over there for a couple of minutes. I've been busy painting the frames at the front this afternoon.'

Diane sat up straight, alarm bells beginning to jangle, questions clamouring for answers. Was she missing something here? Had she been paying too much attention to the man at work and neglecting the one at home? Pete was vulnerable to the advances of needy women, especially when he was low or stressed himself. She knew the pain of an unfaithful husband. 'Why did you go over there, Pete?' she asked, watching his face, trying to read him.

He looked her straight in the eye. 'For a cup of tea, Di, that's all. Seriously, love, there's nothing to worry about.'

She nodded and sighed. 'I know, but you're a sucker for a damsel in distress, aren't you? Just be careful, Pete, please.'

Pete gave her a reassuring nod and went into the kitchen to pour them both large glasses of wine.

'Bit early for this, isn't it?' she grinned, when he returned and handed her one, from which she immediately took a substantial sip. 'So, tell me about your day,' she invited.

Only too happy to be off the subject of Rosie, he related everything their daughter had said about her friendship with the town recluse and her suggestion that he give Haydon some work.

Diane laughed despite an underlying concern for Christie. 'That's typical of her! Do you remember when she befriended that little gipsy girl in primary school because she was getting bullied? And that time she visited old Mr Hope, daily, until he was back on his feet again? I actually think she drove him crazy! She's a born carer, that one. I'm a bit worried she'll get hurt, though. I don't mean physically – from what I've seen of Haydon Rouse, he's harmless enough – but you know how emotionally entangled she can get.'

Pete nodded, thoughtfully twisting the stem of his wine glass and staring at the light patterns it made on the white wall. 'What should we do?'

'Well, nothing. She's a grown woman so she has to make her own decisions and mistakes. We'll always be here for her but it's her life – her friendship. Have you seen him?'

'I think I got a glimpse of him a while ago down by the edge of the pier. It was early in the morning, no one else around, the tide was out and he was collecting driftwood. I watched him for a while and thought him a bit odd, given that it was warm and he was wearing some kind of parker.'

'That sounds like him,' said Diane, stretching her legs out to the sun. 'How old do you think he is?'

Pete drew his breath in through pursed lips as he cast his mind back and considered. 'Difficult to tell with all that hair. Forty five? Fifty?'

'Try twenty nine!'

Pete's expression matched his astonishment. 'Twenty nine! You're kidding me!'

'Nope. He's twenty nine, Pete. Actually, when you're up close you can see it, if you can make out his face under the grime.'

Pete considered this in silence whilst draining his glass. At least if Haydon was working for him, he could keep an eye on him. Christie might be all grown up, but he was her father and that meant life long protection as far as he was concerned.

Christie's mind was racing as she marched up the hill, alongside the cliff edge towards the bend in the road that took her home. The urge to write was burning inside her and she had mixed feelings about what she may find out. Without intending to, she had allowed her compassion for Haydon to begin developing into something deeper. It had hit her the moment she saw him standing on the opposite side of the road, all young, fresh and gorgeous. The idea of Haydon being gorgeous had not figured in her perception of him, until the sight of him had got her pulses racing.

It was like everything else about this situation: things didn't fit, or make sense. There were the peculiar sensations she'd experienced while she was in his house; there was his mother's bedroom, so pristine and polished when his was nothing more than a dirty hovel. And why was the vicar paying a visit? Was that a regular occurrence? It was all so confusing as to be exhausting, including the overwhelming eagerness to get to her laptop and allow the words to flow.

She ran up the stairs to her room, closed the door and drew the curtains to cool the room before switching on her laptop. While she sat on her bed, breathing slowly to calm the turbulence inside her, it hummed to life and obligingly settled its booting up on a blank Word document. That was odd, she thought to herself, dismissing the idea as soon as it entered her head – everything was odd so why should it surprise her that her laptop seemed to know what she wanted to do on it?

The words came like cool rain on a muggy day and as she wrote, so her mind started to calm and a feeling of ease came over her.

You know, my darling, the love of a mother is like no other: it is unconditional, unbreakable. The love we feel for our chosen partners in life is often transient. It can feel all consuming, passionate like fire and never ending, but on another day it can seem lifeless and no longer wanted. The love of a mother for her child, however, never ends, whatever the circumstances.

Bringing a new life into this world is the most precious gift imaginable and neither distance nor time can quench the binding flame of love that exists. To be separated from that love may shroud the feelings that lie deep inside, but the cords of that unique connection can never be broken – bent, stretched and twisted, yes; but never broken.

You must feel that my darling, surely you do, wherever you are. You must feel the magnetism drawing you back along those cords. It cannot be fought or ignored forever, my love. The hold between mother and child is eternal. I know this.

I know you are out there, my darling, and we wait for a sign of your presence amongst us. It is time now. We watch and wait, ready to embrace you.

Abruptly, Christie stopped, suddenly aware of the sound of purring hammering in her ears. Warm fur brushed against her naked ankles, but she didn't look down: she knew that nothing was there. The purring ceased as soon as it had begun.

Her eyes skimmed the words she had written that had not come from her imagination, and she sighed. There was so much she needed to talk to Haydon about. She could deal with her feelings for him, complicated though they were; it was this extra dimension – this third being in their relationship – that on the one hand seemed completely fanciful, and on the other, a burden that felt monumental. She looked up from her laptop and stared emptily into space. How could she cope? How could she find the strength to carry this through, whatever 'this' was? Would she crumple and fail? Just as she felt about to disappear into a pool of panic and helplessness, the purring started again; at the same time the heat rose in her body and she was reminded that she was not alone. Someone was guiding and protecting her; all she needed to do was trust.

She heard her mother calling that the tea was ready and was glad of the mundane interruption. She ran down the stairs and settled herself in her usual place at the table, facing James.

'Where's Dad?' she asked.

'He's outside, just finishing off something that can't be left,' said her mother. 'He tells me you know Haydon Rouse. Why have you never said?'

'I've had stuff on my mind,' Christie said evasively, 'and we're all so busy.'

Diane let that go, for the moment. 'And you want Dad to hire Haydon to help him with this work on the house,' she said, as they all helped themselves from a plate piled high with sandwiches.

'It makes sense, Mum. Dad needs help and Haydon needs work.'

James looked at his sister over the top of his mug of tea. 'He's the guy I saw you with a few weeks ago, isn't he?'

'I expect so,' nodded Christie. 'To be honest, so much has happened since then that I can hardly remember one day from the next. It's been a bit of a roller coaster ride.'

'Christie, I'm really not sure about this.' Diane had been mulling things over and although she felt sorry for Haydon's plight, she did not feel at all comfortable about bringing him into her home. For a start, he looked such a mess and didn't smell too good either.

Christie's eyes rose to the ceiling and she sighed. 'Mum, Haydon has spent his whole life being judged by other people, and you've just gone and done exactly the same thing. Look, I've got to know him quite well. He's making changes and he's ready to take the big step of getting a job of some description. How is he going to do that if no one will give him a chance?' She looked from her mother's face to her brother's, seeing anxiety on the one, mild amusement on the other.

'I vote we give him a chance,' announced James.

Christie smiled gratefully.

Diane sighed in resignation. 'Okay, okay, I give in! We'll give him a chance, but if anything goes wrong, Christie, you'll have to deal with the fall out. Agreed?'

Christie stood up to give her mum a hug. 'Agreed!' she said in triumph.

As arranged, Christie arrived at Haydon's cottage shortly after six that evening. She found him sitting nervously at his kitchen table and again wondered whether he was going to back out. She also marvelled, all over again, at the physical change in him and had to remind herself that this was the same ramshackle individual who had shuffled into her life just weeks previously. Each time she saw him, now, she noticed deep, sensual eyes and a mouth that she could imagine kissing. Her attraction to him was growing from all different angles, which was exhilarating, but was it, she wondered, wise. And then he smiled at her and she melted. Laughing at her own misgivings, she held out her hand to him.

'Come on, then! Let's go!'

They were all waiting in the sitting room with the television burbling away in the corner, no one really watching it. Diane had made a pot of tea and it sat under its cosy on the coffee table, awaiting the guest's arrival. She jumped when she heard the back door open, and when Christie walked in with a young man following closely behind her, she frowned in confusion: this was not Haydon Rouse – it couldn't be. But then she looked more closely, saw the large brown eyes and recognised with astonishment the man she had interviewed.

James was equally puzzled, at first, as he had seen the tramp-like character out and about in the town on a number of occasions. He soon clued in, however, to the fact that Christie had obviously tidied him up a bit – or a lot, actually – and James was impressed. He admired the close cropped beard and sharply styled hair. He certainly was a 'looker'! Who would have thought such a transformation could take place? He looked like a different man altogether.

Pete was the only one who hadn't seen Haydon close up before. He stood up and offered his hand to Haydon. Shaking hands was not something Haydon was accustomed to and he looked to Christie, who nodded encouragement, as he uncertainly took Pete's hand.

'Nice to meet you, Haydon,' Pete said, breaking the silence. 'Come and have a seat.'

Haydon sat down next to James and gave both him and Diane a small smile and a nod as he did so. Having recovered from the shock of seeing such a different Haydon, Diane smiled warmly at him and offered him some tea. As she poured, she sent Christie a dagger of a look that said: *Why didn't you warn me?* She was answered with a bright smile and raised eyebrows.

'Christie tells us that you're looking for work and she thought you may like to get some experience working with her father,' said Diane when everyone was settled with cups of tea.

'Yes, that would be nice. Thank you.' It was the first time he had spoken and he looked at Christie as he did so, as though he was drawing strength from her. Diane noticed this and hoped that the pressure that this man was putting on Christie wasn't too much for her. Looking at her daughter's face, however, she could see that she was not just helping Haydon out of the kindness of her heart: she had true feelings for him. That worried Diane even more.

Chapter 13

Someone whose voice he recognised was calling his name. Hands were touching him, making sense of his life. There was a face – such a familiar face. The voice was reaching in even as the hands were receding in the strange netherworld between sleeping and waking. James reached for them, reached for that feeling of wholeness and safety they had given him, trying to hold onto it as his eyelids fluttered open.

  The morning sun was shining through a gap in the curtains and throwing splashes of gold across James' tiny room as he reluctantly woke up, realising that he had been dreaming about Vince again – Vince, who had promised to keep in touch, and hadn't. Had he ever believed that Vince would keep that promise? Not really. He had not wasted his days waiting for the phone to ring or looking for an email like a love-sick schoolgirl. Vince had left and James had moved on. But there were times when his subconscious allowed him to wallow in that most perfect of nights when his life had changed forever.

  'James! James! Wake up, mate!'

  The intrusive voice was coming from the street and James sat up, feeling for his phone on the bedside table to check the time. Eight thirty. Lurching to the foot of his bed, he pulled the curtains back and peered out. Ollie was standing on the doorstep of the house opposite, waving and just holding a towel rather than his usual collection of surfing gear.

  'Coming for a swim?'

James nodded and gave Ollie the thumbs up sign before he swung his feet to the floor, where they landed on yesterday's shorts and T-shirt which lay limp and uninviting with most of his other clothes. Within minutes, he had washed, closed the front door behind him and was walking towards the beach and an embracing swim with Ollie. Rather than turning right to go towards the town and the harbour, however, Ollie led James in the opposite direction. They passed a collection of cottages of all shapes and sizes, all wedged onto the cliff face. A sturdy wall, facing them on the opposite side of the road, gave way to metal steps that zig-zagged down to the sandy beach below. The tide, made choppy by the Atlantic breeze, was coming in and half way down the steps a red warning flag was indicating that it was not safe to swim.

'Ollie?' said James, pointing to it as it flapped in the wind. Ollie shrugged and remained unperturbed, so James assumed that, as he virtually lived in the sea, he must know what he was doing. In no time at all they had flung their towels and T-shirts onto the ledge that ran along the length of the sea wall, and were running wildly into the surf, laughing and screeching as the freezing water met their warm skin.

Ollie immediately swam strongly out away from the beach. James was following, although not feeling quite so confident, when he felt a tugging sensation on his ankles, and then his calves and knees. He tried to shout out, but salt water immediately filled his mouth and deprived him of breath. His body began spinning out of control as his arm was dragged to one side and his legs felt like they were being twisted and turned. He tried to clear his lungs but it seemed that every time he coughed, more water filled his windpipe. Panic and helplessness enveloped him as, once more, his arm was twisted from under him. By now, he had lost all sense of direction and could see neither the beach nor the horizon, let alone Ollie. His world became cold, menacing and completely fluid as he got weaker and more resigned to his fate. All became quiet, complete calm and serenity came over him, fighting whatever was trying to claim him seemed pointless and unnecessary, and he ceased struggling, surrendering to a soft, engulfing blackness.

'James! James!'
There is was again: the voice that had started his day.
'Fuck! James, you moron! For fuck sake! James!'
He opened his eyes to blinding brightness. He could just make out the shape of a head with a body attached, looming over him. As his eyes adjusted, the face became clearer and he could distinguish the handsome, tanned features of Ollie blocking the glare of the sun. Coughing, he sat bolt upright and vomited salt water that burnt the back of his throat.

'Shit, man!... Shit, James!... I thought you'd bought it!... Christ!' Ollie was kneeling beside him, his hands on his knees, dripping wet and panting like a thirsty dog on a hot day.

James struggled to take it all in. What had just happened? He just sat looking at Ollie, who was obviously distressed and suddenly flung his arms round James' neck, hugging his thin body against tanned Cornish skin.

'I thought you'd fucking died, man,' he choked, continuing to hold James close.

James was enjoying the feel of Ollie so close to him when another wave of vomiting put an end to the emotional embrace. Ollie sat back on his haunches and wiped tears from his wet face, laughing at the ridiculous scene they were creating, before standing up, grabbing James' towel and wrapping it round his friend's bony shoulders. 'I should never have let you come in with me. You were so close to copping it out there. I'm a fucking idiot.'

James patted Ollie's forearm. 'My choice Ollie.' His voice was scratchy and thin, and it hurt to speak. 'What happened? It felt like someone was dragging my arms and legs and whipping them round. It felt like someone was trying to drown me.'

'That, my friend, was the current. It's a killer. I'm used to it but it got hold of you and you panicked. That's when it can all go horribly wrong.' Ollie shook his head and looked down at his hands on his knees. 'God, I feel terrible! I'm so sorry, man! I'm so sorry!'

'So that's why the red flag flies: to stop idiots like me drowning.' Even in his distressed state, James could not help but notice the intensity and beauty of Ollie's dark eyes. He felt stirrings but looked away before things became too awkward; this was something he didn't know how to handle.

'Come on,' said Ollie, jumping up like a young gazelle. 'Let's go and get some breakfast. We need to get you warm, though. Shall we go back to your house?'

James nodded. The house had been empty when he left and would be still as his dad was working on a new shop front in the town, and he remembered his mum talking the night before about going with Christie into Hayle, where Christie had a job interview. 'I can get us some tea and toast,' he offered as they slowly made their way back up the steps, passing the flapping red flag on their way.

Pete could feel someone watching him as he worked and, sure enough, when he turned to look, Haydon was sitting on the harbour wall quietly observing his soon-to-be boss. Pete wiped his hands on an old cloth tucked into his belt and looked back at Haydon, who carried on his silent vigil. Pete was mystified by the sad recluse. Working with him was likely to be awkward with communication being difficult. The meeting the previous evening had been brief, even pleasant, but Christie had done most of the talking for Haydon, who had seemed happy to just sit and watch her animated face as she chattered on nervously. They had left together after half an hour, and Christie had returned home a couple of hours later. Pete wondered how far their relationship had gone, but he quickly dismissed the thought; it was not the sort of thing a father liked to contemplate in relation to his daughter.

He felt uncomfortable just carrying on with his work knowing that Haydon was staring at him so he called over, 'Fancy giving me a hand?' and was astounded at the broad grin that broke out on Haydon's face, transforming it.

Haydon jumped down off the wall and walked over to Pete with his hands firmly planted in his back pockets, as though he didn't quite know what to do with them. He really was like an awkward teenager. Pete patted him on the back in a fatherly fashion and guided him over to the shop front, gave him a piece of sandpaper and a block of wood, and showed him how to gently rub down the peeling paint on the window frame.

The two men worked quietly together, Pete keeping a close eye on Haydon. He was pleasantly surprised at the care and skill with which Haydon worked, and he could see the pleasure Haydon was getting out of such a simple task; he wished Christie could be there to see it.

An hour later, Pete left Haydon working on the door frame while he went off to the baker's on the corner to get two large pasties, one of which he offered to Haydon on his return. Wiping his hands on his trousers, Haydon looked at the hot pasty with hungry eyes and hesitantly reached for it, like a cautious animal. He nodded and quietly thanked Pete, the first words he had said to him all morning. They sat side by side on the harbour wall, looking out across the tops of the colourful little fishing boats to the restaurants and market stalls on the opposite side. Pete wanted to make conversation, but Christie had said that it would take a while for Haydon to start to talk freely; it was a matter of trust, she had said, so Pete just chewed amicably and waited.

'Do you always work on your own?'

It was a simple question, asked in barely above a whisper, but it nevertheless startled Pete.

He turned to look at Haydon, who promptly looked at his pasty, apparently embarrassed, so Pete just talked about his life in Manchester, the people who used to work for him, the vans they used to drive around in, the house that he had provided for his family and the fact that everything was lost when the business failed. For some reason, he found it easy to talk to Haydon, who sat eating his pasty and occasionally looked up to meet Pete's glance with a nod. He realised that it was the most he had said to anyone about his previous life since he had moved to this peculiar little place. He felt cleansed and calm.

Without a word, Haydon suddenly hopped off the wall and disappeared along the road. Pete was mystified and slightly miffed: he couldn't have that if Haydon was going to work for him; he'd have to speak to him about it. But then as he readied himself to carry on working, he spotted Haydon approaching with two steaming cups of tea he must have bought from the supermarket.

'No sugar,' he said, handing one to Pete.

Pete raised his eyebrows in surprise. 'That's right. How did you know?'

'I watch everything,' Haydon confessed, setting down his cup and picking up his sandpaper.

Christie had been pleased to get an interview and she was happy with how it had gone, even though working as a bank teller was not her idea of an ideal job. But that would come eventually, she was sure, and everyone always said it was easier to get another job if you were in employment rather than out of it, so, if she got this job, she would have made a good move in the right direction.

As she approached the coffee house she could see her mother sitting waiting for her as arranged. She had her netbook open and her phone pressed to her ear, having, it seemed, a somewhat difficult conversation. Christie slid into the seat opposite and waited for the call to finish. The fact that her mother looked strained and tired triggered Christie's concern about the long hours her mother had been working, lately, without even getting paid any extra. Although, given the situation, she knew her parents had to make sacrifices, for the time being, and she sighed, knowing her mother was just doing her part.

'Well?' Diane closed her phone, smiled and peered expectantly into her daughter's face.

Christie laughed. 'Yes, it went well, Mum. I don't think it could have gone any better, so we'll see. It's not really what I want, though. I'm good with words – not numbers. But it's a start and getting interview experience is always good.'

'Absolutely right! So now it's time for a little treat. What would you like?'

Christie glanced at the menu. 'Elderflower water and a piece of apple cake, with cream please,' she grinned.

Diane grinned back. 'I'll have the same,' she said, beckoning to a waitress.

'Do you think Haydon will be all right working with Dad?' Christie asked as soon as the waitress left with their order. Now that it was all out in the open, she was eager to talk about her concern for the strange friend she had unexpectedly made.

'Well, I can't think of anyone more patient than your dad.'

Christie nodded in agreement. 'You're right. Dad's the perfect first boss for Haydon, so I hope it works out.'

Diane decided to come straight out with the question that had been playing on her mind.

'Chris, what is your relationship with him?'

Christie frowned, annoyed at her mother's intrusiveness.

'Don't look all affronted, darling,' Diane continued. 'I know you're a grown woman and it's not really any of my business, but I'm concerned for you. If I understand how you feel about him I can support you both more. He's just not the most obvious choice I would have made for you, that's all.'

Christie sighed loudly and sat back with her arms folded protectively across her chest, letting her gaze drift out of the window. How could she explain her feelings for Haydon to her mother when she didn't understand them herself? How could she say: 'Well Mum, at first I thought he was a drunk, then a ghost, then a tramp, then a mad person; and then I started to get to know him and I thought he was a sad, lost soul; and then I saw how he lived and how resourceful he was; and then he scrubbed up and I started to fancy him; and now I think I may be falling for him.' She couldn't, she decided, looking back at her mother. 'It's complicated, Mum,' she said.

'You do have feelings for him though, don't you?'

She nodded, relieved to see their cake and drinks arriving to interrupt a conversation she was now finding uncomfortable.

Diane accepted Christie's evasiveness, knowing she had no choice if she did not want to alienate her daughter. It was more important to her that Christie felt she could come and talk to her parents if she needed to. 'Well, why not take things slowly and see what transpires,' she said with a smile, digging into her cake and making appreciative noises.

The full shock of what had happened to him had not hit James until he was sitting in the kitchen, sharing a pile of buttered toast with Ollie. All of a sudden he had started to shiver and feel nauseous, prompting a worried Ollie to immediately put more sugar in James' tea and encourage him to sip it. Eventually the shaking had subsided, to be replaced by overwhelming tiredness, and James had just wanted his bed and sleep. Ollie, still visibly upset, had not wanted to leave him on his own, but James had insisted, assuring him that he would be fine, until Ollie had reluctantly left.

Waking around lunch time, feeling a lot better, James lay thinking more about Ollie than his own potentially fatal mishap. He was powerfully attracted to the young Cornishman but inexperience prevented him from knowing whether or not his feelings were reciprocated. *Could* Ollie be interested in him? From his reaction to Christie, James had assumed Ollie was straight, but, thinking back, that was the only time Ollie had shown any interest in the opposite sex.

Closing his eyes, James relived their embrace on the beach, skin against skin, asking himself if the ferocity of Ollie's affection was just relief that James was alive, or the beginning of something deeper than friendship between them. Finding no answer, he finally exhaled through puffed cheeks, ran his hands through his light brown hair and got up to look at himself in the mirror hanging on the wall at a slightly crooked angle. Weeks of being out in the Cornish sun and wind had turned his skin a pleasing caramel colour, and his face, which had been pimply and pale in Manchester, was now smooth. His blue eyes sparkled as he smiled at his reflection and judged himself to be not bad looking.

'Your dad's working at the art shop on the corner of Pepper Street. Shall we park down in the town and go and find him?'

Christie nodded, her attention on the passing countryside as her mother drove towards the south coast and home. They had passed a pleasant few hours shopping and Christie had been pleased to see her mother unwind and relax, happily chatting about the possibilities if Christie were to be selected for the position at the bank. Although she was looking forward to entering the world of full time work for the first time, on the drive home Christie's mind reverted back to Haydon, feeling she already had a full time occupation helping him adjust to the outside world.

The town was busy, as usual, with tourists ambling up and down the two streets that bordered the harbour, yet it was unlike anywhere else Christie had been: a deeply relaxed atmosphere was all-pervasive amongst workers and holidaymakers alike. Porthtreval held a special magic; she could feel it and it felt like home.

Having found a parking spot, they were making their way to Pepper Street when Christie spotted the grey-haired vicar she had met at Haydon's cottage. She guessed him to be well into his eighties and admired how tall and straight he was, with his air of gravity and calm. He caught Christie's eye as they passed and gave her a small smile, a hint of a nod and a look that seemed to intimate that they shared a secret. Taken aback, Christie wondered why she should have intuited that from him, and then promptly forgot about it as she caught sight of her father in the street, hands on hips, looking back into the building where he had been working. As she got nearer, she could see that he was talking to someone who was closer to the shop window and currently blocked from view by throngs of holiday makers. Then she saw that it was Haydon, covered in dust, smiling back at her father. Her heart jumped in her chest and she felt herself blush.

'Well, hello you two!' Diane called. 'Haydon! Have you started already?'

Haydon stepped back with his usual uncertainty and nodded as his eyes went to Christie. She smiled shyly at him, aware of awkwardness now between them, as though their relationship had transcended friendship and moved into something deeper but as yet unclear. Whilst Pete showed Diane the work that he would be doing inside the shop, Christie had the chance to speak to Haydon alone.

'How did this happen?' she asked, indicating the newly rubbed down paintwork.

'I don't know really. Your dad just asked if I wanted to help, so here I am. He bought me a pasty and I bought him tea. He's nice, Christie. You're really lucky.'

Christie nodded and smiled. Although it had not been discussed, as far as she was aware Haydon didn't know his father.

It was one of the many subjects they had not talked about and the complexity of them made Christie's young head spin.

Her parents re-emerged from the coolness of the art shop and it was obviously time to let the men get on with their work.

'I'll come round tonight and we'll go for a walk, shall we?' she suggested to Haydon, who nodded. 'Oh, and I'll bring Dad's beard trimmer so you can keep this under control,' she added, affectionately grasping hold of his chin.

Diane and Pete exchanged glances, but said nothing.

Chapter 14

That evening over tea, Pete was full of praise for Haydon and the care he took with his work. 'He's not the fastest, I'll grant you that,' he said between mouthfuls of shepherd's pie, 'but he's thorough and I'd rather that than speed any day. He needs to get the electricity back on in his house, though,' he advised looking directly at his daughter. 'He hasn't had electricity in there for ten years or so, apparently. God knows how he's managed.'

'Could you help him with that, Dad?'

'He'll have to pay for the reconnection, and an electrician will need to check the wiring and so on.' Seeing Christie's worried expression, he smiled encouragingly. 'I'll go down at the weekend and have a look and we'll go from there.'

'Thanks, Dad,' she said, relieved to be able to share some of the burden that was Haydon with her family.

'What does he eat? Does he have any money?' asked Diane.

Christie nodded. 'His mum put quite a lot of money in his savings account, apparently, and every now and then she puts more in. He doesn't spend much, though, not knowing if she'll continue to do that.' She put her knife and fork down. 'You know, he's still waiting for her to come home!' she burst out.

Her family stared at her, waiting to hear more.

'Her room is still as she left it,' she continued. 'Haydon must look after it because it's clean and tidy. Her clothes and everything are still there, which makes me think she didn't plan to leave him, and I'm wondering if something may have happened to her. But then she still gives him money so she must be all right. It's all very confusing and just so sad: he's had no one and has spent all that time alone, waiting for her to come back.' Christie could not hold back the tears and covered her face as pent up emotion overwhelmed her.

'Hey, hey, sweetheart, don't upset yourself,' said Diane, getting up to go and comfort her. 'He's okay now, isn't he? Things are getting better. He's just got some catching up to do, but he seems perfectly capable of doing that. Maybe he just needed a friend like you to help him move on from that place of sadness. Don't you think so, Pete?'

'Definitely,' said Pete, patting Christie's hand. He was happy to help out with the practicalities of Haydon's life, but he wasn't sure how to handle this outburst.

James just carried on eating; he had other things on his mind and wasn't overly interested in his sister's strange relationship with the odd guy who lived without electricity.

Having shared some of her feelings and being more at ease with her involvement in Haydon's complicated life, Christie searched out her father's beard trimmer and made her way to Haydon's cottage, where she found him washing at the kitchen sink. His T-shirt was draped over the back of one of the kitchen chairs and his pale skin glinted with soap and water as he rinsed around his neck and chest. Leaning against the back door, she chatted about her job interview, as if seeing him half naked for the first time was the most natural thing in the world.

Then came the beard trimming. He left his shirt off and sat on the edge of the kitchen table so that Christie could reach, and then he watched her face intently as she worked out how to attach the plastic guard to the trimmer and switch it on to the right speed. She could feel a current of energy between them, and a level of excitement she had not experienced before; she felt flushed, slightly giddy and certainly aroused. She had enjoyed a few sexual encounters during the three years at university, and there had been someone special for almost a year – a music student a year ahead of her – with whom she had learned about young love and intimacy. That had fallen apart when he had gone to work in Essex after graduating, and Christie had been philosophical about it, concluding it was not meant to be.

With Haydon, however, as they stood face to face in the quiet of the little yellow kitchen, there was no comparison with anything that had gone before. There was a communion between them that was not about experience or permission: it was simply to do with instinct and the spiritual need that seemed to link them. Christie's pulse was racing and she saw Haydon's breath quicken as she moved closer and he spread his legs slightly apart so that she could position herself directly in front of him. His hypnotic gaze did not move from her eyes as she switched on the trimmer, placed a steadying hand on his face and slowly ran the vibrating machine across his cheek and chin with small downwards movements. Had he ever been this close to a woman before, she wondered, as his eyes moved to her mouth. She glanced at the tiny specks of hair that had fallen onto his bare chest, aware of his breath on her face, and as she tipped his head back to trim under his chin and down onto his neck, she noticed his eyes close. The whole process had become seductive; she knew they were both aroused by the intimacy of what she was doing. It was difficult to focus as she trimmed the other side of his face and finally moved to his top lip, which hardly needed any attention, but she still took her time over it, not wanting to stop touching him. She knew he was aroused and she shared his now almost palpable heat.

She put the trimmer down but remained standing between his legs, unwilling to draw back, locked in a burning visual embrace. This was their moment and she knew she would have to initiate whatever came next. How would he react? Slowly she raised her hands and placed them on his chest, intimately, delicately, without impropriety. Haydon drew in his breath at her touch, momentarily closed his eyes, and then looked back at her, opening his mouth slightly as his breathing became more urgent. A tiny moan escaped his lips as her palms brushed over his nipples, and Christie could wait no longer. Cupping his handsome face in her hands, she moved closer and brought her lips towards his. He tipped his head to one side to meet them. Heat propelled her as she ran her fingers through his hair and slowly parted her lips, feeling an inward groan of pleasure as Haydon let nature take its course, opened his mouth and entered hers with his tongue. She responded by massaging his tongue around and around with her own, and he finally put his hands on her hips and pulled her to him. His excitement was delicious to her as she felt him revelling in feelings new to him. When they broke from the kiss, Haydon held her fast against his body, at which Christie breathed in deeply, closed her eyes and tipped her head back, exposing her neck for him to kiss as he ran his hands across her back and buttocks. Once again, he brought his lips to her mouth and her lips played over his as she teased him with the tip of her tongue, smiling as she enjoyed every moment of his induction.

Leaning back from him, she looked into his face, so alive and beautiful, the care-worn and weary, grey shadow of a man, now gone. 'Well, this is nice,' she smiled, and was treated to the rare event of a beaming grin in return.

But that was all. Haydon was clearly in no mood for talking. Reaching behind her head, he gently pulled Christie's face to his and continued his exploration.

Twenty minutes later they were walking hand in hand up the hill towards the quiet of the lake. They drew little attention because few people in the town knew that Haydon had undergone a physical transformation; all they saw was a young couple, like any other, out enjoying the summer evening.

As they passed the pub, Christie heard someone calling her name and looked around, searching the faces for one she recognised. A waving arm turned into Ollie, who was pushing his way through the crowd on the pub patio.

'Oh, hi, Ollie! Good to see you. Is James with you?'

'No,' he said, casting a brief glance at Haydon, who still had a long way to go when it came to being sociable: he had walked over to a nearby wall and hitched himself up to watch proceedings from a safe distance. Ollie nodded to him but Haydon just stared back.

Christie decided not to complicate matters by introducing them or trying to draw Haydon into the conversation. Whether or not Ollie recognized the new Haydon, she didn't know, and it mattered not, since Ollie's attention was firmly back on her.

'No, it was James I wanted to ask you about,' he said. 'Is he okay?'

'Yes, of course. Why?'

'Oh, no reason,' said Ollie, realising that perhaps James did not want his family to know about the near death experience on the beach that morning. 'I just didn't manage to catch up with him as planned and wondered if everything was okay.'

'Well, he certainly looked okay when I saw him earlier on this evening. Why don't you go and find him? I think he's at home. Our broadband is all fixed up now so he's probably chatting to some geek somewhere.'

'Maybe I'll do that,' said Ollie. 'Have a nice evening,' he added with a small wave as he backed away.

'You too.'

Christie walked towards Haydon and he fell into step beside her, slipping his hand around hers. Ollie watched them, wondering who the guy was, but then remembering that James had said she had a boyfriend. *Shame*, he thought, as he watched them disappear around the corner, *she's a really nice looking girl*.

As Christie and Haydon carried on towards the lake, she glanced at his silent profile and saw a striking, fascinating, almost brooding man – someone with a strange past and an unplanned future. She tried to imagine how he was feeling. He had more colour in his cheeks than before, but the individual air that sometimes made him impossible to read was still there, even though, in the blink of an eye, he could then look so vulnerable. Nevertheless, his response to her in the kitchen, when all inhibitions had evaporated, had been that of a healthy, hot blooded male with all the usual urges. She wondered if she was his first sexual encounter; the thought that she probably was excited her all the more.

She chattered to him about safe subjects like job and family. Haydon's past, his feelings about his mother, the strange vicar, whom Haydon had yet to mention to her, the deep, dark side of Haydon that slightly intimidated her, could all wait until another day. This evening was about their relationship taking on a new dimension; they had crossed a line from which there was no going back and Christie was totally smitten, her young heart full of love.

Chapter 15

The weather closed in the next day in a way peculiar to the south west coast. It was as though winter had arrived overnight: wind rocketed up the narrow byways; driving rain emptied the streets and people packed into steamy coffee shops and restaurants.

Pete stood naked in the bedroom, peeping out between the drawn curtains at the wet streets and gushing gutters. 'Shit!'

Diane turned over in bed to be met with a pair of taut buttocks at her eye level. 'Pete! What exactly are you doing? I hope you're not flashing at Mrs Carmichael again. She's already told me that you've exposed yourself to her twice since we moved in!' she giggled as she slipped out of bed and into her soft, pink dressing gown. 'I'll make tea,' she sighed, getting no response from her disgruntled husband.

'It's bloody disgusting out there,' Pete moaned, turning and getting back into bed. 'That's another day that I won't be able to get the front of the house finished.'

Diane popped her head back round the door as she was leaving the room. 'What about sorting out Haydon's electrics?'

Pete lay back with his strong arms behind his head and nodded. He wanted to get Haydon's house all arranged for him before the winter came. The man was certainly a puzzle, but there was something about him that intrigued Pete, and he could easily see why Christie was smitten: he was a handsome fellow and had depth to him that did not become apparent at first. His downfall, of course, was his lack of social skills, which could easily give the mistaken impression that he was a bit slow. That had, obviously, all started in childhood and been exacerbated by his withdrawal from everyday life for over a decade. Christie probably knew more than she was letting on, which reminded him: he would have to mention to Haydon that it wasn't right for Christie to walk home alone after a late evening with him, as had happened the previous night; he wasn't happy about that.

He heard a door slam on the other side of the road and assumed it was Rosie's bully of a husband going off to work at the boat yard. He was a nasty piece of work. It made Pete livid to think that he frequently raised his hand to Rosie. She was a lovely woman – so warm – and there was something about her that made him crave her company, despite knowing he shouldn't and Diane having warned him against it. But how could he refuse to share a coffee and a piece of cake with her without seeming rude? Nevertheless, he was well aware that their chats were becoming more personal and intimate, and although he had not touched her, there had been many occasions when he'd wanted to take her in his arms and feel her warm breasts pressing against him as he explored her sensual mouth with its ready smile and soft lips. He remembered the moment when he had found her in her bedroom after Steve had hit her. She had felt softly voluptuous as he'd held and comforted her. He could feel himself getting excited under the covers and felt guilty when Diane returned with two cups of tea; guilt which soon disappeared when he folded her into his arms and made love to her while the wind howled and rain lashed the windows.

Rosie looked around her familiar kitchen, loving this time of the day. It was such a relief when she heard the crash of the front door closing on her husband as he left for work. She bit her lip, feeling just a little guilty for being exhilarated by the thought of nine hours of solitude in which to focus her thoughts on the delicious fantasy that lived just feet away from her. Pete was everything she would have loved her husband to be: solid, dependable, kind, thoughtful and oh, so sexy. He had not been inappropriate in the least, but that made him even more attractive and she was just happy to be in his company when they shared a tea-break; he had an indescribable aura about him that made her feel young and desirable again. He didn't talk about himself or his family much, but his previous life as a business owner often came into the conversation. Rosie could see the pain in his eyes when he listed with pride some of the contracts he had worked on; to suddenly see it all disappear had hurt him terribly. Rosie couldn't help but wonder how Diane had supported her husband through such times and what kind of marriage they had, but Pete was tight lipped about it and she didn't want to pry. She had hardly spoken to Diane since they had moved in because Diane never seemed to be around. Pete just said she was working long hours with the local newsgroup and Rosie had to be content with that.

That Saturday she was working at the two cottages overlooking the sea. It was generally a change-over day, when holiday makers left and new ones arrived, so there was pressure on her to get both cottages thoroughly clean and restocked for 4pm. Pulling her coat around her, she went out, bending her head into the wind, to walk the fifty yards to the first cottage. They were separated by a small garage in which all the bedding, supplies and cleaning equipment were stored. Gathering up the bedding, she unlocked the front door and kicked it open, tutting at the sight of dirty dishes on the table, rubbish and newspapers all over the floor and a broken standard lamp leaning limply in the corner.

For the next two hours she worked with practised speed and finished in time for a quick cup of tea at home before starting on the second cottage. As she left, the wind caught the heavy wooden door, sending it back to crash against the wall behind it, the force of which shattered the porthole window in the door into multiple pieces, and a shower of fragments narrowly missed her as she jumped back in fright. 'Oh hell!' she exclaimed as she stepped over the mess and back into the narrow hallway to catch hold of the door.

'You okay?' It was Pete, walking past on his way to get the newspaper and a pint of milk.

'Thank god, Pete! Can you give me a hand? I need to get this ready for four o'clock and now look what's happened: the flippin' wind caught it and that was that. What the hell am I going do?'

Pete put his arm round the distressed woman. 'Panic not, my dear! It's a ten minute job. I'll go down into town for a piece of glass and get it fixed in a jiffy, so don't fret.'

As he stood in the confines of the hall looking at the broken shards with his arm around Rosie, he became acutely aware of her warmth and femininity, and on impulse he tipped her head back and put his lips to hers. Time stood still as a tingling sensation ran through his body and Rosie responded, running her hand up the contour of his upper arm. He could feel her heat through his clothing as she caressed him and he could not hold back any longer. Everything was telling him *no* but his arousal was urging him on. Without breaking away from the magic of her lips, he kicked the door shut and backed Rosie into the living room where he pressed her against the wall and pushed his body into hers, inwardly groaning as his growing erection nudged her soft thighs. Rosie ran her fingers through his hair and planted small kisses all over his lips and cheeks, and he smiled as she lavished an abundance of love on him, drinking him in as if drinking from the stream of life after years of drought; she was alive, seductive and wanting him – really wanting him. He began kissing her neck and she tilted her head to one side as he moved wisps of hair away and continued to move hot lips over soft skin.

When they momentarily pulled apart, needing to come up for air, they looked at each other. Pete saw lust in her eyes and fear gripped him. Where was this going? He felt trapped by his own desire as his conscience screamed at him to stop *now*, before he went too far. But even as his previous affair ricocheted round his brain, the heat of excitement was overpowering common sense. Rosie was touching him in such a way that he knew he would not have the strength to draw back if he did not put a stop to it immediately. He groaned as she cupped his erection and gripped his hardness. This was the moment of no return. He was ready to lay her down and crudely take her, here and now, on this windy, wet Saturday morning in somebody else's cottage. His heat was increasing and her grip tightened. He had to have her, *now*.

    The sudden noise of a car door being slammed coincided with a flash of Christie's shocked face in his mind, and Pete finally managed to drag himself from the physical abyss into which he was about to plummet. His breath was coming hard and fast, but he grasped Rosie's shoulders and moved their two hot bodies apart. 'Rosie, we have to stop now. I want you so much, but we can't do this. In any case, you deserve better. You're worth more.'

    She put her finger to his lips and stopped him. 'Shhh! It's okay. The last few minutes have given me so much, Pete – so much.' She ran her eyes over his body and searched every inch of his face, before reaching up, softly kissing him and slipping away from him, back out into the hallway. 'I need to get this all cleared up. Is it okay for you to help me with the glass? I can pay you in coffee and walnut cake.'

    Pete went out to her, smiling uncertainly. 'Of course,' he nodded. 'I'll just go and get what I need to measure up.' Still looking deep into her eyes, it took all his willpower to walk past her and out of the door to make the short, uphill journey home.

    As he disappeared from view, Rosie went back into the living room and sat down, weak with excitement and shock. Looking at the wall against which Pete had pressed her, she took in what had just happened. She had thought that he was attracted to her, but she hadn't been certain until now. He had kissed her; she had aroused him – felt him. She laughed out loud, hugging herself and standing up to do a little twirl around the room. She felt sixteen again and nothing was going to spoil this moment. He had kissed her and she had felt his desire! She pictured where this could lead: maybe they were destined to be together. Then again, she chided, maybe that was a step too far, too fast!

A lifetime in sleepy Porthtreval had not provided her with many opportunities for affairs of the heart. Even as a young girl, her choices had been limited and Stevie had seemed like the best of the bunch, so she had orchestrated a marriage as quickly as she could. Her life as a teenager had been blighted by an abusive stepfather and she couldn't get out quick enough. It hadn't been long into their relationship, however, before she'd realised that she'd swapped one bully for another. Painful as that realisation had been, she'd loved Steve and accepted that the beatings came with the territory. She had simply done her utmost not to aggravate him, but now that drink was ruling him there were days when it mattered not what she did, he still bullied her.

It was no secret, either, that Steve was unfaithful to her. He had been seen with several women over the years, usually a lot younger than him, and she accepted this with as much grace and dignity as she could muster, holding her head high when she walked through the town, even when she knew she was being pitied. Her sunny disposition also got her through most of the time, and when there were bruises she just didn't venture out.

The relationship with Pete was the most exciting thing that had ever happened to her, and she hoped that he hadn't thought her brazen; she could hardly believe the way she had touched and caressed him so intimately. His excitement had been evident, though, and now that she had momentarily possessed his passion, she wanted and expected more. It never entered her head that Pete might be devastated by his own wanton behaviour. As far as she was concerned, this was the start of something wonderfully illicit and she relished the thought of the next stage.

Back in his own home, Pete was experiencing very different emotions. He sat on the edge of the unmade bed where he had earlier made passionate love to his wife, and put his head in his hands. Diane was downstairs working on her laptop, so engrossed she had hardly noticed him come in, and, for once, Pete was grateful for her all-consuming job. He felt like crying and punched his thigh, cursing his weakness, his sex and his inability to control himself. What was wrong with him? He was like an out-of-control youth.

He stood up and looked out of the window. 'Shit!' he said out loud to the grey sky. As he stood there he saw Rosie bustling up the street, her coat wrapped around her and a pile of linen under her arm. The everyday scene, almost shocking in its mundaneness, belied the drama of moments before when they had been grappling like rampant teenagers. He was amazed by Rosie's unbridled passion and he felt stirrings once more as he recalled how she had touched him.

Turning away from the window, hands deep in his jeans pockets, he gazed emptily up towards the ceiling. Not only had he just been unfaithful to his wife – again – but he had also given false hope to a lovely woman who was already being mistreated by an arse of a husband. His self loathing at that moment was all-consuming.

In the dining room below, Diane was trying her best to focus on her work. She needed to write up an interview she had carried out the day before but her mind was wandering. She looked at the feeble two hundred words on the document and angrily punched the delete button, removing the lot. 'Not good enough!' she said aloud, sitting back in her chair and looking out at the huge, pink hydrangeas, animated by the blustery wind and bobbing up and down against the tall, sash window, as if jeering at her. She knew she was acting immaturely: her crush on Brian had not diminished; in fact, it had increased. It wasn't that she didn't love Pete, the father of her children and the man with whom she wanted to spend the rest of her life. It was all about the fantasy. She was a writer. She was creative and she made up stories all the time or embellished that which was factual. Brian was just another story, she told herself to ease the niggling guilt, especially when she remembered whose face she had been picturing when Pete had made love to her that morning.

Her mind flitted to Rosie, who lived over the road with the abusive husband. She was obviously sweet on Pete. Who wouldn't be? He was a handsome man with a sexy, rugged air about him that women often found attractive, if not irresistible. His looks had actually improved with age: he was permanently tanned and his five foot ten inch frame had filled out through constant physical work outside in the elements; as for the grey flecks in his close-cropped brown hair, they only enhanced his dark grey eyes. She smiled to herself as she remembered the skinny, smooth skinned twenty one year old who had pulled up in his Ford Escort and blatantly asked her to be his girlfriend. She had laughed cruelly in his face, at the time, and walked off with her friends, giggling and throwing furtive looks back at him as he sat absorbing the rejection. His ardour had not been cooled, however, and his persistent phone calls and visits to her parents' house had finally paid off for the patient Pete Styles. Within eighteen months they had been planning a wedding, and Pete and his friends had been restoring a small 'two up two down' in the back streets of Salford.

Pete was someone you could always rely on to pick you up when you needed a lift, mend anything that broke and be there with a comforting arm if you were upset. But he wasn't dynamic. He was just Pete. Not that Diane thought of that as a fault; it was just the way he was. There was, of course, a wayward side to Pete, as well. Diane's butterfly brain flitted off to the time when she had found out that Pete had been unfaithful to her. It still amazed her that she had known that something was going on, because there had been no particular clues, such as discarded clothes in the car or suspicious phone calls – well, not that she'd noticed anyway; no one had said anything to her at the school gate as she waited for

Christie and James; no well-meaning friend had thought it her duty to make her aware. All it was, was that Pete just changed. He hadn't become less attentive to her sexually – quite the opposite, in fact: their sex life had moved up a gear, especially once Diane had gone back to work. But he had been suffering stress at work, caused by issues he was having with two of his employees, and by losing a lot of money when a client's business went to the wall. At the time, he hadn't shared his concerns with her; it had all come out later, when she had found out.

    She remembered the day vividly. It had started out like any other wet and windy Saturday in October, but Pete had seemed distracted and angry, snapping at the kids and flinging a few unkind comments at her, which she had found perplexing as it wasn't like him. Both Christie and James had been invited to a birthday party that day, so Diane had decided to treat Pete to lunch at the pub, it being a rare opportunity to have some time to themselves. He had not been against the suggestion, exactly, but he had not been particularly keen either, and Diane's sixth sense had been ignited: suddenly she had known that something was significantly wrong.

    Watching the bobbing hydrangeas, she recalled the sick feeling, lying like a heavy rock in her stomach, dragging her down and making even normal conversation impossible. After she had dropped the children off, she had come back home to find Pete just sitting, staring into space. Alarm bells rang and she had known she had to get to the bottom of whatever it was. She had asked him outright if he was having an affair, and to this day, she had no idea how she knew that to be the truth of the matter. The way Pete's eyes dropped to the floor and he put his head in his hands had confirmed her misgivings, and it had been a moment in time when her world had stopped turning. The emotions had been so overwhelming that nausea had sent her rushing to the bathroom. She hadn't been sick but she had taken a few minutes away from him to calm down and gather her composure.

Going back into the room she had quietly sat down opposite him. He hadn't looked up, and had reminded her of a badly behaved schoolboy, sitting in the corridor after having been thrown out of class. All this being new to her, she hadn't been sure how to handle it, so she had just taken a deep breath and asked him whom he was seeing. He had answered in monosyllables whilst twisting his hands together in a wringing motion. Diane would never forget how the scene had played out: her emotional outpourings had ranged from quiet controlled enquiry to almost manic accusations. The pain had been deeper than she had ever before been subjected to, and she hoped she would never have to go through it again. Pete had sat like a wounded animal and taken everything she had thrown at him. In a way, he had seemed almost relieved.

And here she was, thinking about another man! She was no better than Pete had been! But then, she hadn't done anything, had she? Even as the thought formed, a part of her posed another question: if she had the chance, though, would she?

Pete needed to get out of the house. Grabbing his car keys, he popped his head round the door to speak to his wife. 'All right, love? I'm just popping into town to get a piece of glass. One of the holiday cottage doors has smashed. I shouldn't be gone long.'

Before Diane could react, he was gone, banging the back door behind him. She watched him through the window. Was he okay? Was he sensing something was wrong with her? Had she let her guard slip? Something about his exit had screamed 'avoidance' at her. Sometimes she wished she was not so sensitive to the feelings of others. It was a trait that her daughter had inherited from her and it was definitely not always a blessing.

Rosie was vacuuming up the last of the glass when he got back to the cottage. With hardly a word and a sweat breaking out on his forehead, announcing his stress level, he took the necessary measurements while she went to clean the kitchen.

'See you later,' he called, hurrying away as soon as possible without a backward glance. Driving through the narrow Cornish streets, he suddenly felt as though he were living a nightmare and, once more, cursed his inability to control his urges. He had come close on previous occasions over the past ten years or so since his affair, but this was the first time he had succumbed and now he was having to cope with overwhelming feelings of failure and unadulterated weakness. He would have to avoid Rosie, now; their friendship would have to end because he had pushed it beyond that into something unacceptable. He felt great sadness for her: he knew she was the victim of a thoughtless thug and now he had destroyed a perfectly lovely friendship – something she had little of in her life. He smashed his palm against the steering wheel in frustration and almost hit a metal dustbin standing innocently at the side of the road. As he drove on, his mobile phone bleeped in his pocket, making his heart skip a beat; he knew who had sent him a text. After parking the car, he checked and found he was right.

'That was unexpected and very nice. R'

The text stared at him and seemed to explode like a distress flare in his brain. He knew what Rosie was referring to, and it wasn't his help with the window. And she was correct: it was certainly unexpected, and yes, definitely very nice. But it could also ruin his life. He groaned, knowing he would have to broach the subject with her and get things sorted out. It was the only way. It was also easy to think that way, he realised, when he wasn't within reach of her voluptuous femininity and could be objective. The problem was he found her so irresistible. Nevertheless, he had to be strong for the sake of his family. Hadn't he cocked things up enough already with the way he'd handled his business affairs?

Thoughts continued to swirl around in his head like a whirlpool of unsolvable emotional puzzles that actually had no answer and made little sense. Needing the antidote of activity, he got out of the car, locked it and made his way into the masculine environs of the builders' merchants, pushing all thoughts of Rosie and the way she made him feel to one side, for the moment, and focusing instead on glass, putty and wood nails.

Chapter 16

The following day the town burst into life again as a bright sun appeared over the horizon in a blue sky punctuated with soft, white, wind-blown clouds which scudded enthusiastically over the harbour mouth. It made ideal surfing weather and already there were die-hards out riding the waves before most had even put the coffee on for breakfast. Ollie lifted his face and breathed in deeply, savouring the familiar salty fragrance. Days like this made him feel glad to be alive, despite the worry that was presently occupying him. It had been several days since he'd seen James and, at first, he had been concerned that the near-drowning had affected his friend more that it had appeared at the time; but then, he would have heard if something was amiss, he thought. They had texted a few times but James' replies had been non-committal and evasive. Now Ollie was wondering if James was angry with him. Had the trauma damaged their friendship? Ollie had been surprised at how quickly his feelings for James had developed, and he'd wondered why he was so drawn to a pale, shy, geeky Mancunian. But having got to know him better, he found him engaging and interesting. He would have liked to get to know his sister better too, but, for the time being, she seemed to be all wrapped up in her sullen boyfriend.

As he started to pull on his wet suit, he had the feeling he was being watched and glanced up over the roof of his car. James was looking down at him from the alleyway leading from the top road. They just looked at each other for a surreal moment, before James waved and started to make his way towards the cobbled road where Ollie had parked. The two boys spontaneously hugged and Ollie was thrilled to see that their relationship had not suffered. In fact, the warm hug confirmed for him that something had happened between them that day on the beach; he wasn't sure what it was but it had formed some kind of bond between them that was more than just casual friendship.

Ollie held James' shoulders and looked into his clear blue eyes.

'So, you're okay, then?' he asked. Despite the hug, James seemed quite shy, this morning, and Ollie felt he needed to ease the situation.

James nodded. 'Sure,' he shrugged without conviction and tore his eyes from Ollie's to look out across the bay. 'Good day for surfing?'

Ollie sprang to life like an excited puppy and drew James to the open boot of his car. 'Yes! You coming? I brought your wet suit, just in case,' he said, looking at James with eager hope written all over his face.

James grinned at his animated friend. He had been keeping himself to himself since the incident on the beach and had felt quite nervous about seeing Ollie again, partly because he had mixed feelings about going in the water again, but mainly because of his growing attraction to Ollie. One minute he wasn't sure if it was mutual, and the next he was sure there was a spark between them, which, in turn, terrified him because of his lack of experience. He had opted not to see him for a few days in case his imagination was playing havoc with him; now, the impromptu hug they had just shared was adding to his confusion. 'Thanks,' he said to Ollie, 'but I'm going to give it a rest for a few days – feeling a bit wary, you know?'

Over Ollie's shoulder, James spotted Bruce and two other surfers making their way along the harbour side towards them, boards under their arms and half-donned wet-suits slung low across their hips. Unwilling to deal with unfriendly comments from surly Bruce right then, he jovially slapped Ollie on the shoulder and turned to go, but then, on a whim, turned back. 'Fancy a drink tonight?' he asked.

'Sounds great!' Ollie nodded in surprise. 'I'll see you up at the top about seven, then?'

'Sure thing,' replied James with a little wave as he turned and jogged off, feeling truly happy for the first time in what seemed like a lifetime.

Christie had reluctantly decided that it was time to speak to Haydon about matters that made no sense to her. In all the excitement of their deepening intimacy, she had ignored the question of the spirit being who seemed to be in contact with both of them, and simply enjoyed getting to know the man under the beard. She was hesitant about bringing up painful subjects for fear of putting their fragile and utterly precious relationship at risk, but she needed answers.

For the past couple of days they had simply taken walks around the lake, or sat chatting on a bench. Christie did most of the talking and Haydon seemed happy to just sit holding hands and watching her. There had been no repeat of their sensual encounter against the kitchen table, although the opportunity was consistently and tantalisingly present, because Christie was keeping the brakes on. She felt responsible for making sure they took things slowly, being aware that although Haydon was older than her, he was much less emotionally mature.

As she pushed open the cottage gate, feeling slightly anxious about the prospective conversation, Haydon's neighbour, Mr Chritchley, greeted her from across the fence with a cheery 'hello'. 'Where is he?' he enquired. 'Young Haydon? Has he gone somewhere?'

Christie was perplexed for a moment as Haydon had been in and out of his house as usual. Then she realised that no one was recognising him now. She threw her head back and laughed out loud, while Mr Critchley stared at her as though she had completely lost the plot.

'I'm sorry young lady, but I really don't see what's so funny. The wife and I are worried about him. Have they taken him away? Have you moved into his house?'

As if on cue, Haydon came out into the garden, smiled and nodded to his neighbour and put his arm round Christie.

'Well, I'll be …' the old man gasped, his expression changing from indignation to delight. 'Bridget! Bridget! Come 'ere, love! Come and see who it is!'

Christie felt Haydon tense and she reached behind and took his hand firmly in hers. Being sociable was a lesson he needed to learn and now was as good a time as any. She knew he wanted to back away but she held fast and wouldn't let him go.

Mrs Critchley popped her head round the door and smiled at Christie. 'Hello, love? You here again? We've seen you going in and out, haven't we Jim?'

Jim was just staring at Haydon and nodding blankly in response to his wife.

It was then Bridget Critchley's turn to do a double take. An astonished grin broke out across her face. 'Well I'll be buggered! It's young Haydon, isn't it, Jim, isn't it?'

'It is, love! It most certainly is!' Jim could not tear his eyes away from the young man who was now shifting uncomfortably from one foot to the other.

Christie finally came to his rescue. She smiled sweetly at the gawping Critchleys and looked up at Haydon. 'Lunch?' she suggested. Relief flooded his face and she couldn't help but reach up and give him an affectionate peck on the cheek, to the further delight of the Critchleys, followed by a jaunty wave as she led him back into the cottage and shut the door on the world and on those who judged. Walking through to the kitchen, they turned to each other and burst out laughing.

'Well done, lovely man!' she said, softly kissing his mouth. Immediately his arms encircled her and they shared a few blissful moments before Christie broke loose, knowing where this was leading if she didn't. Haydon let her go and leant back against the sink to watch while she busied herself with food preparation.

They decided to take their lunch and sit on a bench overlooking the harbour. Virtually the whole of the town's activity could be witnessed from there, and they sat for a while just enjoying the view.

For a change, it was Haydon who spoke first. 'You have something on your mind, don't you?'

Christie turned to him and decided to wade right in. 'Yes. How did you know?'

Predictably, he shrugged. 'I can feel it. I can feel what you're thinking.' It was an odd thing to say but Christie didn't find it so, coming from Haydon; in fact, it gave her an ideal segue into the awkward topic of conversation.

'We feel a lot about each other, don't we?' she began. 'It's like we don't need to speak to communicate. Does that make sense?'

Haydon just squeezed her hand in agreement. He might not be good with words but after years of being invisible and observant, he could pick up on communication better than most.

'I want to always be honest with you, Haydon,' Christie continued. She felt him tense a little, probably wondering what was coming, she surmised. 'I was in your house looking for you, the other day, and I went upstairs. I honestly wasn't prying …'

Haydon let go of her hand and nervously leaned forward, his elbows on his knees, and studied the ground; he obviously knew what she was going to talk about and Christie had no wish to prolong the torture with preamble.

'What's happened to your mother? You have to tell me, darling. We can't go on with questions hanging between us. Do you understand?' She put her arm round his shoulder and moved in closer to him, encouraging him with her body. She had to know the truth if she was to help him, and if she was to have any kind of future with him. 'Haydon, we're good friends – best friends, actually – so please open up and let me in. I really like you – well, more than that – which you can tell, can't you?'

He nodded and gave her a sideways glance, but then looked down again.

'What's happened to your mother?' Christie persisted. 'Is she still alive?'

'I don't know.' Haydon looked up and out across the harbour, as if he might find the answer there. 'I think she must be all right because of the money in my account.'

Christie could see the tension in his jaw as he once more revisited the pain that had shaped his life for so long.

'I haven't seen her since the day when I came home from school and she wasn't there.'

'Go on,' she encouraged when he hesitated, obviously distressed. She then had to bite her lip to stop herself from saying anything else that might halt the intermittent flow altogether.

He straightened up and Christie took her arm away from his shoulder, taking hold of his hand instead. 'I waited and waited,' he finally said. 'I sat at the window every day after school. I didn't know what else to do. We didn't talk to anyone in the street and I was scared to say anything to anyone at school. I had my bus pass so I just kept going to school and waiting. It was horrible.' His voice cracked and he swallowed hard.

It might have all been long ago, but Christie could see the hurt in him was as raw, now, as it had ever been. She desperately wanted to put her arms round him and hold him close, but that would have to come later. 'Did she contact you, at all?' she asked.

'No, not in person. The money in my account was the only contact. I just took bits out for food but there wasn't enough for the bills, so eventually everything got cut off.'

'Did anyone at all know what you were going through?'

'Only Reverend Gilmore, the old vicar who's been here all my life, I think.'

That must be have been the one who spoke to me at the cottage gate, thought Christie. 'How did he find out?'

It was an obvious question but not one that Haydon had, apparently, ever thought about, because he looked puzzled and his brows knitted together as he considered it. 'I don't know,' he said. 'He just knew. He came to the house the weekend after she went and I said I was fine because I didn't want him going round getting people involved. I was afraid they'd take me away and I wouldn't be here when she came home. I made him promise not to tell anyone. He said I could go and live with him and his wife but I didn't really know him, and even though he was kind I didn't dare trust anyone.'

Christie felt like she was interrogating him but she had to go on. 'How did your mother know him?'

'She used to do some cleaning for him sometimes. She said he was very kind, but she felt odd being there so didn't often go. Mum wasn't very good with people – same as me, really. And she had panic attacks – you know, when you can't breathe properly – so she didn't like going out much, except to buy something for our tea.'

'What about your father?'

Haydon shrugged. 'I don't even know his name. I did ask Mum about him once but she just went into one of her fits and made me promise never to ask about him again. She was very … er … sensitive.' He stared into the distance, lost in his own thoughts.

Christie studied his profile, trying to imagine him as a frightened youth with no one to guide him but a neurotic mother, who deserted him, and a cleric, who offered to befriend him. It was a sad, empty story. 'You've kept her bedroom nice and clean. Do you know if she was going anywhere that day – a dentist appointment, or anything?'

'No, not that I know of.'

'Would you like to find her?' Christie asked gently.

He fidgeted with indecision. 'I suppose so, but it doesn't seem so important now.'

This was not the answer Christie had expected. 'Really? What's changed? You've always wanted her to come home, haven't you?'

Haydon tensed and then made her jump as he abruptly turned to fully face her and grasped her hands. 'I always dreamed about her coming home – walking in the door and calling my name,' he said earnestly. 'The first year was the worst because I spent every spare minute at the window, watching for her. But then you came and everything changed. My life began again the minute you walked into the launderette. I've thought about that: my life ended when my mother walked out of the door and never came back; it began again when you walked through the door of the launderette, and you've stayed with me.' He stopped talking suddenly, as if someone had flicked a switch, apparently as surprised by his own outburst as Christie was; his eyes flickered uncertainly away from her face and he let go of her hands.

'What a lovely thing to say!' said Christie, and then took his face in her hands and kissed him soundly, taking pleasure in the tickle of his stubble.

'It just sort of came out,' he said with a shy smile and eyes down like an embarrassed youth.

Christie retrieved their lunch from the bench, where she had put it down while they talked. 'Well, let's eat and you can have a think about finding your mother,' she said. 'It's up to you, but it would be good to know what happened and why, just so you can understand, at least.'

Haydon just nodded.

Pete parked his car, took his toolbox out of the boot and walked the short distance to Haydon's house, Christie having texted that morning to remind him that he had promised to have a look at Haydon's electrics. His daughter's whole life now seemed to be consumed by this introverted young man and his brow furrowed with concern that she could get hurt. He appeased himself with the thought that she was helping a man forgotten by life, and she was having a profound effect on his progress. He was proud of her, and maybe this was all meant to be.

He ran a practised eye over the place as he opened the creaky gate: the small front garden was just a piece of scrub ground, untended and neglected; the single glazed, wood-framed sash windows were weather beaten and in need of attention; slate tiles on the roof looked as though they may be coming loose in a couple of places, and the chimney stack definitely needed re-pointing. Pete sighed and wondered what was waiting to greet him on the inside. 'Hello, anyone home?' he called through the open front door.

'Hi, Dad! We're out back.'

Pete walked through the dark, unwelcoming front room and was pleasantly surprised by the sunny kitchen, where he found Christie and Haydon sitting at the table looking like any other young couple sharing a meal of bread, cheese and large, shiny, red tomatoes.

'Come and join us,' Christie invited while Haydon went into the front room for another chair, which he placed at the table for Pete, who smiled and sat down, relaxing into the everyday normality.

'Help yourself, Dad,' Christie said, passing him a plate and pointing to the tomatoes. 'These are from Haydon's garden. Aren't they a gorgeous colour? They taste lovely, too. You have to have one.'

Looking out into the tiny yard, Pete could see what Christie referred to as 'Haydon's garden'. It was certainly full of all sorts of vegetables. *He's a strange one*, Pete thought, as he buttered the bread Christie had cut for him and Haydon sat back watching him. It was slightly disconcerting to be examined in such a way, but Pete was getting used to the ways of this odd, but likeable fellow.

Awkward silences were a rarity in Christie's presence and today was no exception. 'So Dad, Haydon and I have been talking and he'd like to start improving his house so that he doesn't get cold in the winter. With what he'll be earning from you, he can buy what he needs, so can you show him what to do?'

Pete looked at her animated face and wondered if this Haydon realised just how lucky he was to have captured her heart. 'I don't see why not, sweetheart. How about we have a good look round today and make a list of all the things that need doing and then we can prioritise. Haydon, you'll be starting with me properly tomorrow, okay?'

Haydon nodded, his eyes bright and attentive.

'We'll be working on our cottage tomorrow if the weather's good. You'll be preparing and painting the window frames, like you did at the shop the other day. That's definitely a job you'll need to do here, too, from what I saw as I came in.'

Christie and Haydon smiled excitedly at each other, and as the broad grin spread across Haydon's face, Pete was again struck by how unusually handsome he was.

After a quick snack, Pete did a complete survey of the house and made the promised list. The first task was to get the electricity back on. The sockets seemed to be in reasonable condition but Pete wanted to get an electrician round for an expert opinion. In the meantime, he would contact the electricity board the following day to get the reconnection underway. He noted the contrasting conditions of Haydon's room and the room at the back of the house – obviously the mother's room – but he just made a few notes and moved on to the bathroom to check the immersion tank. When he came back downstairs to report his findings, Haydon was tending his vegetable patch and handed Pete an old tin bucket full of salad ingredients when he came out into the yard.

'This is for you,' he said, speaking for the first time since Pete had arrived.

Pete looked into the bucket, which held two huge Romaine lettuces, spring onions, a bunch of radishes and six large, rosy tomatoes. He clamped his hand on Haydon's shoulder. 'Thanks!' he said. 'This is great! You certainly have a skill with plants, don't you?'

'I like making things grow. I always have done. I used to grow things for Mum. I even had flowers growing then.'

It was Pete's turn to just nod, as he didn't really know what to say. Inspecting the contents of the bucket, he picked out a big tomato and comically took a huge bite out of it, scattering juice and pips down his shirt. Haydon laughed a big wide-mouthed laugh and they both enjoyed the moment, during which Christie happened to return from the shops, where she had been buying cleaning products.

Her aim was to help Haydon get his whole house – beginning with his squalid bedroom – clean and hygienic, and to encourage him to take as much pride in his home as he did in his garden. She was surprised to find the two men laughing like drains, but understood when she saw the state of her father's shirt. If it wasn't for that, she would have hugged him for making an effort to get along with Haydon and put him at ease. Instead, she shook her head in mock disapproval and grinned all over her face, quite sure that Haydon could not want for a better role model than her father.

They gathered in the kitchen to share a pot of tea and a packet of chocolate biscuits while Pete tried to establish Haydon's exact situation so that he could properly advise him. It soon became clear, however, that Haydon couldn't answer Pete's questions. He didn't know if his mother owned the cottage, if there was an outstanding mortgage or she had rented it and there was a landlord somewhere. All he knew was that he didn't pay any rent or mortgage.

'What about council tax?' asked Pete and got a blank look in response.

'Do you get any letters from the local council at all?' Christie asked, by way of clarifying.

Haydon shook his head, beginning to look agitated as the realisation dawned that he had no answers to what sounded like important questions.

'Don't worry, we'll sort it all out,' said Pete, seeing Haydon's growing concern. After all, the man had lived in the house for years so there must be someone taking care of business. No doubt Christie could look into all that, while he concentrated on knocking the house into shape. 'Walk round the house with me, Haydon, and we'll think about the best way to heat it.'

Haydon immediately brightened up, happy to be relieved of complicated issues. There was no central heating in the house but there was a fireplace in the living room and in the main bedroom, so Pete thought the most economical option was have the chimneys swept, which he would arrange. Haydon was in full agreement and led Pete to the outhouse, where he stored neat stacks of driftwood and logs that he had collected. Pete marvelled at his self-sufficiency, something which, in his opinion, was unfortunately dying out in the general population.

He then left the two young people to get on with the cleaning and drove home, having enjoyed the time with them; it had taken his mind off himself and his misdemeanours. He hadn't responded to Rosie's text. In fact, he had immediately deleted it, determined to put distance between them and naively ignoring the fact that he was not the only one involved; in actual fact, a fire had been lit that would not be easily extinguished.

Chapter 17

Christie felt slightly guilty about heading off to the library the next day to check up on Haydon without his knowledge, but she thought it best not to burden him with too much information too soon; especially since he seemed happy with how his life was progressing. He had arrived bright and early that morning to start work, and she had welcomed him with a warm hug when she'd opened the door to him. Her feelings for him were growing daily and she treasured the trust he had in her. She recognised that they might seem an odd couple, but to her, their relationship was new and exciting and she was not in the least interested in what other people might think.

She was astonished to find Haydon's name on the electoral role for the little house in The Nip. She would check with him, but it was a safe bet that he would not have completed any of the forms that regularly dropped through the letter box to update council records. She was also certain he would never have voted. She had already come to the conclusion that someone was looking out for Haydon and she had a good idea whom to go to for some answers.

Surveying the library with its bright posters and rows upon rows of colourful books, she felt the sudden urge to write. With it, the inner heat began to build and she knew that she just had to sit quietly for a while and breathe slowly. Luckily, she had her laptop with her, so she sat at one of the large tables in the reference room and closed her eyes whilst the wave of heat crested and then slowly abated. All was calm around her as she opened a document and allowed the words to flow through her.

I know you are hurting, my darling. That is why I yearn to reach out and comfort you. Your pain is mine also and I understand why the hurt is unbounded and all encompassing. I fear that you live each day unaware of the truth that invisibly surrounds you. I have tried to reach you, but you are deaf to my call.

The joy of having a child is absolute. There is no other emotion that can surpass it. Further to that, the first born to any mother is the most exquisite experience that can be imagined. It is the time when a woman moves into another sphere of her life – she becomes a different person altogether. I had that joy for three short months; without warning, it was then cruelly ripped away from me. I am so thankful that you have not had to go through that trauma and that you were able to watch your own flesh and blood grow through the stages of childhood. How I would have loved to enjoy your progress, and nurture and love you every step of the way.

I am now far out of reach, but I see all and I know what must come about for all our sakes. I understand your inability to hear my call, my darling, so I am trusting in another to heed my anguish and to bring me peace. I tire now and need to rest, but I will not do so until you are filled with the love that should have been yours all along. There is love waiting for you and soon you will discover it and come home to revel in its warmth and safety. Then, my darling, I will rest.

Christie stopped in awe, re-reading the confirmation that she was, indeed, being used as a kind of conduit. She was starting to fit the pieces together, like doing a jigsaw without knowing the final picture, and there were still many pieces missing. Nevertheless, it was quite apparent that the spirit was talking through her and that the whole story was connected to Haydon in some way. It had to be, because the synchronicity was so strong: they had met, were together and he had also experienced some kind of sixth sense communication at the same time as she began receiving these messages.

As she sat quietly absorbing all this, out of nowhere came the awareness that *the spirit was talking to Haydon's mother.* As if to confirm her insight, she suddenly felt warm; not heated, as before – just warm and safe.

Now that she had an important piece of the puzzle, she saw her connection with Haydon as far more than happenstance – it was destiny. She immediately wanted to talk to him, but then hesitated. She was sure he would readily understand and accept her experience, but she had also seen how he had reacted the previous day when she had spoken to him about his mother. Maybe she needed to do a bit more digging before she started to give him false hope. With a firm purpose in mind, she packed her laptop away and quickly made her way to the bus stop and Porthtreval.

Pete was thankful to have Haydon working with him, that day. He had not spoken to Rosie since the passionate incident in the holiday cottage, and Haydon's presence would hopefully discourage her from inviting him over for cups of tea. That was all very well and gave him some kind of a breathing space, but there was nothing to put a similar brake on his desires: he couldn't stop thinking about how she had felt when he'd kissed her and how she had been so ready for him. In bed at night, he pictured her laughing face and the soft, rounded body that he now knew more intimately. There was no doubt that if circumstances were different he would want nothing more than to make love to her. But he was married; she was married; they were both mature people in their late forties who should know better than to behave so inappropriately; he loved his wife dearly and valued his family above all else. In spite of constantly reminding himself of these facts, however, he could not stop the feelings he had for the sensual Rosie. Being on a diet didn't stop a person wanting to eat chocolate, he told himself wryly.

Turning round on the scaffolding tower on which he was standing, he looked over at his new assistant. Working solidly and with great care, Haydon was giving the window frame of

Christie's bedroom its first coat of paint after spending the morning preparing the wood. *He's such a gentle soul,* Pete mused, smiling to himself.

The gate on the street below made a chinking sound as someone opened it. He knew who it would be, and like a naughty school boy, he pretended he hadn't heard and carried on painting the metal down pipe with black anti-rust paint.

'Pete?'

He closed his eyes, feeling inadequate to deal with the situation, as butterflies started in his stomach. Nonetheless, he turned and smiled down at Rosie, who was shielding her eyes from the sun and probably only seeing his silhouette against the bright blue sky.

'The kettle's on. Can we please talk?'

Pete looked over at Haydon, who had stopped and was looking back at him. 'Are you okay for a few minutes?' he asked. When Haydon nodded, Pete gave Rosie the thumbs up. 'Five minutes?'

She nodded and made her way back into her kitchen.

Pete finished the area he was working on, and though he didn't need to explain anything to Haydon, guilt made it seem necessary. 'I'm just going to speak to Rosie about some work on the cottages down the road,' he lied.

Haydon shrugged and Pete immediately regretted the lie, feeling as if the younger man could see right through him.

She was cutting cake and had put an extra piece for Haydon in some foil. Typical, thought Pete, thinking how stunning she looked in a vivid green sundress. Was he imagining it or was he noticing more cleavage than usual? He accepted his tea with a smile and she sat opposite him at the breakfast bar, sipping her own tea and quietly regarding him. The silence seemed to stretch out between them until Pete felt obliged to speak, even though he did not want to say what he knew he must. 'Rosie … ' he began hesitantly.

'I don't like the sound of that,' she said, something in his tone alerting her to the fact that he was about to destroy her happiness. Before he could continue, she got up, walked round to him, took the cup out of his hand, placed it on the table and kissed him.

It was as if time stopped. Pete felt powerless. This woman had something magical about her. She was warm and wild like the Cornish breeze. She smelt of heady meadows on a summer day – fresh, sensual and everything feminine. She was a drug that he knew could destroy him, but he still wanted to take her and experience the high. He pulled her hips against him as her mouth drove him deep into the abyss.

It was Rosie who pulled away first and gently stroked his face before going and sitting back down opposite him. Pete's eyes followed her, knowing he was putty in her hands and she was in control. Her hands were curved around her mug, her eyes never leaving his face. Pete was at a loss: he didn't know what to say, what to do, or how to cope with his burning desire to whisk her upstairs and make love to her. He was spellbound and terrified, all at the same time.

'Who's your new apprentice?' asked Rosie, sipping her tea and lowering the temperature in the room to something closer to normal.

There was a pause and Pete blinked, as if not comprehending the sudden change of subject and atmosphere. 'Ah! That's Haydon,' he said, feeling as if his voice belonged to someone else. 'You know – the recluse. Christie's taken him under her wing, so I'm giving him some work.'

'Haydon? Haydon Rouse?' Rosie was wide-eyed with surprise.

Pete nodded, relieved to be sinking back into the mundane and talking about something that didn't affect his testosterone levels. 'Yes, that's him. He's gone through quite some transformation thanks to the care of my little girl.' Pete realised how proud he was of Christie, his own words bringing home to him the enormity of what she was doing for another human being.

'Wow! I'm pretty amazed at that. I used to worry about that boy – well, man, should I say. He must be in his late twenties, now, surely?'

'Yes,' agreed Pete, swallowing a bite of cake. 'We're just getting the electricity reconnected for him. It's a miracle how he's managed all these years.'

'I'm really pleased to see him like this. I always worried about him and I did try to speak to him a couple of times, but he wouldn't have it. Everyone round here will tell you he never lets anyone near him, so it's incredible what your lass has done.'

Pete saw the opportunity of finding out some more about him. 'Did you know his mother?'

Rosie sipped her tea and thought for a minute. 'I knew who she was,' she said. 'Everyone did, but you couldn't get to know her, if you see what I mean. She was a nervous soul and very protective of Haydon, as though she was afraid someone would take him away from her. I was a teenager when he was born, and I remember there was a lot of curiosity about how she was managing because she didn't work, or couldn't work. She didn't really have the wherewithal to hold down a job. I suppose she must have lived on Social Security. Anyway, when she had Haydon, she wouldn't even let the midwife in to see him. Eventually, social services had to force their way in, and she was allowed to keep him as long as she agreed to have regular visits. After that, everything calmed down and Haydon seemed to be growing up healthy. I got married and had Archie and didn't pay much attention. Years later, I found out that she just went off and left Haydon when he was still a lad, and no one knew for the longest time, apart from Reverend Gilmore, of course; he was the only person either of them ever allowed into the house.'

'Reverend Gilmore?' Pete's interest was piqued.

'Yes, the old vicar of St Mary's. Bridget Critchley said he was a regular visitor – not that that was really surprising as he's the type of vicar who always makes house visits.'

'So he's still there?'

'Oh, yes. He's well into his eighties now and has a lot of help from other preachers in the diocese, but he's still fit and healthy and very with it. I believe he was actually born here, although he left and then came back when I was a little girl. I remember seeing him at Sunday school. He used to terrify me because he was so tall and looked huge in his black robes.'

Pete smiled. 'I can imagine. Do you know who owns Haydon's cottage?'

Rosie shook her head and flicked a few crumbs of cake off her lap. 'No idea. But listen, Pete, take care. Haydon is a damaged soul, and you may need to look out for your Christie; you wouldn't want her getting hurt.'

Pete got up to put his mug in the sink and looked up at Haydon through the window; he was still working on Christie's window frame. Rosie wasn't saying anything he hadn't already thought himself, and Haydon was certainly difficult to assess, but for some reason he wanted to believe in him. He turned from the sink and thanked Rosie, feeling slightly self-conscious walking to the door under her scrutiny.

'Come round again soon, yes?' she called as he went out into the sunshine.

He turned back and nodded, although his intention was to keep some space between them. But then, hadn't that been the plan earlier that day?

Christie walked through the town and up the hill away from the harbour, having just got off the bus and popped into the newsagents to get directions to St Mary's and the rectory, which she now knew was situated to the rear of the church.

The vicarage was a large Georgian building with a majestic driveway and an imposing front door sporting a bold, brass knob in the centre. Christie yanked on the bell pull to the side of it and heard a ring somewhere deep inside the building. A heavy silence settled as she stood patiently waiting, the stillness intensified by the afternoon heat.

'Can I help you?' An elderly woman, removing gardening gloves, approached Christie from the direction of the side gate, her face shaded by a large sun hat tied down with a filmy chiffon scarf.

Christie immediately walked to meet her. 'Hello. I'm sorry to disturb you. I was looking for Reverend Gilmore.'

'Is he expecting you, dear?' asked the woman in a cultured, kindly tone.

'Oh, no. Sorry. Perhaps I should have rung. I wanted to have a chat with him about a friend of mine who lives near the harbour. I've seen Reverend Gilmore visiting him so I thought he may be able to throw some light – '

'And who is your friend?' the woman interrupted.

'Sorry. His name is Haydon Rouse.' Was that a shadow of concern on the older woman's face or was she imagining it in her nervousness? Christie wondered in the ensuing pause.

'I see,' the woman replied slowly and somewhat thoughtfully. 'Well, I'm afraid my husband is currently at a bible study class and won't be back until at least four o'clock.'

It was obvious that the mention of Haydon's name had caused a certain hostility to creep into Mrs Gilmore's tone, and Christie wanted to know why. 'Do you know Haydon, Mrs Gilmore?'

'I do. Everyone in the town knows him. He's our very own Howard Hughes without the private fortune. But you must talk to my husband about him; there's little I can tell you. Now, if you'll excuse me, I must get on. I have a Mothers' Union meeting.'

With a dismissive nod of the head, she turned towards the front door.

Christie thanked her and walked thoughtfully back down the driveway, glancing back at the house as she reached the road. The door was firmly shut but she could see the vicar's wife in one of the front rooms moving a vase of flowers. She was about to continue on her way when a movement in an upstairs window caught her eye: she could just make out the shape of the white-haired woman looking down at her and raising her hand in acknowledgement when Christie looked up. The woman then retreated back into the darkness of the room. Christie understood: she might not have found out much about Haydon, but she was on the right track.

She went straight home, her mind working overtime creating possible reasons why a vicar might have always been welcome in the Rouse household when the door had been closed to everyone else; and why the vicar's wife did not seem kindly disposed to Haydon when her husband clearly was.

Pete was in the kitchen making tea when Christie got back. 'Hello, sweetheart. Fancy a cuppa?'

'Yes please, Dad, I'm gasping,' she sighed, dumping her bag on the worktop and pulling up a stool. 'Where's Haydon. Have you fired him already?'

Pete chuckled. 'No, he's on the scaffolding out front, doing a good job of your bedroom window frame. He's nearly finished, finally! It's taken him most of the day, but I have to say, he's done a flippin' good job.'

Christie beamed. 'I'll be back in a minute,' she said and nimbly jogged upstairs to her room. She couldn't see him, at first, and then he suddenly popped up with a paintbrush full of dark green paint. She shrieked in fright and delight at seeing him. He was equally startled by her sudden appearance and almost dropped the paintbrush, before grinning from ear to ear. Drawn to the warmth of his smile, she went up to the window and put her hands flat on the glass; he put down the paintbrush and fitted his hands to hers. With the glass between them they gazed into each other's eyes. Christie's stomach flipped and her heart expanded, jolted anew by the miracle of his smile. Did it affect her this way because he was simply a beautiful man, or because he had transformed from something so dark and guarded? she wondered. 'Shall we go to the lake tonight?' she called through the glass. 'Okay,' she continued in response to his enthusiastic nod, 'see you at seven by the clock tower.'

With a little wave she left him to his work and went back down to the kitchen, thinking, as she went, about her feelings for Haydon, which were complicated, given the situation, but also very simple – she loved him. Was she 'in love' with him? she asked herself. She wasn't sure because she didn't know what that was supposed to feel like; not that she cared – she just knew that she loved Haydon Rouse.

'How's your day been?' asked her father, planting a mug of tea on the table in front of her.

'Thanks Dad. Yeah – interesting actually. I went up to see if I could have a word with the vicar of St Mary's and was met with a frosty Mrs Vicar. She was all right until I mentioned Haydon's name and then she went all cold on me and virtually sent me packing, just to add to the general mystery.'

'Hang on a minute, how did you know about Reverend Gilmore?'

'I met him,' said Christie, puzzled by the question. 'He was visiting Haydon a few weeks ago and I met him at the gate when I was coming out. Haydon has mentioned him, too. Why?'

'Rosie mentioned him.'

'Who on earth is Rosie?'

Pete felt his face turn as red as a pillar box. 'She lives over the road,' he said, pointing in the appropriate direction and hoping Christie wasn't noticing his discomfort. 'We often chat and

I've done a bit of work for her on the holiday cottages that she looks after.' *Evasive but not outright lying,* thought Pete guiltily.

'And she knows Haydon?' Christie enquired.

'She's been here all her life. She was a teenager when Haydon was born, and she remembers his mother as being very strange – wouldn't let the midwife in to visit because she was afraid Haydon would be taken away from her, apparently.'

'Did she work, do you know?' asked Christie, trying to piece more of the puzzle together.

'It seems not. Rosie said that everyone wondered how she managed to live, but she kept herself to herself so folk left her alone, apart from the vicar, and then one day she just vanished.'

'Hmm … it's all a fascinating conundrum,' remarked Christie. 'Did you manage to get anything sorted out about Haydon's electricity?'

'They're coming on Friday to get the connection up and running, and I'm getting George Ribbons in to make sure all is fit for purpose, and then at least there will be light!'

Christie moved over to her dad and put her arms round his neck, snuggling in for a cuddle.
'Thanks, Dad,' she murmured into the familiar comfort of his chest.

Pete looked over the top of her head towards the cupboards opposite. Right now he was his daughter's hero. That wouldn't be the case if she knew of his recent behaviour. Pete closed his eyes to the memory of hot lips and soft breasts, and returned his thoughts to the mystery that was Haydon.

Chapter 18

James looked at his phone to see that the familiar 'beep, beep' heralded a text from Ollie. His heart picked up a beat and he felt a slight flutter of nervousness in his stomach.

See you at the pier at 7?

The message was tantalisingly brief and James was excited by that: it seemed to assume a closeness between them that didn't require a lot of words of explanation or invitation. Then again, maybe he was imagining it all and reading too much into it. Maybe Ollie just enjoyed his company or wanted to get near to Christie, he mused. There was no denying the electricity between himself and Ollie, though. He thought back to the night before, when they had sat on a bench on the pub patio, looking out over the vast Atlantic Ocean, and Ollie, being the more demonstrative of the two, had frequently touched James' arm or leg as he chatted and laughed, and their knees had been touching. James had found it all a real turn on.

They had talked a lot, too, and Ollie had confided that he didn't know what he wanted to do with his life and was currently just drifting along, stacking shelves and serving on the till at the supermarket, after leaving school at sixteen. James had asked him about girlfriends, and Ollie had told him that he'd had a few relationships but no one really special. He found Christie very attractive but considered her a bit out of his league. That had grated on James and further confused him about where Ollie's tastes actually lay. He wondered if he was bisexual, but didn't dwell on the subject. They had been surrounded by groups of people enjoying a few drinks, no one taking any notice of them, and James had not wanted the evening to end. He was discovering a deeper, more serious Ollie than the carefree, tanned surfer boy, which made him all the more attractive.

Having answered Ollie's text with an equally brief message, he got up from the patio, where he had been sitting reading a computer magazine, and went into the house to shower and get ready for the evening ahead.

'I want to show you a different kind of surfing beach than we have in Porthtreval,' Ollie explained as he drove towards Port Dennis. 'I haven't been there in a while because it's a good hour's drive and usually a group of us go and camp out in the dunes overnight.'

Ollie was talking quickly, nervously, and James detected a certain tension in the car. He sat quietly, letting Ollie chatter on, and listened to the full tourist spiel as they crossed from one side of the county to the other. It was as if Ollie couldn't bear any silence between them, and James suspected there were things on his mind that he'd probably get round to saying at some point later on during the evening. After his brief but profound experience with Vince, he had a good idea what those things were.

They stopped in a remote little car park at the bottom of a steep road that ran to a dead end at the beach. Ollie was finally quiet but drumming his fingers on the steering wheel. James felt calm and in control of the situation. He reached up and stilled Ollie's jittery fingers with his hand, letting it rest there, over Ollie's, for a few seconds – a tiny action that spoke volumes – while Ollie stared out to sea and the horizon beyond.

'Do you want to tell me what's on your mind?' James asked, removing his hand.

Ollie drew in a breath and exhaled in a rush, as though in preparation for saying something monumental. 'I'm confused.'

'I can see that.'

'Sam wanted me to go for a game of pool tonight and I lied to him: I said I was seeing a girl.' He looked at James. 'Why should I feel guilty about meeting up with you?' Not waiting for a response, he carried on, pushing the words out between clenched teeth. 'When I saw you coming down the hill, I was bubbling with excitement, man! I figured it was because you've changed since you first came here: you've come out of your shell and that hangdog expression has gone. You've turned into this quietly confident person who knows what he wants and who he is. That's … attractive. I wish I could be as certain about life as you seem to be.' He stopped talking and looked back out to sea, clenching and unclenching the muscles in his jaw.

James waited.

'I have feelings I can't understand,' Ollie finally admitted.

'Feelings about what?'

'Feelings about 'who' is more like it,' said Ollie, fixing his eyes on James.

'I know,' nodded James.

Ollie looked away and resumed his horizon watch. 'What do you know?'

'Someone much older and more experienced taught me that we're not born to fit into little boxes. We have to be who we are and it's very much about the energy between two people. It doesn't matter about age, sex, religion, social standing – it's just about energy. Does that make sense?'

Ollie nodded and turned to meet James' eyes. 'Like the energy in this car; it feels like we're both caught in it.'

James smiled and this time took Ollie's hand and held it.

Ollie blinked rapidly a few times, trying to hold back tears. 'I feel the same way as I did when I pulled you out of the sea and thought you were dead: terrified and excited at the same time.' A solitary tear slid unceremoniously down his face. James followed the line of the tear with his finger and both boys laughed. 'Tell me about this other guy,' urged Ollie.

James explained that he had never been attracted to girls and didn't have many friends, so the friendship he had shared with one of his father's employees had been extremely important to him, and he had totally trusted Vince, never realising that the friendship would become physical. 'When it did,' said James, 'it felt like the most natural thing in the world and everything fell into place – I finally understood.'

'Yes, but I *am* attracted to girls, Jay. I'm not rampant, like Bruce – he shags anything that moves – but I enjoy being with girls and I like looking at them, even though I don't want to have sex with them all the time. Now I've met you and I'm all over the place! How does this all work?'

James chuckled at Ollie's frustration, understanding it perfectly. 'There aren't any rules, mate. Just go with the flow. Follow your feelings. It's not as if we're going to rush off and have babies, is it?!'

Ollie grinned. 'Let's take a walk,' he suggested. 'I need to get my head round this.'

'Sure.' James undid his seatbelt and got out of the car, stretching his cramped limbs.

The sun had now virtually sunk below the horizon and there were few people around. Members of a youth group were enjoying a campfire on the far side of the bay and Ollie, knowing the area well, set off in the opposite direction, towards a surfing lodge that stood in the shelter of the rock face. It was closed for the night but the glass covered notice board sported a variety of colour photographs of sunny days and surfing competitions, so Ollie was able to point out what the surfing could be like when the conditions were right in Port Dennis. He then led James round the back of the wooden building and they sat down in the darkness, backs against the wall, which was still warm from the sun. They talked for a while, but then James moved closer to Ollie and kissed him. In the dark behind the shack on the surfing beach that night, he proceeded to show his friend how to love another man with his hands and his mouth, while Ollie simply went with the flow and welcomed the experience.

Chapter 19

Christie saw Ollie and James hug when they met. As she carried on walking towards the harbour to meet Haydon, she thought about her brother. Was she right in thinking he was gay? It made sense of things: he was good looking but he'd never had a girlfriend; he'd hung out with Vince a lot, which seemed odd as he was so much older, and then James had been really upset and become incredibly morose when Vince emigrated. It was probably a blessing for Jay that they moved down to the West Country, but if he was gay he was wasting his time on Ollie, who was obviously attracted to girls – herself included, she suspected. He had been very friendly towards her, but James quite obviously didn't want to share him as he hardly ever let them have more than two words together, as if he was jealous of her having any of Ollie's time. She smiled. They were a nice couple of lads. James had changed beyond recognition, since moving to Cornwall and meeting Ollie. Emotionally, he was happier, less moody, more confident. His body reflected the change: he had filled out, now sported a healthy tan, and had had his hair cut much shorter, as though he no longer needed to hide behind a drooping fringe. The features of his well-proportioned face were male versions of her own, and people often remarked on how alike they looked, which had always annoyed Christie as a child, but now she rather liked having a good looking brother who resembled her.

  Her thoughts were interrupted by the sight of Haydon coming up through the alleyway at the rear of the clock tower. They waved and when they came to within a foot of each other they simply stopped and smiled. Christie delighted in the fact that words were so unimportant to Haydon. He was all about the visual and used his eyes to express himself, his former disconcerting stare at her having now given way to something much more intimate.

As usual, Christie made the first move and kissed him gently on the lips, before stroking his beard. 'Needs another trim,' she said, eyes sparkling.

Haydon smiled and raised his eyebrows, clearly remembering the last occasion when she had trimmed his beard. Christie's stomach flipped with excitement as she returned his smile, the wordless communication between them as clear as ever: their relationship was progressing and they were both ready to step into the unknown together.

The lake that evening was rippled by a spiky breeze that rolled in from the Atlantic. Christie shivered as they sat on the little bench that had become their own, and Haydon took off his sweatshirt to put it round her shoulders; a life without central heating had hardened him to the cold. Christie gently caressed his bare arm and he closed his eyes, enjoying the touch of her soft fingers on his skin. She wondered what it must have been like in his world – a world virtually devoid of human contact or interaction. Had he suffered intense loneliness, or was that what he had wanted, given that he'd probably had many offers of help over the years? He was an odd one, her Haydon.

When he opened his eyes and looked down at her, she had a sudden, wicked idea. Grinning at him impishly, she checked that no one was around and then jumped up and straddled his lap, putting her arms round his neck and kissing his deeply and passionately. Haydon returned her kiss with equal fervour and pulled her closer as she began grinding herself against him. He moaned as sensation ran through his mounting excitement, and his breath quickened as he broke away to run his hands through her shoulder length hair and push it off her face in order to kiss her neck and around her ear. She groaned as she felt his hot breath and thought she heard him say 'I want you', but didn't react, preferring to just enjoy the obvious effect she was having on him. She, herself, was so aroused by this man that she wanted to drag him off into the bushes and make him take her there and then, but she realised that their love-making had to be sensitive and gentle, and not a quick hump up against a tree. She pulled back, smiling, and dismounted to stand in front of him.

He stood up, uncomfortable with what was going on in his pants, and Christie took his hand, knowing she was the experienced one and so had to take the brunt of responsibility for how their relationship developed. Haydon was not one of the boys at university – he was different, precious and vulnerable.

'Haydon,' she said, looking deep into his eyes. 'I want you … I so want you. Do you feel the same?'

He nodded awkwardly, clearly having no idea how to deal with this beautiful young woman standing in front of him doing physical and emotional things to him that he had not experienced before.

Christie put her arms around his neck. 'There's no rush,' she murmured, kissing him on the cheek. 'It needs to be special.'

For the next few days Christie put the investigations into Haydon's situation to one side and concentrated on improving his house. She was thrilled once the electric wiring had been checked, replaced where necessary and some extra sockets had been added. Now he would be able to do all the things that she had always taken for granted. She would not soon forget the look of anticipation on his face as her father put bulbs in all the light fixtures after the electrician had left, and she was impatient for darkness to fall so that she could share his enjoyment in simply switching on a light.

Like excited children, they watched the sun set, and then Christie presented him with two table lamps as a 'return of electricity' gift; he put one in the front room and one in his bedroom. To the accompaniment of much laughter and sheer glee, they had their own little lighting up ceremony.

They spent most evenings cleaning and painting and, one evening, as they were sitting at the kitchen table, planning what else they needed to buy to get the house up to scratch, Christie broached the subject of money. Haydon reached across to one of the drawers in the dresser and took out his Post Office book. When he handed it to her, she smiled at his unconditional trust; her smile changed to shocked surprise and her eyes widened in disbelief on opening it.

'Haydon! You have forty seven thousand pounds in here!' she exclaimed, staring at him with her mouth agape.

Haydon shrugged in his characteristic manner.

The next day was Saturday and he was not due to work with Pete, so they first went to the Post Office, where Haydon withdrew a substantial sum of money, and then they took the bus into Penzance where they spent the day buying a new bed, linens, towels and a host of other things that Haydon had managed to live without for years. Christie loved every minute of the day, even having to coax and encourage Haydon, who was finding shopping a harrowing experience. She couldn't help laughing at the relief on his face when, juggling countless bags, they clambered back on the bus for Porthtreval.

An evening meal with Christie's family ended his very full day and, feeling drained, he flopped back on the sofa beside Pete, who had switched on the TV. James had gone straight out after they had eaten and Christie and Diane were having a girlie chat in the kitchen.

'Christie tells me you've been out buying stuff for your house.'

Haydon nodded.

Pete was now completely used to always having to initiate conversation with Haydon, or not, as he so chose. He no longer felt awkward in the silences or attempted to fill them; he simply said whatever he wanted and left it at that. 'It'll be better for you when winter comes.'

Another nod.

'Electricity working okay?'

'Yes. And Pete – thanks for all you've done for me.'

It was a long sentence for Haydon in Pete's experience, and he was pleasantly surprised because he knew Haydon must genuinely mean what he said. 'That's all right. No problem at all.'

Haydon went back to watching the television – still a novelty and a rare treat for him.

Brian was in the office early and was already jacket off and shirt sleeves rolled up when Diane arrived on the Monday morning. The smell of coffee percolating in the kitchen greeted her, first, as she walked in through the back door, and then came Brian's voice, calling, ''Morning!'

''Morning to you. My god, you're early!'

'You too, which is good because I got a call late last night that I want to talk to you about. I need you to go up to Southport to interview the guy who was wrongly arrested for the Elliott murder. He's agreed to do an exclusive for us. Seems he's got a big downer on the nationals. You okay to cover that?'

'Sure. No problem at all. I'll go home and get my stuff ready after I've checked my emails and then make my way up there. What time is the interview?'

'Nine a.m. tomorrow.' Brian was searching his emails. 'I'll forward on his details. Brenda will book your hotel.'

Diane was thrilled to have been given this opportunity after a relatively short time at the paper. It was a major story for a local newspaper and it showed Brian's confidence in her ability. She would not let him down; in fact, she hoped this was her chance to shine.

Later, on the drive home, she planned what sort of questions she would ask. The guy would obviously want to have his say and was quite likely to be very angry, so it would have to be dealt with sensitively. As she parked alongside the cottage gate, she heard a text message come through and rummaged in her handbag for her phone. The text was from Brian: *Have had further call from guy in Southport. Will be coming with you. Still want you to carry out interview though.* Diane felt the blood rise to her cheeks and heat suffuse her body. What did this mean? Was Brian picking up on her interest in him? Was he still interested in her after all these years, or was the reason he was coming totally work related? Was she over-reacting? Probably! Pulling herself together, she quickly texted back: *OK. Will be back in 45 mins.*

She looked around for Pete, but he wasn't working on the cottage. She knew he'd given Haydon the day off to get his own house ready, as Christie and he were having a special dinner that night to celebrate her 2:1 degree, the results having come through that week. *Pete must have gone down to the town,* she thought, dashing in and straight up the stairs. Pulling her overnight bag out from under the bed, she packed an outfit for later that night and a change of clothes for the next day. Minutes later, with her wash bag packed and slotted in, she remembered she hadn't packed a nightdress. Rather guiltily, she picked out a red, silky one that she rarely wore and quickly stuffed it into the bag, refusing to dwell on her choice. She was looking around the room, wondering if she had remembered everything, when she heard the sound of a gate opening and absentmindedly glanced out of the window; the sight of the top of Pete's head as he emerged from Rosie's front garden made her do a double take. Rosie was leaning against the back door frame in a way that only a woman with passion on her mind would. Pete turned and Rosie give him a seductive little wave. There was no mistaking what was going on there! 'Oh god!' Diane said aloud. 'Please, no!'

Pete didn't come into the house, but instead walked down towards the holiday cottages that Rosie looked after, while Diane, with hurt and anger spilling over, began pacing the floor. She wanted to scream but thought better of it and grabbed her overnight bag, ran down the stairs, picked up her keys and handbag and slammed the door shut behind her. Sitting in the car, breathing heavily with the up-swell of emotion, she remembered that she had meant to leave a note for Pete and the kids. Well, she didn't trust herself to write anything at that moment. Her heart felt like it was bursting out of her chest and she concentrated on taking deep breaths to calm herself before driving off.

Unbeknownst to her, Pete had picked up the keys for the cottage, that morning, in order to finish off the work on the damaged door. Rosie had got permission from her manager to get the work completed following the temporary repair to the smashed window, and it was the first time Pete had seen her for a few days; he had spent just five uneventful minutes in her company.

Diane was, however, regaining perspective by re-assessing what she had seen and admitting to herself that she had probably jumped to conclusions. Although there had been plenty of opportunity for Pete to spend time over at Rosie's house, her own work having taken her away from home all day, every day, and the evil Steve being out from eight in the morning, all she had, in fact, witnessed was Pete coming out of the woman's house. She had no proof whatsoever that there was anything going on, apart from that look on Rosie's face. There was no mistaking that! But Diane could see why Rosie would find her Pete attractive. He was the exact opposite to Steve, who wore a permanent mean and angry look. She always made sure she gave him a wide berth – she had nothing to say to men like him. It made no sense to her that Rosie stayed with him, but then love was a funny thing. And loving Pete, she decided to give him the benefit of the doubt. It was the least she could do, given the man she was now driving to meet. What would the next twenty four hours bring as far as her relationship with him was concerned? She felt bubbles of anticipation rise in her stomach and, for the time being, she pushed all thoughts of Pete away, in order to enjoy her own fantasy.

She left her car at the office and joined Brian in his plush Audi, sinking back in the seat and trying her best to relax. Pete came, unbidden, to her mind, but since there was nothing to be done about him, at present, she gave herself permission to forget about home and enjoy the brief sojourn out of her normal life.

Brian seemed pre-occupied and didn't say too much for a while. But then, as the A30 became the M5 he seemed to lighten up and they chatted about the interview and how they would deal with it. It was decided that Brian would start off, to get an idea of how the story would pan out, and then Diane would take over with Brian filling in any gaps.

'I'm a bit suspicious about why he doesn't want to sell out to the nationals, to be honest, Di. It doesn't make much sense, although money isn't everything, I suppose.'

'I agree it's a bit odd. We'll just have to see what he has to say.'

'Well, how are things in your world?'

'Oh, okay thanks. We're getting by quite nicely. Pete's work is picking up and the kids seem happy enough. They're both looking for work. It's not easy for youngsters down in the West Country, is it?'

'What does your Christie want to do with her future?'

'She's really a writer, very much like me in that way, but right now she'll consider anything to get herself on the employment ladder. A degree these days rarely leads directly to a dream job.'

Brian nodded, 'I know. Tell you what: I'll see how things are in the office once the summer's over. The work experience undergrads will have gone back by then and I may be able to take her onto the editing team. How would that fit with you?'

Diane looked out of the window. Why was she hesitating? Would having her daughter around cramp her own style? How selfish that was when it would be such a great opportunity for Christie. 'That would be fantastic, Brian,' she said, pulling herself together. 'Thank you. I'll chat to her about it, if the opportunity comes up.' She smiled at him and he gave her a smile in return, making her heart leap. 'In all the rush, I didn't see Pete before I left,' she said, slightly flustered. 'I'd better call and let him know what's happening.' She rummaged in her bag for her phone. 'Do you mind?' she added.

'No, of course not. We can't have the poor man worried and sending out a search party for you.'

Pete accepted her explanation of where she was going, why and with whom, with his usual easy going grace. 'Okay love. Have a good evening and take care. See you late tomorrow night,' he said, sounding not the least bit concerned that she was staying away for the night in the company of another man, and arousing her suspicions once more. Her mind promptly threw up images of her husband putting the phone down and immediately stepping out of their home and into the home and arms of the ever-present neighbour. She refrained from comment, however, and they just said their goodbyes.

Brian soon noticed her subdued manner and asked if she was feeling all right. She assured him she was and relegated Pete, once more, to the back of her mind, determined that her suspicious mind would not interfere with this trip. After that, the seven hour journey went by in a flash for her. The further she got from home the better she felt and she was enjoying being in Brian's company, despite the fact that he was such a private man, who avoided mentioning his family or anything about his life outside work. That puzzled her, but spoiled nothing, so intent was she on living out a little of her fantasy.

The bed was delivered while Haydon was out at the launderette, washing his clothes this time and not just warming up and sitting there staring. While he was doing that, Christie was busy arranging his bedroom so as to surprise him when he came back. Her mother had given her a rug and some curtains from their previous home, and though the curtain rails were old fashioned some extra hooks enabled her to create a pleasing result, after which, she stood back to survey the freshly painted room now sporting a double bed. The lamp on the chest of drawers provided a nice finishing touch and she nodded to herself, satisfied, before going downstairs to start the special tea of sausage and mash that she would have ready for the man she loved when he came home.

When she first heard the front door opening she assumed it was Haydon coming back, but the sound was followed by an unfamiliar voice.

'Hello? Anyone at home? Haydon!'

Realising who it was, she dried her hands and went through to the front room. His height dominated the dark space and it was difficult to see his features, but the dog collar round his neck made him unmistakable. 'Hello, Reverend Gilmore. Haydon's not here at the moment but he won't be long. Would you like a cup of tea?'

For a good few seconds, Reverend Gilmore didn't answer. He just stood staring around the room, stunned by the change in it. The peeling 1970's wall paper had gone and the whole room was painted white; a pine framed picture of the nearby lake hung over the fireplace; a pine book shelf in the corner held a neat row of novels; the little table was now dressed in a lacy tablecloth and a bowl of fruit; and there were cushions on the armchair, as well as a lamp on the shelving in the recess.

'Well, well!' was all he could say. 'Well, well. I'll be ... well!'

Christie had to laugh, which brought his attention to her.

'I met you at the gate a while ago, didn't I?' he said through narrowed eyes. ' And you must be the young lady who spoke to my wife the other day.'

Christie nodded. 'Yes, I'm sorry I haven't been back to see you. I just haven't had a chance. As you can see we've been pretty busy.'

The reverend gave a small, tight smile. 'So you have. It's certainly very different. How did you get Haydon to agree to all this?'

Christie's brow furrowed. 'What do you mean? I don't understand.'

'Your name, dear? I've forgotten.'

'I'm Christie.'

'Well, Christie, how much do you know about Haydon and his past?'

Christie felt her cheeks redden. She knew Haydon had lived a strange and complicated past, but all that had changed now and she was not happy with the reverend's condescending tone. He had obviously recovered from the shock of seeing the newly decorated house and was trying to take control of the situation. His power came over her like a heavy blanket, and she began to feel like an unwelcome stranger. Standing a little straighter and taller, she mustered her confidence to reply. 'Enough to know that he needs support and help and someone to love him,' she said, speaking, as always, from the heart. It was the only way she knew.

She turned and walked into the kitchen, refusing to see the patronising smile that was breaking over the vicar's face. 'That's very sweet,' he commented, following her, 'and I can see you're quite taken with Haydon. But my dear girl, you don't understand what you're dealing with here.'

'Dealing with?' Christie retorted, swinging round to face him. 'I don't like that expression, at all. Haydon and I are close. I'm not 'dealing' with him, as you put it.'

'Let me ask you this,' said the reverend, looking down at Christie with something resembling pity. 'How long have you known him? A few weeks? A few months, at the most. What do you really know about him, about how his childhood shaped his early adult years, and about his mother disappearing?'

'Tell me, Reverend Gilmore, what is *your* interest in Haydon?'

Now it was the vicar's turn to colour and Christie felt she was regaining some ground as he seemed unsure how to answer.

'I think your tone is a little accusatory, young lady, and you're being rather difficult, all of which is unnecessary. Suffice to say that Haydon is a member of my parish so, of course, I'm interested in his welfare. It's my vocation to care for others; it's what I am called to do.'

With its usual unexpectedness, Christie suddenly felt the heat begin to rise in her. *Oh no!* she thought, *not now*. However, instead of feeling faint, she experienced a sense of righteousness and power: this time, the heat was giving her energy and a kind of faith that she was right to say what she was about to suggest to this domineering man of the cloth. 'Reverend, I'm not accusatory,' she said with confidence, 'and I apologise if I've come across that way. There are things I want to say to you, but first, please know that I love Haydon. I love the man I see before me, the man I hold in my arms and the man I want to spend the foreseeable future with.' Christie had the impression she was being spoken through, as though she was not in control of her own soul: someone else was guiding her and giving her wisdom way beyond her years.

'How can you love him, Christie? I'm sure you're fond of him but you don't know the real, deep Haydon. You really do only know what you see before you.'

'Well that's enough for me. I love Haydon Rouse with all my heart and I would do anything for him – anything. And guess what!' She was now shouting, so great was her passion. 'I know that you absolutely understand this, because the truth of the matter is, you love him too!' Almost spitting the last few words at him, she stood back and folded her arms in total defiance. The man in front of her suddenly no longer seemed intimidating: he had almost shrunk before her very eyes, and he shakily moved to sit down. Christie could see that she had hit a nerve and must finish what she had to say. 'Haydon is your grandson, isn't he?'

The silence in the room throbbed with emotion. Christie waited for the vicar to speak, but he simply sat, staring at the floor, visibly aged. She began to feel sorry for him, but at least she had gathered a couple more pieces of the puzzle.

'How on earth did you know?' muttered the reverend.

'If I told you, you probably wouldn't believe me,' she said, relaxing slightly and moving over to the sink to fill the newly acquired electric kettle.

'Who else knows? Someone must have told you. Dear girl, you have to understand that my whole reputation – everything – is at stake here!'

'I'm not interested in destroying you or your family. But I do want to be part of Haydon's future and the one thing that's holding him back is the hurt of being abandoned by his mother; it's a shadow over his life. You can help with solving that problem.'

'I'm not sure how raking up the past can help anyone.'

'Does Haydon know who you are?'

The reverend shook his head and looked Christie in the eye. 'No, and he mustn't know. It could send him over the edge. I'm not sure you realise just how delicate he is. Like his mother, his mind is fragile. Surely you can see that.'

Christie could see what he meant and simply nodded. Sighing, she turned and poured water onto teabags, gazing out of the window for a moment, before adding milk. 'Does your wife know?' she asked, looking back at the old man.

'No one does,' he said brokenly, staring at the tea she put in front of him, as if it could somehow help him. 'Haydon's mother was born out of wedlock and the shame was too much for my parents, so they banished me abroad for a few years. By the time I came back, the only woman I've ever truly loved and the child we made out of that love had both gone. I lived my life the only way that seemed possible – in the Church. It was the only way I could make it up to my parents. Their disappointment still cuts like a knife even though they are, of course, long gone.' He stopped for a moment, frowning suddenly. 'I can't believe I'm talking this way to a virtual stranger,' he said.

'Please, go on,' breathed Christie.

He looked past her into the distance, remembering. 'One day, a timid little bird of a woman came to the vicarage to clean for us. I didn't take much notice, but as she worked I saw something in her: it was as if I recognised her, but I didn't know why. Then she stopped coming and I heard that she had just disappeared, so I went in to see Haydon to ask if he wanted to come and stay with us, but I couldn't reach him. He had started on his road to self-destruction and all I could do was make sure he had money to live and that his rent was paid. I wanted to call the Social Services in, but he made me promise not to. I accepted that because he was sixteen and legally able to make that choice.'

'So you've been paying his rent all these years, and his council tax?'

'Yes. Obviously, it's not usual for me to financially support my parishioners, but even before I realised who he was I felt compelled to help him, and money was the only way: he wouldn't let me do anything else; he didn't seem able to bring himself to trust me. I rationalised my actions by telling myself it was my Christian duty, but I'm not sure I ever believed that.'

'When did you realise that his mother was your daughter?'

'It was most peculiar. It was Christmas Eve, six months after his mother had vanished, and I was sitting in this room with him. As usual he wasn't speaking very much. Then I just felt there was someone else here with us, and I felt warm and safe and … sort of… well, right – it felt right for me to be here. I can't explain it any more than that. And then I felt Haydon staring at me and when I looked at him I saw her eyes – I saw Edith's eyes. And then he smiled – such a beautiful smile. It's the only time I've ever seen him smile. Then he looked away and everything went back to normal, but I had seen her eyes and her smile, and I knew who he was. The torment I felt, knowing my own daughter had been cleaning my house and I didn't recognise her. I wanted, so much, to tell Haydon he wasn't on his own, but how would that help him when I couldn't tell my own family? It's been torture watching him live like this, in squalor and self-imposed poverty. Haydon has always had enough money, but he wouldn't spend it. I tried to persuade him but he just wouldn't. He's always believed it was his mother putting the money into his account.'

'But it was you?'

He looked at his untouched tea. 'Time went by and I just had to keep the lie going.' Tears rolled down his face and plopped onto the table as he pulled a handkerchief out of his pocket to wipe them away and then, finally, he took a gulp of tea.

Christie understood the enormity of the situation. She was now equipped with life-altering information about Haydon's past which could affect his future and could well affect his emotional stability. Unless she could find a way for him to understand the truth, it would lie between them like a huge but invisible wedge.

She and the aged vicar were sitting in silence, each considering from their own perspective what might be the consequences of the conversation they had just had, when Haydon returned with the washing. Christie heard the door and leaned across the table to whisper urgently, 'You need to tell him, Reverend. He needs to know.' She put her hand on his forearm, desperately searching his expression for agreement.

He quickly placed his hand over hers. 'Not yet! Please, not yet!'

Haydon's smile faded when he saw the vicar sitting in his kitchen with Christie.

'Reverend Gilmore likes what we've done to the house,' she said brightly, hoping she wasn't overdoing it and sounding slightly false.

Haydon acknowledged the reverend with a small nod and the old man seemed to gather himself before standing up to his full height and walking over to place a hand on Haydon's shoulder.

'You've both done wonders with the place,' he said. 'I'm very pleased for you. And now, I'm going to leave you two young people to enjoy your evening.' He stepped towards the door. 'I'll call in and see you soon,' he added, looking back and smiling at the young woman who had not exposed him. 'Christie is a wonderful young lady, Haydon. You're a very lucky man.'

With their attention on her, Christie looked from one to the other and felt her heart would break. For a second she wanted to blurt out everything she knew, but she fully understood the devastation she might cause if she acted on impulse. She smiled sweetly and said nothing.

Reverend Gilmore walked slowly back up the hill to the vicarage, his mind in turmoil. Until now, there had not been a living soul who knew that Haydon Rouse was, in fact, his grandson. Not only was there another who now knew the truth, but she was emotionally involved. His whole world could turn upside down: a scandal in a small community such as Porthtreval would finish him, once and for all. It would be the end of all that he had known and built over the years. He would have to retire – and what an ignominious reason for leaving his post. His whole life would be considered a sham. Nor would he be the only one hurt: Cynthia would never forgive him for keeping a skeleton such as this in the cupboard.

He could not face going home. Instead he walked into the churchyard and made his way round to the rear of the building, where he let himself quietly into the vestry and sat in the still silence of his little office. Closing his eyes, he asked for help.

'Come on. I've got something to show you.' Leaving the new revelation lying unspoken in the kitchen, Christie took Haydon's hand and led him through the front room and up the, as yet, uncarpeted stairs. Pausing outside the bedroom door, she turned to him and smiled mischievously, twisting coyly from side to side before straightening up and meeting his gaze. There was fire in his eyes, burning into her soul, entering her thoughts, her heart, her whole being; the spiritual power she drew from him was exquisitely unique and sensual. She reached up and tenderly touched his cheek and then traced her finger over his mouth. Opening his lips, he met her fingertip with his tongue and her eyes widened as a shared energy coursed through her.

    Haydon broke the spell with a knowing smile and looked towards the bedroom door. Christie opened it and led him in, watching his smile broaden as he scanned the room with its low lamplight and brand new bed. The curtains were drawn and she gave him a few moments to take everything in before slipping her arms round his neck.

    'Do you like it?' she asked expectantly.

    'It's lovely,' he smiled with an affirming nod. 'Just how it should be. There's love in the room.'

    Christie stood back in amazement. 'Haydon! That's really lovely! What makes you say that?'

    'Well …' A frown creased his brow as he searched for the right words. He was obviously struggling and Christie cursed herself for pushing him.

    'Never mind, I'm just thrilled you like it. And you're right: there is love in this room, but that, my darling, is because you and I are in it! Now, come on. Let's have a celebratory dinner. I bought some ice and there's a bottle of champagne chilling in a bucket in the shed.'

Christie's culinary repertoire was limited, to say the least, but she felt confident with sausage and mash. She had peeled the home grown potatoes and carrots earlier in the day and now lit the gas under the two saucepans while lining up the sausages on the grill pan, tutting to herself as she realised she hadn't bought gravy granules. *Oh well,* she thought, *I'll add a tin of peas and we can have ketchup.*

Haydon was in the garden, pulling out a few weeds and watering his vegetables. He brought in a large onion and handed it to her with a smile. 'Shall we cook it in some butter to have with the sausages?'

Christie was slightly surprised and flustered: playing house was all so new to her. 'Lovely idea,' she agreed, taking the onion. A spasm of worry hit her stomach as she watched him go back out into the garden and her mind sprang back to the earlier conversation with the vicar. Haydon was happy and she didn't want to be the one to destroy that. Despite the fact that, in truth, it had nothing to do with her, she felt that, in one way, it actually had everything to do with her: she was the catalyst bringing it all out in the open, thanks to communications from someone beyond the grave. Plus, from her own point of view, Haydon was now, inextricably, a huge part of her life.

She thought about the latest pieces of the puzzle to come to light: the spirit now had a name – Edith; the face at the window, the source of energy she experienced as heat, was Haydon's grandmother – Reverend Gilmore's own true love. How sad, confused, scared and upset he must be feeling. Underneath the stiff upper lip and ecclesiastical inflection, he was a man who had loved, lost and then lived a lie for more than half a century. Compassion demanded that she get in touch with him and offer her support. But he must be the one to tell Haydon, and maybe he knew more than he was letting on about Haydon's mother.

A loud spitting sound from the grill brought her mind back to the present. Here she was, cooking for her man! Such a simple thing and yet it excited her so much. Calling out of the door, she reminded Haydon about the champagne cooling in the rapidly melting ice. A refrigerator was definitely next on the list. One step at a time, though.

She waited while he stood outside, wrestling first with the foil, then the wire and finally the cork, and laughed when the cork popped out suddenly and shot off into the Critchley's garden, accompanied by a loud 'Whoa!' from Haydon. He brought the bottle triumphantly into the kitchen, and poured the champagne into the two mugs Christie was holding ready. They toasted each other, laughing at the clunking sound of the two mugs as they brought them together, and then gazed at each other as they sipped.

'I love you Haydon.' There, she had said it, without thought, preparation or doubt. Now, she held her breath, waiting for Haydon's reaction.

He tipped his head to one side, somewhat quizzically. 'I know you do,' he said.

It was dusk when they sat down to a candlelit dinner; the novelty of electricity in the house could not outweigh the romance and sensuality of candle light. Haydon had stuck to one glass of bubbly and then reached over to the cupboard for a can of beer. He was about to drink from the can but glanced at Christie and checked himself; Christie giggled when he poured the contents into his mug. She was feeling light headed, the bubbles having taken delicious effect.

After lemon cheesecake and a cup of tea, she sat back in her chair and observed the fascinating man across the table. She was ready, she wanted to take him upstairs and give herself to him. But she couldn't tell if he was ready. He had certainly seemed to be whenever they were physically close, but was he ready emotionally? She was fairly sure that she would have to lead the way, but it could all go wrong. Her own inexperience may well let her down and ruin what they were building.

She was brought out of her drifting thoughts by Haydon saying her name. Once again, she felt his eyes penetrating her psyche. Incredibly, as he looked into her, it was as if he was making love to her without moving, speaking or touching her. He stood up, took her by the hand and they slowly mounted the stairs. As though he had been reading her thoughts, he was taking the lead, showing her his readiness. Christie's heart was pounding with excitement

The bedroom was softly lit by the single lamp. Haydon pushed the door shut behind them and took her head in his hands, slipping them under her hair. Bringing his lips to hers, he kissed her with extreme gentleness, making Christie want to cry, so sweet was the tenderness. Haydon was telling her without words, which so often eluded him, that he loved her. He pulled back and looked deep into her eyes, almost breathing the words, 'I want you.' She backed towards the bed and pulled back the new, crisp covers. Everything was plump and inviting. Outside, late summer holidaymakers could be heard chatting and laughing as they made their way back to their cottages and apartments dotted around the town. A dog barked a few houses up the road and a car started up in the high street, just a few yards away. Christie heard it all but registered none of it. Haydon was watching her, his face wearing the obvious desire he was feeling as she undid her checked shirt and slipped it off her shoulders, letting it fall to the floor. Undoing her jeans, she wiggled them down over her hips and stepped out of them. He still stood motionless but she could feel his energy, and her own – the heat now rising in her was desire. Unhooking her bra and slipping off her panties, she stood before him. 'I'm yours,' she whispered as she reached out for him to come to her.

He felt a tiny moment of hesitation. This was it. Everything she did fascinated him; she had become his everything; he existed only to look at her and hear her voice. In contrast to that fateful day, when the only person he had ever loved had left him, and he had thought he could never trust another woman again; when he had allowed himself to become dirty, uncouth and undesirable so that no one could get near and hurt him – in contrast to all that, this magical creature had unveiled herself and was standing in front of him, offering herself to him. How perfect she was, her skin pale and smooth, like porcelain, her body lithe and firm with small rounded breasts topped off with nipples just waiting to be kissed. How he wanted her! His blood was rushing through him like an express train, yet he felt powerless to move. He allowed her magnetism to pull him to her, feeling the heat of her arousal. He touched her shoulders and ran his fingers up and down her arms, delighting in her gasp at his touch. She smiled, closing her eyes, and he kissed her neck and shoulders, breathing in the fragrance of her – lavender and dewy mornings. She was intoxicating and so soft – how could anyone have skin that soft?

  Now she was reaching up and helping him off with his T-shirt. It was her turn to touch, and she traced patterns across his chest, running her fingers through his dark chest hair. He felt on fire and wanted to join her in her nakedness. He quickly undid his shorts, which were becoming restrictive, and removed all his clothing. Now they stood naked, just inches apart, their shared anticipation exquisitely seductive. He drew her body to his and they both moaned in ecstasy as skin touched skin, and he trembled as she gently stroked and coaxed his growing erection. Instinctively, he kissed her deeply, with primal passion.

Christie turned and got into bed, looking at her man, naked, for the first time. She took in his slim, firm torso, his dark body hair and the well-defined muscles of his arms and shoulders. 'You're really beautiful, Haydon,' she said. 'Come and make love to me.'

  He slid in beside her on the cool sheets. She took his hand and showed him how to pleasure her. She was ready for him and he increased her mounting desire with his fingers as she lay back, tensing and relaxing in time with his touch. He moved in between her legs and she opened to him, aching as she was for him, and totally at one with the moment. All protective thoughts of ensuring Haydon's well-being had disappeared – dispersed by pure physical lust: she had to have this man inside her. Haydon reached down to guide himself into her, his instincts more than making up for his lack of experience. Her hips rose to meet him and their bodies rocked and rose like the Atlantic waves. They fed on each other's mouths and caressed and massaged everything within reach, until Christie's arousal was at its height and she clamped her arms around his neck as her climax crashed through her. Haydon was a bit confused about what had happened but it felt right and so he went with it. Christie relaxed under him, mewing like a kitten, but then she came to and brought her attention back to him. Moving her hips up against his, the motion once more began and Haydon felt an indescribable feeling mounting in his whole body. As he ejaculated inside her, he forgot everything – the past, his abandonment, his pain all dissolved into nothing as his mind exploded and he called out Christie's name.

    Christie held him close, feeling him trembling and wondering if he was all right. When he turned his face to her, she could see from his blissful smile that he was just fine. His body was damp with sweat, but his breathing was becoming even as the adrenalin running through him abated. Throwing the covers off, he rolled over and lay beside her, stoking the soft skin of her belly. Christie guessed what was about to happen, and she was right: with the smile still on his lips, his eyes slowly closed and within minutes, his hand on her stomach had stilled and he slept.

Chapter 20

Diane had dressed carefully and taken extra care with her makeup. Her emotions were in turmoil and she had the surreal sensation that it was another version of herself now walking down the stairs of the hotel to join Brian in the bar. They had decided to have a drink first and then go out for dinner as the hotel menu was unappealing, and the receptionist had given them directions to an Italian restaurant just a few minutes' walk away.

Brian was standing waiting with two glasses of white wine. 'Wow! Look at you!' he said appreciatively, kissing her blushing cheek in welcome. 'I took the liberty of ordering a dry white. Is that okay?' he asked, pushing the glass towards her.

'Lovely, thanks, Brian,' she nodded.

'Come on, let's sit down over there,' he suggested, indicating a secluded corner on the opposite side of the room.

The wine tasted like nectar and Diane immediately began to relax after feeling totally out of sorts. She couldn't work out if it was Brian's proximity or the uncertainty about whether or not her husband was straying in her absence; or, indeed, the sheer oddity of her situation – fantasizing about one man, while insecure about her husband. Was she guilty of a double standard?

Brian was again asking her about her family and how she was finding the workload he was giving her.

'You really are asking a lot of questions, Brian. I'm flattered that you're interested but is there a specific reason?' She looked at him with hooded eyes. It was the first time she had given him any kind of signal that she was attracted to him.

He wriggled uneasily in his seat and attempted an explanation. 'It's just a good opportunity to make sure that everything is going well for you, because I know you've been through it over the past few months. I'm fond of you, Di. I want to make sure you're happy.'

Diane sipped her wine and wondered what he was playing at. Was he interested in her as a friend, a colleague, her boss, or were there other thoughts on his mind? She sighed and looked around the bar, watching a solitary man in the corner working feverishly on his iPad, as the silence between her and Brian lengthened. Finally she just came out with the thought she had been battling to ignore. 'I think Pete may be having an affair.'

Brian's eyes widened in surprise. 'Really? I'm shocked, Di, I really am. He's always seemed such a steady character – well, from what you've told me about him, anyway.'

'And that's the case, most of the time. Pete is one of the nicest people in the world, but he's a sucker for any woman who's vulnerable and having problems. He's a great shoulder to cry on and constantly gets himself into situations where he gives out the wrong messages. But this time, I can tell that the interest is mutual. He's done it before and I recognise the signs. Pete has a very large self-destruct button and I think he may be about to press it – if he hasn't already.' Diane took a large gulp of her wine to calm her emotions.

'I don't really know what to say. I'm so sorry. If I had known I wouldn't have suggested you come away on this job. I could have covered it on my own.'

'No, I'm glad I'm here. It's probably just what I need right now. Anyway, let's not talk about Pete. Let's change the subject. '

Brian leaned forward and momentarily covered Diane's hand with his own. She felt a warm glow at his touch and she looked directly into his eyes. The look she received back showed friendly concern rather than anything else she might have wanted to see.

'I'm sorry things aren't too good for you, at the moment. I'm sure it will all be okay in the long run, though. Maybe you need to have a good chat when you get home.'

Diane shrugged, feeling mildly irritated: the conversation was not going how she wanted.

The crowded restaurant was obviously a popular venue. Brian and Diane were shown to a corner table next to the window. With soft music playing in the background and more wine, Diane soon let thoughts of home and Pete slip away into another world, while she focused fully on Brian's animated face as he told her of his plans for the online aspect of the newsgroup. He was explaining that he knew they would have to constantly innovate to keep up with the competition and not get left floundering on the side-lines like so many other regional news groups.

Diane laughed and joked with him at every opportunity, thoroughly enjoying herself as the wine clouded her senses and she felt her more reckless side emerging. As he was talking, she was imagining his lips on hers and his hot, urgent hands on her body. She pictured them falling onto the bed in the hotel room, tugging at each other's clothes. She wondered what it would be like to feel his full body weight on hers as he entered her. She found herself looking at him with longing eyes, hoping he would pick up on her lustful feelings.

After paying the bill, he took her arm, guided her out of the restaurant and back to the hotel. The cold night air did little to sober her up; she was unable to walk straight and incapable of not giggling. She noticed Brian roll his eyes at the receptionist as she was manoeuvred into the lift but she didn't care and grinned up at him as the doors closed and he put his arm round her, holding her fast until the lift stopped on the eighth floor.

'Where's your key, Di?'

'Dunno. Can't remember what I did with it. I'll have to come to your room. Take me to your room,' she pleaded with glazed eyes.

'Come on, let's have a look.' Taking her bag and checking in the side pocket, Brian located the electronic key and opened the door, holding Diane upright as she almost fell into the room and laughing at her antics. 'Let's get you into bed,' he chuckled.

Becoming suddenly quiet and compliant, Diane plopped down on the bed and kicked off her shoes, and then allowed Brian to slip her jacket off. Reaching behind her he unzipped her dress, then helped her up and slipped it off her shoulders. Now standing in her bra and panties, she made a concentrated effort to stop swaying and lean towards Brian with her face raised for a kiss. This was the moment she had been waiting for – the moment all of her fantasies had been built around. Brian took her face in his hands and looked into her eyes, which she closed, waiting for the touch of his lips on hers; instead, Brian kissed her forehead. He then pulled back the covers and gently steered her onto the bed.

'Lie down,' he said quietly.

Diane did as she was told, expecting him to join her.

'Sweet dreams,' he said, pulling the duvet up over her. 'I'll call you at seven to make sure you're up.'

Diane promptly sat up. 'Brian!' she said, holding her hand out to him.

'Di, you're very lovely, but you're also very married. It would be oh so easy to get into bed with you and take advantage of you, but that's not what friends do. So I'm going now. You have some issues to sort out with Pete, remember?'

Diane nodded like a little girl.

'Well, I hardly think us jumping into bed together is going to help that, is it?' Brian continued.

This time she shook her head.

'Some years ago, I was at a low point. You may remember a hot kiss at a hotel door.'

She nodded.

'You did me a favour that night. You didn't know it but I was going through a similar thing to what your Pete may be going through, now. I was well and truly pressing my self-destruct button and your rejection made me come to my senses. I'll be honest, I wasn't happy about it at the time, but it changed me. I was used to getting my own way and you made me think twice about my behaviour.' He sat down on the bed beside her. Tenderly moving a piece of stray hair from her cheek, he bent and lightly kissed her. 'I'm returning the favour.'

After leaving a glass of water on the bedside table, he tiptoed out of the room and left an already snoring Diane to sleep her way through to a hangover.

The phone call at seven o'clock the next morning was not the first thing to wake Diane up: a pounding headache had done that an hour earlier. She had taken some strong pain killers and drunk at least two pints of water, and the worst feeling she was now experiencing was acute embarrassment. Picking up the phone she gave a little sigh of a hello.

''Morning. Feeling like crap?'

'Spot on, Brian. I've been up for an hour, though, so I'm starting to feel more human. I'm so sorry about last night. I behaved badly and I hope you weren't offended.'

'Offended? Hey, more like flattered!' he laughed. 'Get yourself downstairs and let's have some breakfast.'

She was relieved by Brian's obvious lack of concern over her sad attempt at seduction, but she was still mortified. And how could she get things back on a professional footing, now that boundaries had been crossed, not once but twice? It just wasn't going to be possible. They were even, now, though, at least.

As it turned out, they worked seamlessly together, as if they'd been doing it for years. With the interview taped and all the details collected, they started the long journey home. As the miles sped by, Diane found herself seeing Brian in a completely different light and, with his help, was able to laugh at her juvenile behaviour. Vowing to sit down with Pete and give her marriage the respect and attention it deserved, she felt confident she could get it back on track and all would be well.

Chapter 21

Christie lay looking at Haydon as he slept. What an enigma he was. He certainly intrigued her and she felt blessed to have been guided to him, albeit in such an unconventional way. Her mind drifted back to the conversation with Reverend Gilmore. The spirit, whom she was now assuming was Edith, had been guiding her to get involved with this disjointed family and Christie now believed that her task ahead was to solve the mystery and bring them all together, if that was possible. Being contacted by the dead certainly was a surreal experience, but as she lay there with Haydon she realised that at no stage had she ever felt afraid, which really was very odd.

Her next step would be to speak to Reverend Gilmore again. She would be sensitive but she had to find a way for Haydon to know the truth about his mother and that would definitely involve the vicar. Sighing, she stretched over to her jeans pocket to find her phone and check the time. Eleven fifteen. She really ought to be getting home. Staying the whole night with Haydon, much as she would like to, was not yet an option. For one thing, her father would be worried if she wasn't there in the morning, and she didn't want to complicate the working relationship that Haydon had with him, either.

She looked back at the man whose life she had helped turn around, to find his sleepy eyes were on her. As she leaned over to softly kiss him, his arms immediately scooped her to him and she found herself lying back against the pillow with his face above her. She relaxed into the love in his eyes and allowed him to take delectable charge. He pulled back the covers and ran his hands over her naked body while kissing her neck and shoulders;

she moaned with pleasure and left all thoughts of going home aside for the moment.

It was approaching one o'clock in the morning by the time they started the short uphill walk back towards her home. The night was cool and Haydon held her close to keep her warm. At the top of the hill and in sight of the cottage, Christie stopped and Haydon turned to envelope her in an embrace. They kissed, not wanting to part, the intensity of new love binding them together.

'You go back now, darling,' she said. 'I don't want to wake Dad and I'll be fine from here. I'll see you tomorrow.'

'I wish you could have stayed,' he murmured against her lips as he kissed her.

'Soon. It will be soon. I love you,' replied Christie, pulling herself away from him.

He watched as she approached the rear gate and then, as she went out of sight, he turned and walked back down the hill, ducking in between two cars to let a van pass as he went.

Christie, meanwhile, had stopped alongside her father's newly acquired works van to find her back door key, and she stepped into the driveway to allow the same van to pass. She didn't notice it stop a few metres away and its lights go off, so engrossed was she in searching her handbag for her keys. Nor did she hear the van door open or the soft footsteps approaching her from behind, so she had no time to scream when a foul-smelling cloth was clamped firmly over her mouth and nose, sending her into initial panic and then unconscious oblivion.

The next morning dawned bright and clear with a hint of autumn breeze in the air. A fine dew had gathered and Haydon noticed that the leaves on his vegetables glistened with a layer of moisture that would burn off as the sun rose. The summer was coming to an end, and soon the holiday cottages would be battened down for the winter, leaving a rapidly diminished population in the town. Haydon walked with a spring in his step, just like any other young man in love, and especially so since it was his first love. He had slept well, lying on the side of the bed that Christie had occupied, her fragrance still on the pillows stirring memories of their love-making and causing him to marvel at the wonder of having sex.

It was just approaching eight o'clock when he reached Pete, who was loading his van with the tools they needed for the day.

'All right, Haydon? Christie still down at yours, then?' said Pete.

Haydon was perplexed. He didn't know what Pete was talking about and he didn't know what to say. So, in true Haydon style, he said nothing.

'You okay?' asked Pete, looking up in response to silence.

Haydon pulled himself together. 'Pete, Christie came home last night. She's not with me.'

'What?! But she's not here! Her bed hasn't been slept in.'

Fear churned in Haydon's stomach. How could this be? He had seen her go home with his own eyes.

'I'll look again,' said Pete, leaving his tools at the side of the van, 'but I'm sure she hasn't been home, unless she got up ridiculously early and went out before I woke up. What time did she come home?'

'Late,' Haydon replied, feeling guilty about that. 'It was gone one.'

Pete's face was etched with worry as he rushed into the house and straight upstairs to Christie's room with Haydon close on his heels. Both men stood looking at her neatly made bed. Ignoring Haydon, Pete went straight to James' room and flung open the door. 'James. Have you seen Chris?'

James stirred and peered at his father through bleary teenage eyes. About to react angrily to the sudden intrusion, he changed his mind when he saw the concern on his father's face. 'Not since yesterday morning. Why? What's wrong?'

'She didn't come home last night. Christ! What the hell has happened to her?'

'Dad! Calm down! She's a grown up! She'll have stayed the night with Haydon. It was bound to happen sooner or later.'

'Haydon is here,' said Pete, drawing back so that his son could see Haydon on the landing behind him. 'He said she came home after one.' Pete turned once more to Haydon. 'Did you walk her home?'

Panic rose in Haydon's chest. 'Yes. Well, to the top of the hill. She said for me to go but I watched her get to the back gate.'

'Did you see her go in?' urged Pete, grabbing Haydon's arm.

'No, not through the gate, but she was right there. She wouldn't have gone anywhere else. I don't understand.'

Pete could hear the fear rising in Haydon's voice and took a breath, remembering that the young man was vulnerable. 'Okay,' he said, trying to keep his voice calm, 'there has to be a reasonable explanation. Come and show me where you last saw her.' The words 'last saw her' made Pete feel sick and, for a moment, he thought he was going to vomit. Taking deep breaths he followed Haydon back outside, and as they went out of the gate, Pete saw it: wedged down between the wall and his parked van was Christie's handbag. 'Oh no! Dear god, no!' he cried as he lifted the handle of Christie's small red handbag. The contents seemed to all be there, including her phone, and for a few seconds Pete and Haydon just stood staring at each other in horror.

Without speaking, Pete rushed back inside the house. Haydon did not know what to do. His mind was in turmoil. He couldn't believe it was happening again: someone he loved had just vanished. But this was not like before: Christie would not have simply run away – left one day, never to return; she must have been taken. But by whom? He followed Pete into the house and found him on the house phone giving his details to someone, presumably the police. Waiting for him in the kitchen, Haydon played back in his mind the moment when he had parted from Christie. It was so late that he had not seen anyone around, apart from whoever was in the white van. He wracked his brain. Had he seen that white van before? Panic was scrambling his memory but if there was one thing that Haydon was good at it was watching and noticing things. He knew most of the permanent residents in the town. Whom did he know who had a white van? It could have nothing to do with it, but it was all they had.

The police car arrived at the cottage within fifteen minutes of Pete's call, having been parked up in the next town when the call came through. PC Bromsgrove and PC Steel were both fathers of teenagers and shared Pete's anxiety. PC Bromsgrove had met Haydon several years before, when he had been attacked by a group of local youths. The officer had been polite enough to Haydon but he had not enjoyed dealing with the rather pungent recluse. Because Haydon now looked so different, PC Bromsgrove had yet to recognise him. That all changed when he took down Haydon's details.

'I think we've met before, haven't we?' he asked, his face suffused with recollection and surprise.

Haydon nodded.

'You're certainly looking different these days. So tell us about your relationship with the young lady in question.'

Haydon looked to Pete for guidance but Pete was staring out of the window as if about to rush out and start looking for his daughter. Haydon could understand that as he wanted to do the same. Not getting any clues as to what to say from Pete, he quietly stated, 'Christie is my girlfriend.'

Both officers glanced at each other and shifted in their seats, causing Haydon to feel as if a huge finger of blame was pointing directly at him. They started asking questions, but then PC Bromsgrove stopped the direction they were going and asked Pete if he could have a word with him outside.

'Sir, can you tell me more about Haydon Rouse's relationship with your daughter?' the officer asked once they were outside in the yard.

'What do you want to know? They recently got together and Christie has helped him transform from a bit of a recluse into the man you see today. That's it really. He works for me as a labourer.'

'How long have you known him?'

'Just a few months – since we moved in earlier this summer.'

'Are you aware of his circumstances?'

'What do you mean?'

'Well, the fact that he's a recluse who let's no one near him; someone who's not, perhaps, mentally stable.'

'Oh, he's odd, I grant you, but he's a gentle soul who wouldn't hurt a fly. You know him then?'

'Yes, some years ago he came to our notice and is well known amongst the officers who patrol Porthtreval. I'm not sure he's as trustworthy as you make out. We'll need to question him and search his house.'

'I don't care what you do, officer. Just find my daughter.' Pete's eyes filled up and PC Bromsgrove put a reassuring arm on his shoulder.

'We shall certainly do our very best, sir.'

By midday there were approximately fifty officers in the Porthtreval area and the police helicopter could be seen scouring the coastline. Pete had thought about calling Diane but decided there was little she could do and it seemed pointless to worry her. Officers with sniffer dogs were searching the rocky hillsides on both sides of the town and the Under Water Search Unit had been deployed to search the lake. Christie's phone and handbag had been taken for forensic examination and the police had searched her bedroom, but found little to help them.

Haydon's cottage was a hive of activity. While he sat in his kitchen with PC Bromsgrove, his house was being examined by two forensic officers, and his garden and shed were being searched by two other officers.

'Haydon, I'm going to ask you some very personal questions,' said PC Bromsgrove carefully. Having met Haydon before he considered him something of an unknown quantity, and, despite what Christie's father had said, thought that there was a strong possibility that he could have got carried away with Christie and gone too far. 'We're just gathering information so that we have all the facts necessary to find Christie. Do you understand?'

Haydon nodded mutely.

'Okay. So when did Christie become your girlfriend?'

Haydon took his time considering the answer, since it had just sort of happened and it was difficult to pinpoint a specific day. He decided it was the day he'd had his hair cut, because she'd hugged him that day. 'About two months ago,' he finally said.

'And have you had sex with Christie?'

Haydon blushed and said he had, while PC Bromsgrove watched his face closely.

'How many times?'

'Two,' muttered Haydon, as though it was something to be ashamed of.

'When was that?'

'Last night.' Haydon could see that he was under suspicion, but did not comment or prematurely protest his innocence.

'Did Christie have sex with you willingly, Haydon?'

'Of course!' Haydon's eyes blazed with indignation. How dare this policeman sully their beautiful love making!

PC Bromsgrove held his hand up. 'I'm sorry I have to ask these questions, Haydon, but it's important we consider every possibility and eliminate anything that won't help us to find her.'

Haydon calmed himself but was now angry as well as frightened.

The forensic team came down with bags full of things they had taken from Haydon's bedroom.

'Don't worry, you'll get everything back,' PC Bromsgrove assured him, seeing the distress on Haydon's face as he watched the officers leave the house with the bags.

Back at the station, later that afternoon, PC Bromsgrove was briefing Detective Chief Inspector Williams about his interview with Haydon. 'To be honest, sir, he comes across as a bit simple … Well, maybe simple is the wrong word … He lacks normal social skills and he may be slightly autistic, in my opinion, although I don't think that's ever been diagnosed.'

DCI Williams briefly perused the interview notes. 'Is he violent, do you think?'

PC Bromsgrove shook his head. 'That's one thing he does have going for him – no history of violence. But then, who knows? He hasn't had a girlfriend before, by all accounts, so he may be dealing with overwhelming emotions for the first time – at nearly thirty years of age.'

'We obviously don't have enough to arrest him, at the moment; maybe forensics will come up with something. Did he say anything else of interest?'

'He openly admits that they had sex last night, so it's not likely that forensics will come up with much we don't already know on that score. He did mention that he walked her home, left her in sight of her back gate, and a white van passed him – the only vehicle he saw on his way there and back. He didn't notice it stop, but it was going towards the place where Christie should have gone into her house.'

'Did he get a registration number?'

'No such luck, but he did know of several vans in the town. Haydon Rouse watches everything; he was known for staring and upsetting people, in the past – all part of his odd behaviour. The good thing, of course, is that he doesn't miss much.'

'Okay. Check out the vans and get back to me.'

Haydon was asked not to leave his house, for the time being, and although he wasn't under arrest he felt powerless and thought he may as well have been. From his window he watched the house to house enquiry instigated by PC Steel and wondered what his neighbours were saying about him.

He need not have worried as the general consensus was, yes, they had known Haydon for a long time; yes, he was a bit odd; yes, he appeared to have gone through a dramatic physical change but, no, he was unlikely to have harmed Christie.

As time passed, Haydon became frustrated, trapped in his own house and unable to go out looking for Christie. The police didn't seem to be getting anywhere and every hour that passed could mean that Christie was in more and more danger. He felt tremendous guilt that he hadn't seen her right to her door. If he had done that one simple thing, she would be here with him now. What a contrast this was to the previous day, when he thought he had regained his life and had a future, after all. Now, his self-loathing was at an all-time high. A police woman had come to sit with him and had made tea for them both, but Haydon was so sick with worry he couldn't drink it. When PC Steel came into the house to question him, he was glad of the opportunity to, perhaps, be of some help.

'Who else would know that Christie was with you yesterday, apart from her family, of course?' the officer asked.

'No one really,' said Haydon. 'The neighbours may have seen her come in. Oh, and Reverend Gilmore was here talking to her when I got back from the launderette.'

PC Steel raised his eyebrows. 'And you didn't think to mention this?'

'No,' said Haydon, thinking it a pointless question.

'Are you referring to the vicar at St Mary's?'

'Yes.'

'Do you know what they were talking about?'

'No, Reverend Gilmore left as soon as I got home and Christie didn't mention anything.'

'And you didn't ask?'

'No, the reverend often visits to see how things are.'

PC Steel clenched his teeth in frustration.

It was past three o'clock in the afternoon by the time PC Steel drove up to the vicarage and repeated Christie's earlier actions at the front door, hearing a faint tinkling sound way off in the bowels of the house in response to the bell pull, and waiting. Eventually, he heard footsteps approaching the imposing oak door, which almost immediately creaked open.

'Mrs Gilmore?'

'Yes, how can I help you?'

'Good afternoon, ma'am. Police Constable Steel,' he said, showing her his ID. 'Is your husband at home?'

'He is. May I tell him what it is you'd like to see him about?'

'It's a delicate matter, Mrs Gilmore. If you could just tell him that I'm here to talk to him about a missing person.'

She invited him in and showed him into a pleasant sitting room where a semi-circle of antique chairs were set out.

'Before you go Mrs Gilmore,' said PC Steel as she moved to close the door, 'can I ask you: do you know Christie Styles?

She's the girlfriend of Haydon Rouse, one of your husband's parishioners.'

Cynthia Gilmore's face clouded over and she seemed uncertain about how to answer. 'Erm … I'm sorry, officer, but you really will need to talk to my husband about this.'

PC Steel recognised evasion when he saw it. 'And I will, Mrs Gilmore, but at the moment I'm asking you. It would be most helpful if you would just answer the question. The young lady has gone missing in extremely suspicious circumstances and we're very concerned for her safety. It's imperative that we gain as much information as possible to help us understand Christie that little bit more.'

Cynthia was obviously anxious and PC Steel could see that she was hiding something. He was, thus, all the more determined to find out what she knew. She was staring at him as if tongue tied, and then gave her head a little shake.

'Of course,' she said. 'I'm so sorry. I didn't realise the gravity of the situation. I believe she came to see my husband a few weeks ago. I'm not sure what she wanted, but it concerned that Haydon Rouse fellow – a peculiar character, if ever there was one. My husband was out, at the time, and I told her she would have to come back another time, so she left'

'I see,' said PC Steel, jotting down a few things in his notebook. 'And you haven't seen her since?'

'No, I haven't.'

'Has your husband seen her since then, do you know?'

'I have absolutely no idea, officer. You'll have to ask him.'

PC Steel nodded and Cynthia Gilmore left the room with a swift, tight smile and a nod of the head. She returned with her husband, who was wiping his hands on a tea towel.

'Excuse the wet hands, officer. I was washing up.'

'Sorry to disturb you, Reverend Gilmore, but I want to talk to you about the disappearance of Christie Styles. Could you tell me how you know her and what dealings you've had with her?'

The colour drained out of Alan Gilmore's face and he turned to look at his wife, who was standing behind him looking equally pale. 'I'll deal with this, my dear. It doesn't need to concern you. Perhaps you could finish the dishes?'

His wife was about to turn and go, apparently relieved to be no longer required, when PC Steel interrupted. 'I'd rather Mrs Gilmore stayed, if it's all the same to you, sir. She may be able to be of help.'

'I very much doubt it, officer.'

'Nevertheless, I would rather she stayed.' PC Steel had no intention of budging on this. He could sense an underlying tension in both the vicar and his wife and wanted to know what they were hiding – from the world, from each other, or both. 'Shall we all sit down?' he suggested, indicating the numerous chairs. As the couple settled themselves nervously on the edge of seats, the seasoned police officer sat opposite them and decided on a direct approach. 'I've been a police officer for over twenty five years,' he began, watching their faces, 'and I can always tell when people are hiding something, or perhaps feel unable to speak out of loyalty or affection for another. In this instance, a young girl is missing, possibly dead; at the very least, she is almost certainly in grave danger, so I'm asking you to put all other considerations aside and be completely open and honest. Am I making myself very clear?'

'Very clear, officer,' Reverend Gilmore replied.

PC Steel noted that the old vicar looked suddenly very tired, defeated almost, his manner that of a man who wanted to get something off his chest and tell the truth. 'Haydon told me you were at his home yesterday, talking to Christie. Is that right?'

'Yes.'

'And can you tell me what you were talking about?'

'Well, about Haydon and her relationship with him.'

'What, exactly, was discussed?'

The reverend faltered for a second, glancing at his wife. He then appeared to make a decision, straightened his shoulders and announced with some dignity, 'Haydon Rouse is my grandson.'

The stillness in the room almost vibrated with his words. A tiny gasp escaped Cynthia's lips.

'Did you know of this Mrs Gilmore?'

The vicar and his wife looked at each other. 'Yes, I did,' she said, keeping her eyes locked on her husband, informing him rather than the policeman. Alan Gilmore simply gaped at this latest bombshell.

'I take it neither of you was aware that the other knew,' observed PC Steel.

Tears gathered in Cynthia's eyes as her husband swallowed and found his voice.

'How did you know, Cynthia darling?'

'Oh Alan, I've known for years. I just wasn't aware that you did, too. I thought you were just looking after him out of the kindness of your heart.'

'How did you find out?' he asked, taking her hand in his.

'I realised when I went to visit Kathleen in the residential home over on the north coast.'

'Kathleen? Haydon's mother?'

Cynthia nodded. PC Steel kept silent as he felt that more information was likely to come out that way. He knew about Haydon's past and the way he had turned his back on the world when his mother had upped and left him. Why had Cynthia kept this information from Haydon? Things could have been so different.

Reverend Gilmore was obviously thinking the same thing. 'Cynthia, why did you keep all this to yourself. Haydon was broken when his mother left. It's only recently that he's started to get well again, and that's all due to the love and strength of this young woman, Christie. And now she has gone from him it seems. Oh my! This is a merry mess.'

'It couldn't come out, Alan,' wept Cynthia, dabbing at her tears with a lace-edged handkerchief. 'Not after all these years. Don't you see that? The scandal! I was terrified that it would besmirch your name and we would lose everything we had worked so hard for over the years. I couldn't let it happen to you. I'm so sorry, Alan, I just couldn't.'

Reverend Gilmore sat looking at his wife agape. 'Kathleen is alive?' he spluttered.

'Alive, but not mentally stable,' nodded Cynthia, delicately wiping her nose. 'She's looked after by nuns at St Agatha's home near St Ives. She has little memory of her life, although she often talks about her baby boy. I see her every month and have done since I found out she was there.'

'But how did you find that out, and that she's my daughter? I can't work it out Cynthia. It's beyond my comprehension.'

'I found out by chance that she was at the home when I was at a fund raising event there, some years ago. But I've known who she was since the time she was working for us. You're obviously not aware of this and I never said anything to you, but on numerous occasions, when she worked for us, you called out the name Edith in your sleep. It sounded like this Edith was haunting you – quite heart breaking, it was. Then one day, you and Kathleen were sitting side by side in the kitchen while I was making coffee, and you know how you always pull at your left ear when you're nervous about something? Well, you were both doing it at the same time. You looked like two peas in a pod.
Kathleen was a funny little thing and always very nervous, but as I got to know her there were things about her that constantly reminded me of you: the set of her shoulders, her habit of sitting bolt upright in chairs, certain expressions on her face. At first, I thought I must be imagining it, but the more I paid attention, the

more I realised how like you she was in all sorts of subtle little ways.' Cynthia stopped abruptly and looked hesitantly from her husband to the police officer.

'Please go on, Mrs Gilmore,' PC Steel encouraged, not sure how this was connected with Christie's disappearance but certain that the revelations should continue.

'This will sound odd, but I came into the drawing room one sunny day when we had the French doors open to the garden, and Kathleen was sweeping the patio just outside. She didn't know I was there, and she was talking to someone in a very different tone to her usual timid one. I heard her say, "Oh, don't scold, Mother! Haydon is fine; he's with Mrs Critchley today." There was clearly no one with her, so I called her in and asked her about it. She told me she was talking to her mother, who wasn't happy that she didn't have Haydon with her. I knew her parents had moved to the north years ago and she rarely saw them, so I questioned her more and she said it was her real mother she was talking to – the one who gave her away when she was a baby.' Cynthia paused with a far off look on her face. 'I remember those words distinctly: "the one who gave me away when I was a baby",' she said. 'It was such a sad thing.' Cynthia paused again, reliving the moment in her mind, before giving a little shudder and continuing. 'It was then that I asked if she knew her mother's name. "Edith," she said. My whole world stopped turning, and it suddenly made sense why you resembled each other. I talked to a few of the local old folk who would have, at least, remembered an Edith who became pregnant or left the town, and it was confirmed. No one had put all the pieces together, of course, but I knew there would always be that risk if Kathleen were to return, so I just kept a watchful eye over her. The nuns don't know her relationship to me or my husband: I pretend I'm just a local visitor who got to know her there, in the home. Unfortunately, her health, both in general and mentally, has deteriorated, and ...' Cynthia let out a huge sob. 'Oh, Alan, I've been so evil and I am so very sorry.' She continued to sob into her handkerchief and Alan, in a shocked daze, held her hand.

PC Steel sat quietly trying to make sense of it all and working out how it affected the missing person case. 'So, let me get this straight,' he said. 'Haydon's mother, who has been missing for nearly fifteen years, is in a residential home in St Ives. Her name is Kathleen and she is your daughter Reverend Gilmore, which of course makes Haydon your grandson. You both knew all this, but neither of you knew that the other knew. Is that right?'

'Yes, except that I didn't know where Kathleen was,' the old vicar corrected.

'Okay, so let's get back to the main issue: what was your conversation with Christie about, yesterday?'

'She knew Haydon was my grandson. When I asked her how she knew, she said I wouldn't believe her if she told me. I didn't press her on it. I'm ashamed to say that I was more concerned about it all coming to light. I asked her not to tell Haydon, but she said I would have to tell him soon as it was his right to know. I knew she was right, but I had to think about how to deal with it and how I could bear Cynthia finding out after all these years.' The reverend patted his wife's hand. 'But it seems she already knew,' he said with a wan smile.

This was not helping PC Steel. 'Reverend Gilmore, let's focus on Christie. I really don't want to be coming up here and telling you we've found a body. To be blunt, do you think Haydon could have had anything to do with her disappearance?'

'Good heavens, no!' Reverend Gilmore exclaimed. 'He couldn't hurt a fly, and from what Christie says, they're very much in love. I really think including Haydon in your investigations as a possible suspect is a waste of your time, constable.'

'You may be right, reverend, but we have to consider anyone who might possibly want to harm Christie or hold her against her will. To that end, could you tell me where you were around one o'clock this morning.'

The elderly vicar's face turned a sickly shade of grey and his mouth fell open in dismay. 'You cannot seriously think that I have anything to do with the child's disappearance! That's preposterous!'

'Actually, you both have a motive for preventing Christie from telling what she knows. So I'm afraid these questions have to be asked, however uncomfortable they may be. If I don't ask them, CID will be along to do so later today.'

The elderly couple looked at each other in horror as the realisation sunk in.

'I'm sorry, officer. I can see your point, now that you mention it,' conceded the vicar. 'My wife and I were in our beds at one o'clock this morning, although I don't pretend to have been asleep: that eluded me far into the small hours. I had a lot on my mind, as you can imagine.'

'Of course. Maybe you could help me with something else. A white van was seen in the vicinity of Christie's home at the time of her disappearance. Do you know of anyone in the town who has a white van? It was quite large – a transit-type van – no markings as far as we can make out.'

The Gilmores sat for a moment with brows creased in thought.

'Goodness, now let me think …' Reverend Gilmore began. 'I often see one early in the morning near the public conveniences just up from the library; I've always assumed it was the cleaner's van. Then there are a couple owned by builders up on the council estate, but I believe they may have writing on the sides. Oh, and the boat yard has a van. I know that one doesn't have writing on because we use it for all the tents and luggage on the scouts' annual camping trip.'

It had been a gruelling interview for the elderly couple, and, being of the opinion that he had probably got as much information as possible, for the moment, PC Steel stood up to take his leave and get back to the temporary incident room that had been set up in the town hall. 'Thank you. You've both been most helpful,' he said.

Chapter 22

Blissfully ignorant of all that was happening, Diane arrived home at eight thirty that evening to find Pete at the end of his tether. She had seen several police cars parked in the pub car park just up the road from her home and had wondered what was going on, never dreaming it was anything to do with her family. When she walked into her kitchen and saw a police officer through the open door of the lounge, however, her stomach somersaulted with fear. 'Pete!' she called in a panic, just as he came into the kitchen to her. He seemed to have aged ten years since the previous day, and the wretched Rosie was in attendance, except Diane hardly noticed because the tactful neighbour promptly departed. Pete's face crumpled at the sight of his wife and, wracked with sobs, he fell straight into her arms. 'For god sake, Pete! Tell me!' She pushed him back and held him at arms length, looking into his face.

'Christie's gone missing.'

'Missing?' Diane repeated, as though she had no idea what the word meant. 'Missing?'

'Haydon walked her home late last night and left her at the gate, but she never came in the house. She's just disappeared, Di. I found her handbag outside this morning. Nothing was taken, just her.'

'Oh god, no! Please, no! Not my baby girl!' The strength in her legs began to give way from the shock and she stumbled outside into the fresh air, to sit heavily on one of the picnic chairs. 'What are the police doing?'

'Everything they can.' Pete tried to sound reassuring. 'There have been helicopters, dogs – the lot. If she was here they would have found her. They've even searched the lake. Nothing.'

'Oh god! The lake! No, Pete! She can't be dead! Not our little girl! Not Christie!'

Pete heard the rising hysteria in her voice and gathered her up out of the chair and into his arms. 'We're no good to her if we fall apart,' he said gently but firmly, his own emotions once more under control. Tears poured down her cheeks and he held her as she sobbed.

'Where's Haydon?' she asked when she was calmer.

'At his house. He's not allowed to leave. It's like he's the main suspect.'

'Do you think he should be a suspect, Pete? Do you?' Diane urged. 'After all, we hardly know the man! He could be capable of anything!'

'Sit down, Di,' said Pete, guiding her back into a chair and squatting down in front of her. 'It's not Haydon,' he said confidently, taking Diane's hands in both of his and keeping her focus on him so that she did not lose control. 'I was with him this morning when he came to work. I thought she'd been with him all night, and he was as shocked and upset as me when we realised she was missing. Seriously, if there's one thing that's quite obvious about Haydon: he's no actor.'

Diane had to agree. 'Where's James?'

'He's out with the surfer boys and the police, searching all the farmland and woods surrounding the town. He's phoning in every hour to touch base. They won't be able to search for much longer, though; it'll be too dark, but they'll get back to it at first light.'

Diane slowly got up, feeling exhausted and light-headed. 'I need to be near her things,' she said and walked off into the house. Pete let her go, knowing they both had to deal with this nightmare in their own way.

Diane sat on edge of Christie's bed and picked up her daughter's pyjama top, bunching it up and holding it to her face. She closed her eyes and breathed in Christie's fragrance, thinking about the strong, intuitive or telepathic connection she'd always had with her daughter. When Christie was a baby, Diane would know when she was going to cry five minutes before the child had even woken up; she knew when things were not right at school and would quiz her when she came home; she knew when the latest boyfriend had dumped her and momentarily broken her heart. That connection had weakened in latter years, as Christie's need for her mother's support had lessened, but Diane now wondered if she could activate it at will. For certain, she had to try.

She breathed deeply to calm her mind and relax herself. At first, it was very difficult, given the extreme situation and her level of worry, but she knew any angst would just block her. She closed her eyes and persisted with deep, slow breathing, and as she felt her body relax, she brought to mind an image of Christie and held it there, concentrating her full focus on her daughter. Nothing seemed to be happening, until she became aware of a comfortable sensation of heat rising through her body and with it, the sound of purring. She thought it was her imagination or her mind playing tricks, but the sound was so comforting and the warmth so safe and secure that she did not want the experience to leave her. Nevertheless, the purring abruptly stopped and Diane's eyes flew open. The first thing she saw was Christie's laptop lying open on the bedside table. Surely it had been closed before. Because it seemed like the logical thing to do, she pushed the power button and waited, the calming heat still with her. A moment later, a picture of Haydon and Christie appeared on the screen. They were sitting on the bench on the piece of grass at the head of the harbour, and behind them was the inner harbour, full of colourful little fishing boats, their windows and chrome fixtures glinting in the sunlight. Diane opened up a blank document, deciding that writing a letter to Christie would be a good way to 'talk' to her and strengthen the connection.

My Darling,

I just cannot wait to see your wonderful, smiling face once more, as you come home to the place where you belong. It seems as if several lifetimes have passed, but now you have been found and you are on your way to be with the ones who love you.

Diane cried as her fingers whizzed across the keyboard in practised fashion, not taking much notice of the words she was forming. It just felt good to be with Christie, even in this removed way.

It has been so long since you left those who love you, my darling, though to you it may seem like minutes. Your gentle soul will now be cherished as it should be, and you will know, after all this time, just how much you are loved.

My heart sings as I imagine you walking through the door, your face lit up with expectancy and delight, your arms ready to embrace and you heart open to receive. This is what I have been waiting for, my love. This is what I have wanted for a whole lifetime. It is now, my darling, it is now.

Diane stopped, bewildered by the words she had written. Was it shock and distress making her write such things? What was happening? Whatever it was, the urge to continue was as powerful as the urge to push when giving life to her daughter. So she continued.

But before we go gladly into the light my darling, we must give our attention to another who is in dreadful need; another whom we both will love, in time; another whose kind heart is bruised, stricken and empty. She lies without words or movement, but she has both life and breath. She rises and falls with the Atlantic swell, but she does not travel; she is still. We must help her, my darling, if those we love are to be happy.

Diane had just re-read the 'letter' when, without warning, the document went into hidden mode and the screensaver of Haydon and Christie re-appeared. Diane's attention was not on the two smiling faces, however. Her eyes were on the fishing boats in the background as her mind latched onto something she had just written: *She rises and falls with the Atlantic swell, but she does not travel; she is still.*

'Pete! Pete! Tell them she's is in a boat. She's in the harbour, Pete. Tell them!' Diane was running down the stairs, holding the laptop open in front of her. Pete came running to meet her, closely followed by James.

'What are you saying, Di?'

'Pete! She's alive! She can't call out, but she's alive! Tell them to search the boats in the harbour – these in particular.' She held the laptop out for him to see.

Puzzled and frustrated, he looked at the picture of his daughter's smiling face. Was his wife having a breakdown? 'I don't understand, Di.'

'Do you trust me?'

'Of course I do.'

'Then trust me, now, and tell the police to go down to the harbour and look for Christie in the boats. These boats!' she said, pointing to the coloured shapes behind the laughing couple in the photo.

Pete took the laptop from her, his face alight with renewed energy and hope, and he raced to the pub car park, where a few of the police were still gathered, looking at maps of the area. 'Hey, have you checked the boats in the harbour?' he called as they looked up expectantly at his approach. 'The little boats – these?' He showed them the laptop.

The officers, two uniformed and one plain clothes, looked at him as though he had lost the plot. 'But they're open-topped – well, most of them. We'd be able to see,' one of them remarked.

'Not if she's gagged, bound and under a tarpaulin. Can you please search all of them?'

'We may as well,' the plain clothes detective shrugged, unconvinced. 'Let's cover every possibility. What made you think of this, Mr Styles?'

Pete glanced back towards the house, not knowing quite how to explain. 'It sounds silly but my wife's always had this telepathic thing going with Christie, and she just has a hunch, if you see what I mean.'

The three police officers looked at each other, scepticism written all over their faces, which annoyed Pete. 'Look, it's a mother-daughter thing. I don't know how it works and I really don't care. Are there any other leads? No! So can we just get on with it?'

The detective sprang into action, understanding a parent's sense of urgency. It made no difference if they came up with nothing. But, you never knew.

James went down to the harbour with the police detective, who had radioed in to get the frogmen down to the jetty. Pete stayed with Diane and they were sitting on the sofa, holding hands in anxious but hopeful silence when there was a call at the back door.

'Hello, Pete? Is it okay to come in?'

'Sure thing, Rosie. Come through.' Pete was past caring: his misdemeanours now seemed petty and trivial. 'You allowed out then?' he asked.

'Well, that's the thing, Pete. Stevie hasn't come home and it's not like him. He's usually home by seven at the latest, even if he's gone to the pub. He wants his tea by then.' She looked nervously at Diane. 'I don't know where he is. I called the pub but they haven't seen him, so I called his work and he hasn't been in all day. It's very odd.'

Pete couldn't quite believe what he suspected Rosie was getting at. 'When did you see last him, Rosie?'

'I saw him briefly this morning. He slept on the sofa last night as he had one of his headaches and he finds it easier to sleep alone.' Rosie twisted her hands together. 'I didn't think about it when you mentioned the white van, but there's one at the boat yard. I forgot all about it, but sometimes Stevie brings it home if he has an early start in the morning. I don't know if it's connected. I'm so sorry I didn't mention it before.'

Once more, Pete leapt up to speak to the police, leaving Diane and Rosie alone together. Diane saw an opportunity and took it.

'We hardly know each other, Rosie, but you've got to know Pete rather well over the few months that we've been here.'

Rosie turned the colour of a ripe plum.

'At the moment,' Diane continued, 'I'm not interested in knowing about the relationship you may or may not have been having with my husband. What I really need to know is: would your husband have any suspicions on that score?'

Rosie looked down at her hands and twisted her apron in her clenched fists. 'I admit I've enjoyed Pete's company over the past weeks. He's everything I would love in a husband, but I know he's yours Diane. He's made that perfectly clear. I'm afraid it doesn't stop me fantasising, though.'

Diane understood that very well.

'Stevie pays me absolutely no attention whatsoever,' said Rosie, 'until he wants a bit, if you see what I mean.' In response to Diane's nod, she continued. 'The first day that Haydon was working with Pete, I asked Pete over for tea and cake, and he came. We had become close – just as friends, of course,' she added, with a little too much emphasis. 'When he left, I didn't realise, but my Stevie was watching from the top of the road. He didn't come home straight away, but when he got home later on, he beat me – said it would teach me not to have men in the house when he wasn't there. It might be nothing, but there again ...'

This time, it was Diane who jumped up and ran out of the house to find the officers and tell them Rosie's tale. Pete was still with them and looked momentarily distressed about the two women talking about him, but Diane made it quite clear that they had other things more pressing to sort out than his wandering eye.

Haydon was allowed to leave his home and go down to the harbour with the female officer, to see if Christie was there. He had no idea how or why they thought she might be there, but he didn't care: it was activity and, doing nothing all day, he had been going mad with worry, as well as wondering what he had done to lose the two most important people in his life. In the long, empty hours of waiting, he had lost all sight of a future for himself and had started to remember why he had not let anyone get close to him. It seemed to be happening again.

When they reached the jetty, they found that three police cars and two police vans had gathered there, and the whole area was awash with uniforms and activity. A few reporters had turned up with cameras and microphones at the ready, and Pete and Diane were also there, unable to wait any longer at the cottage. The small fishing boats bobbed around as the frogmen moved from one to the other, finding nothing. As the light was fading fast, hopes of finding Christie were running low. Haydon, Pete and Diane were joined by James and Ollie, and they all watched apprehensively, waiting for news – good or bad.

Meanwhile, PC Steel had contacted the owner of the boat yard at home, to follow up on the lead from Reverend Gilmore. Stuart Smith was happy to help and readily admitted that they had a white transit van, although he wasn't sure if it had been taken out by any of his guys the previous evening. He agreed to ring round and ask those who might have done so. While he was doing that, PC Steel received a message regarding Steve and promptly questioned Stuart about him. Apparently, Steve was known to be a bit of a hot head who also had an eye for young girls and was often seen around the town being inappropriate with women half his age. It didn't seem to matter to him that he had a wife at home and a grown up son. 'What's he working on at the moment?' the PC asked.

'He's been working on a large pleasure boat that's moored over by the harbour wall. It's finished now and I think the owners are due to sail out tomorrow morning.'

'Would it be possible for him to conceal someone on the vessel, do you think?'

'I couldn't really say. I wasn't very involved with it. Steve's an experienced boat-builder so I more or less let him get on with it. He has an apprentice with him most of the time, although I think the lad was on holiday this past week.'

The policeman and boatyard manager looked at each other as they both connected the dots.

'I'll grab a torch,' declared Stuart, ducking into the understairs cupboard of his hill top cottage. The two men then ran down the hill towards the crowd that had started to gather. 'I'll get the keys. Meet you on the jetty,' Stuart said over his shoulder as he ran towards the boat yard offices.

Minutes later, a large crowd had gathered around the steps that led down to the luxury wooden pleasure boat sheltering snugly against the harbour wall. Stuart Smith and PC Steel descended the step ladder leading down onto the swaying pontoon and proceeded to search the boat from bow to stern, to no avail. The light of the moon showed the disappointment etched on their faces.

Diane was devastated. 'I was so sure she was here, Pete. So sure.'

Even as the words left her mouth, she began to feel the warmth rise in her. For no reason that she could fathom, she impulsively reached out and grabbed Haydon's hand. He looked at her and knew what she was feeling; he had seen the same look in Christie's eyes and he knew the one from beyond was in contact. Holding Diane's hand tightly, he locked his gaze onto hers, willing her to be the conduit for information about his beloved Christie's whereabouts. She staggered under the pressure of the heat, but Haydon held her steady, knowing she was sensing something.

The words came back to her again: *She rises and falls with the Atlantic swell, but she does not travel; she is still.* Her eyes widened as she looked down onto the pontoon where the police officer and boat-builder were about to climb the ladder. 'No!' she yelled, starting forward and held back by Haydon and Pete, without which she would have pitched head first onto the wooden platform. 'Don't come up! What's that over there?' She pointed to a huge pile of thick rope that was used to tether the larger boats. 'Go and see what's under it!' she shouted.

The two men looked up in disbelief, but with no other ideas, they did as she bid. Stuart reached the rope first and pulled it out as though to send it into the water to do its job. As he did so, a wooden trunk was revealed under the uncoiled rope.

'Look Pete!' Diane shouted. 'She's in there! She's rising and falling on the swell but she's not going anywhere. She's in that box!'

The rest of the rope was pulled swiftly away by others who had descended onto the pontoon to help. Stuart shone his torch around the box and found that it had been turned to the wall. It took three men to turn it round, the clasp was then undone and the lid lifted. Inside, curled up, gagged, and bound at ankles and wrists, lay Christie, screwing up her eyes against the sudden light of torches. 'She's alive!' shouted PC Steel.

In seconds, Pete and Haydon had clambered down the ladder and were beside her, tearing off the gag and undoing her cramped arms and legs. Whether it was the result of cramp from being confined in a small space for so many hours, or severe shock, or a mixture of both, they couldn't tell, but she couldn't move. She lay in her father's arms as he wept with relief, and her glassy eyes stared into Haydon's as he held her hand and rubbed her arm.

The stand-by ambulance crew quickly took over: she was examined and treated for hypothermia before carefully being strapped to a stretcher, hoisted up the harbour wall and put straight into the ambulance. Haydon stayed quietly by her side and her eyes continually searched for his face. Diane let him go in the ambulance with them while Pete followed directly behind in a police car with James. Pete broke down again as soon as they were out of the town and heading towards the hospital; he sobbed continually while the police officer and James just sat and silently listened to him.

Chapter 23

Drained and exhausted, the Styles family sat with Haydon and PC Steel in the relatives' room in the Accident and Emergency Department, anxiously waiting while Christie was thoroughly checked over. PC Bromsgrove had stayed in Porthtreval to follow the strong lead into who was responsible for the abduction: the hunt for Rosie's husband was underway.

When the house doctor came into the relatives' room and pulled up a chair in front of the anxious faces, Pete could hardly breathe; he felt completely responsible for his daughter's trauma; his lustful, adulterous behaviour could well have destroyed more than his marriage.

'Christie is doing well, physically,' the doctor informed them. She's obviously bruised and her muscles were severely cramped during the time she was kept confined. She's warmed up nicely though, now, and it's lucky she didn't have to spend another night like that.'

'How is she doing emotionally, doctor? Has she said anything?' Diane asked, her hands clasped tightly in her lap.

'No, she hasn't spoken, as yet. She's in severe shock and I think she just needs time, and the love and support of her family. There's no reason why she shouldn't make a full recovery, but the mind is complex, as I'm sure you realise, and we'll have to wait and see.' The young doctor smiled encouragingly at the worried faces in front of him.

'Thank you,' said Diane. 'Can we see her now?'

'Of course. I'll show you where she is. The nurses have washed her and made her more comfortable.'

Diane took Haydon's arm. 'Would you mind if Pete and I just went in first?' she asked earnestly. 'Would that be okay?'

A flicker of concern flashed across his face, but he nodded and awkwardly sat back down again.

'I'll stay with Haydon, Mum,' James offered.

'Thanks,' smiled his mother as she and Pete hurried to follow the doctor down the sterile looking corridors.

Christie was lying in a side ward that was dimly lit by the over-bed light. A drip was attached to the back of her right hand and a nurse stood beside her, checking the fluid levels and marking up figures on the chart. She smiled as they entered the room. 'I'll leave you to it,' she said. 'I'm just out at the nursing station if you need anything.'

Diane and Pete both nodded, their attention fully on their daughter, who looked so small and helpless all tucked up in bed. Apart from the drip in her arm, there were no outward signs of her ordeal. However, there was no Christie smile of welcome, either; she looked at them out of hollow, haunted eyes. Diane sat down on the side of the bed and took her hand, gently stroking the soft skin either side of the needle.

'Hello, darling. Are you feeling better now? Are you warmer?'

Christie was looking directly at her mother, but it was as if she hadn't heard what Diane said. She just blinked and looked from her parents to the door.

'You gave us quite a fright, darling girl,' Pete said gently, leaning forward to place a hand on her leg. Christie looked at him as he spoke, but then her gaze returned to the door.

Diane and Pete looked at each other, not understanding for a moment but then realising what – or whom – she was looking for.

'Shall I go and get him?' Diane suggested.

Pete nodded and returned his attention to Christie, who was still staring at the door. Her face fleetingly brightened as her mother opened it but became blank as it closed. Pete did not know what to say. He took her hand, said her name, and she squeezed his hand as she moved her eyes from the door back to his face. The look in them broke his heart and he bent to kiss her small hand, quietly giving thanks that his precious girl had not been taken from him. Christie's attention returned to the door and her eyes softened as it opened and Diane came back in, followed by Haydon, who moved swiftly to the other side of the bed from Pete. He fell to his knees and took her hand in both of his, his face just inches from hers. Wordlessly, he looked into her eyes and leaned forward to softly kiss her lips; it was as if no one else was in the room.

Diane motioned to Pete that they should go and leave Haydon and Christie to have some time together. Pete gave Christie's arm a squeeze as he got up, but her eyes did not leave Haydon. Out in the corridor, Diane turned into Pete's familiar, comforting arms and broke down. Sobs rattled through her as he held her close and tight, kissing the top of her head and thinking what a complete idiot he had been to risk hurting the people he loved so much. What was wrong with him?

'What can I say to make this easier, Di?' he murmured against her hair.

'Nothing, Pete,' she hiccoughed, pulling back from his embrace and fishing up her sleeve for a handkerchief. 'The only thing that matters, right now, is our daughter. We do have to get our act together, though –both of us. It's time to get a grip and realise what's really important.'

Pete was slightly confused by the intimation that they *both* needed to get their act together, but decided not to pursue the matter. There would be plenty of time for that later.

'Let's go and grab a cup of tea. I could do with something to perk me up,' Diane said. She smiled up at him as they set off down the corridor, and took his arm, pulling it around her shoulders as she nestled into him.

Meanwhile, Haydon was battling with a medley of emotions all jostling for position inside him. He was not a good conversationalist at the best of times – today being no exception – but the tables were turned, and he was the one who must do the talking when all he wanted was to hear Christie's bright, girlish voice. 'Speak to me, Christie,' he pleaded. 'I need to hear your voice.' Tears filled his eyes as he spoke and she mirrored him with a tear running down the side of her head onto the pillow. Haydon wiped it away, kissed her and stroked her forehead, longing for the haunted expression to leave her face. Somehow she looked so much younger, lying there, and anger bubbled inside him. He had suffered insults, persecution and bullying on many occasions and had certainly felt anger towards the perpetrators, but it was nothing compared to the rage he now felt towards whoever had done this. 'I promise you'll feel better soon,' he said. 'And no one is ever going to hurt you again – I promise that too. I'm here, Christie, and I'm staying here.'

Half an hour later, Pete and Diane came back to the room with James. They had brought a cup of tea and a sandwich for Haydon, which he accepted gratefully, not having eaten all day. They hadn't been there long when Diane motioned that it was time for them all to leave.

'We'll be back tomorrow, sweetheart,' she said, bending to kiss her daughter. 'I'm sure you'll be feeling better then, after a good night's sleep.'

Haydon felt Christie's grip on his hand tighten. 'I'm staying,' he said, and no one argued.

A nurse came in to check on Christie and Haydon told her the same thing, so she brought him a blanket and he pulled the footstool close to the chair, forming a makeshift bed right next to Christie.

During the night he heard screaming and thought he was dreaming. The screams persisted and he woke to confusion: nurses were gathered on the other side of Christie's bed, and she was screaming and lashing out with her fists. Haydon leapt up and kicked his chair back, noting that Christie's eyes were glassy and unseeing. 'Let me! Let me!' he shouted above the noise, reaching across the bed and catching hold of Christie's wrists as she fought. 'Christie! Christie! It's Haydon, I'm here! I'm here! I won't let anything hurt you.'

She stopped screaming but continued to thrash about.

'Christie, don't fight me. It's okay, you're safe. I love you, baby, I love you.'

Christie abruptly became still and lay back with her eyes closed. 'Haydon,' she said, curling up on her side, asleep.

It had only been one word, but it was music to his ears.

Some hours later, the sun crept up over the buildings and burst into the little side ward where Christie and Haydon were sleeping soundly. A nurse came in to check Christie's fluids and Haydon woke.

'Cup of tea and a wash?' she whispered on her way out.

Haydon nodded and stood up to stretch his stiff limbs. The sun was falling across Christie's sleeping face and she bore little resemblance to the hysterical young woman he had calmed in the small hours. He bent and kissed her cheek, hearing her draw in a long breath as she began to waken, and then watching as she turned onto her back and stretched her arms above her head, wincing at the soreness in them. She opened her eyes and looked straight into Haydon's.

'Hello you!' she said, reaching up to touch his cheek.

They were the sweetest words Haydon had ever heard.

Christie's family came to the hospital early that morning and happened to run into the doctor who had treated Christie the previous evening.

'Good heavens!' Pete said. 'Do you work twenty four hours a day?'

'Pretty much,' grinned the doctor, the look of him confirming that he was probably not joking. 'I'm glad I've bumped into you. Could I have a word before you go in to see Christie?'

'There's nothing wrong, is there?' Diane asked anxiously.

'No, no. Christie is talking now and seems unscathed by the whole incident. I just wanted to let you know that last night she did have a bit of an episode which could be quite frightening if it happens again. She woke screaming and struggling as if trying to break free, which is entirely understandable given the trauma of abduction. She didn't respond to the nurses' attempts to calm her, but her boyfriend succeeded where they failed: she calmed to his voice and quickly settled. She woke up this morning fully coherent and talking.'

'That's wonderful news!' Pete burst out. 'That she's coherent and talking, I mean,' he added a little self-consciously.

'She has very little recollection of what happened,' the doctor continued. 'She knows she was attacked and remembers being shut in for some time, but no details, or the length of time she was held. Haydon is doing a fantastic job of talking her through whatever comes back to her, though, and I've asked the police not to question her until tomorrow because we need time to fully assess her mental and physical health. So,' he concluded with a smile, 'everything is progressing well.'

'Thank you, doctor,' said Diane. 'Will Christie return to her normal self, do you think?'

'That's not my field, Mrs Styles, but, obviously, an ordeal such as the one Christie has suffered is going to have an effect, to a greater or lesser degree. The good news is that she's young and has her family around her to see her through dark moments. Your GP will refer her to a therapist, if necessary, and I would suggest that she have a couple of counselling sessions as a matter of course.'

Christie was sitting up in bed wearing Haydon's sweatshirt when the family trooped into her room, and the television on the wall was showing a cartoon, although neither Haydon nor Christie was watching it. The smile of welcome on Christie's face immediately reduced her mother to relieved tears and there were hugs all round. In the conversation that followed, little was said about the harrowing events of the day before, since everyone took their cues from Christie and she seemed intent on talking about the changes to Haydon's house, Diane's trip to Southport and James' latest surfing escapades. There would be time enough, when she was ready, to talk about those terrifying hours.

Steve had disappeared from Porthtreval. There had been no official announcement but everyone in the small community knew that the police were looking for him. Rosie sat in her kitchen feeling sick with worry and fatigue. She knew he was a violent and unreasonable man, but she had not realised the depth of his depravity until now. She looked around at the meagre extent of her life – the house and the cramped streets surrounding it – and judged the whole of her adulthood a complete waste, considering she had reached this stage of her life and this was all she had to show for it. Sighing, she stood up and leaned against the sink to look out at Pete's house. They were all at the hospital with Christie. Thank goodness the girl had been found.

A wave of nausea sent her to sit back down, the thoughts that were causing it continuing to plague her: her husband, the man she had slept with every night for decades, had abducted and locked a young girl up in a wooden bin, *because of her* – to punish her and Pete. It was horrific enough to think that he could do such a terrible thing; even worse to realise that it was hers and Pete's actions that had driven him over the edge. The police had told her that Christie had not been sexually assaulted, and physically she was going to be fine. But how does a person get over something like that? she wondered, a shudder running through her at the thought of being tied and locked up, never knowing if anyone would ever find you.

She looked around the place that had been her home for over thirty years, and wondered how she, herself, would ever get over this. Maybe it was time to move on, but where could she go? There was the static caravan they owned in Torquay. They hadn't been for a couple of years, but maybe she could go and live there for a while. No one would know her, she could start again, and it was not too far from Archie.

It came over her like a tidal wave. The caravan! That's where he would have gone! She jumped up and checked the drawer where the keys were kept. They were gone. Picking up the business card that PC Steel had left her, Rosie made the call that she knew would end her marriage.

By mid-afternoon, Christie was on her way home, sitting between Haydon and James in the back seat of the family car, her hand held fast by Haydon, who never wanted to let her out of his sight again. With her hand firmly planted in his, he watched the passing countryside, thinking back to the last time he had been in a car – a police car, as it happened – after he had been beaten by a group of youths and the local police had driven him back home from the hospital. Thanks to Christie, he was no longer that sad, lonely person who attracted ridicule and violence, and now he would protect her always.

Back at the cottage, Christie complained of tiredness and her mother suggested she go and have a lie down, graciously accepting the fact that Haydon felt the need to go with her. As soon as they were sitting side by side on the bed, Christie turned and kissed Haydon with all the passion in her young body.

'I thought I'd lost you,' he whispered as they drew apart.

Christie saw the fear in his eyes. 'Hold me, Haydon,' she murmured, pulling him down onto the single bed and turning in his arms so that he lay directly behind her and moulded his body to hers. With his arms around her, she hugged his hand to her chest and they both fell asleep, lulled by the familiar sound of the sea crashing on the pebbly beach.

James had gone out to meet Ollie, which left Diane and Pete alone. Diane made coffee and they sat in the coolness of the shady lounge, both of them mentally and physically drained.

'What's been happening to us, Pete?'

He stared down at the pattern on his coffee cup as if it was the first time he had ever seen it and it deserved closer inspection.

'Pete!'

'Sorry, love.' He glanced at her and then looked down again.

Diane could see that he was struggling with his emotions and was in no fit state to have an in-depth discussion about their marriage. She sighed and moved to sit next to him on the sofa. Taking his hand in both of hers, she thought how comfortingly familiar it was; she knew every scar and blemish. With that thought came the realisation that she had something with Pete that no other woman could have: a history, and memories that would always be theirs. Whatever foolishness he'd been up to, that shared history remained. And anyway, wasn't she just as foolish and guilty as he was? 'How about we start afresh?' she said.

'Yes,' Pete nodded with a grateful smile.

'It's sad that we both had to come close to losing something precious in order to realise how lucky we are.' She took her husband's ruggedly handsome face in her hands, looked into his grey eyes and softly kissed him. He choked back tears as he put down his coffee and took her into his arms. She stroked his head and let him cry.

The police were still in attendance down at the harbour, and the area where Christie had been held was still cordoned off by police tape. James and Ollie sat side by side on the wall, watching everything that was going on. They leaned against each other, shoulder to shoulder, arm to arm, thigh to thigh. Their physical relationship had developed further, but James was reaching the conclusion that he didn't want free-spirited Ollie to be much more than a friend; their interests and personalities were too different.

'Have you told your parents that you're gay?' Ollie suddenly asked.

Although it dominated James' thoughts most of the time, the right moment never seemed to present itself. 'Not yet,' he replied, giving Ollie's leg an affectionate rub. 'Why?'

'I just wondered how to do it.'

James laughed out loud and had to stifle the urge to lean over and kiss Ollie's handsome face. He was so naive and straight forward – qualities James really enjoyed. 'Isn't that just the million dollar question: how do you tell your parents you're gay? The answer is that I don't think there is an answer. You just have to do what you think is best and then cope with the fallout, I suppose. I've never done it so I'm no expert.'

'Do your parents suspect anything?'

James' brow furrowed as he gave this some thought. 'I don't think so. They're occupied with their own lives at the moment and I'm not really on their radar much, to be honest. Suits me, though!'

'Actually, I've got something to tell you.'

'Oh, yeah?' said James, his curiosity piqued.

'Yeah, working in the shop and hanging out in this town isn't really cutting it, so I've decided to go travelling.' Ollie paused and looked at James, whose face was giving nothing away. 'I'm going to the States – New York. I have an uncle who lives in the West Village and he's asked me to go out there …. Are you angry?'

James initial reaction was shock that someone close was, again, leaving him to go to another country. Common sense followed close behind: he had already decided that there was no future for him with Ollie, so instead of being upset he put his arm around his friend's shoulders. 'Of course I'm not angry. Do what feels right, mate. Be careful, though. You're a dishy guy and great as that is, there will be a lot of men after you, so be choosy - you know what I'm saying?'

Ollie grasped James' hand on his shoulder and gave it a squeeze. 'Yeah, okay. Good advice. I'd still be all over the place if it wasn't for you.' He sent a flirtatious glance James' way. 'You're a great teacher,' he grinned.

James smirked and looked down into the watery depths below him. 'I'm a novice, mate; there's a lot more to learn. Promise me one thing, though.'

'What's that?'

'Stay in touch; don't become a stranger. That hurts more than anything.' Tears stung the back of James' eyes as the one person he trusted implicitly and ultimately loved sprang to mind.

'I'll be on the phone before you know it, asking for help probably! And thanks for everything you've done for me, Jay.'

James strengthened his hold around Ollie's shoulders. 'That's what friends are for, isn't it? Anyway,' he said with a chuckle, 'it really was my pleasure!'

Diane had to rustle up a mattress and quilt for Haydon, that night, as he refused to leave Christie's side. Lying on her stomach with her hand hanging down the side of the bed, Christie, in turn, held onto Haydon's shoulder, as if they had to have some degree of direct physical contact between them.

Chapter 24

Rosie pointed out the lane that led to the campsite and the driver of the unmarked police car stopped at the end of it.

'This is as far as you go,' the officer in the passenger seat said to Rosie, who was sitting in the back with a female police officer. 'It's important that you're not seen, so PC Simon will stay here with you, while PC Blackman and myself go in and take a look around.' He opened the car door. 'Joan, let's go! Number thirty four, you say, Rosie?'

'Yes, go to the wooded area by the toilet block. You'll see about ten static caravans with small gardens in front. Ours is the second one in.'

The officers nodded and walked swiftly away down the track. Watching them go, Rosie felt a sadness flood through her. Whatever he had done, whatever monster he had become, she had loved him, and part of her always would. The past few weeks had made her see things in another light, however, and it was time to take the next step to a different life.

Many miles away, Christie was sitting in her room, the pillow she was clutching wet with tears as sobs juddered through her and she released the pent up trauma that had so far been repressed. As expected, the police had come to take a statement from her and the torturous ordeal had brought back much of the attack that shock had previously blocked out.

With Haydon sitting beside her, she had told the police that she remembered saying goodnight to Haydon and then stopping outside the back gate to look for her house keys. She had then sensed someone behind her, smelt a strong smell and the next thing she knew, she was coming to and finding she couldn't move or call for help because she'd been gagged and her hands and feet were bound. She remembered breathing slowly through her nose to keep herself calm and stop panicking so that she could work out what to do. She didn't think she was injured, although she was extremely uncomfortable; her head was throbbing and she felt disorientated and woozy. By moving as much as she could, which was hardly at all, she had guessed that she was in some kind of cupboard or trunk, which was cold and damp; she had been shivering badly. After that she'd concentrated on keeping herself awake, knowing that falling asleep could be the end for her and she never lost hope that she would be found. She hadn't seen her abductor and she had no idea who could want to harm her.

She realised her statement wasn't overly informative, but she was greatly relieved to have it over and done with. Later that night, when she and Haydon were lying together on her bed, she told him what she hadn't told the police. It wasn't that she had been hiding anything, she just knew that this part of her experience wasn't relevant to the police investigation; besides which, they wouldn't have believed her. She said that there had been a moment in that box when she was at the end of her tether, shaking violently with shock, fear and cold, and about to give up, when, out of nowhere, she'd heard the faint sound of a kitten mewing. It had been so distant and soft that she'd wondered if it was just her imagination playing cruel tricks on her. But then the purring had begun, and this time it was right in the box with her. In fact, she had felt the weight of a cat lying against her back, its warmth penetrating her clothing and oozing right into her core. At the same time, another source of heat had begun in her bound feet, building and building until her whole body was toasty warm. She had stopped shivering and known that she would be all right.

Haydon listened to her without comment and held her until she slept.

The next few days were full of visits from well-wishers as Christie recuperated. Not wanting her upset by anything, Haydon had briefly returned to his cottage to clear up any signs of the police searches, and to clean the second-hand fridge Diane and Pete had bought him as a surprise. The following weekend, he returned with Christie.

He was upstairs fitting a blind at the bathroom window when there was a knock at the front door. Not wanting Christie to answer the door to anyone, he ran down the stairs calling, 'I'll get it.'

Nevertheless, her face appeared round the kitchen door and she followed him just out of curiosity. Haydon taking charge was a new concept for both of them, but Christie was learning to relax into it and to acknowledge that it was just what she needed.

'Hello, Haydon. I thought I should knock and not just walk in as usual. Is Christie at home with you?' Reverend Gilmore stood nervously at the door with his wife hovering behind him. He stepped back and ushered Cynthia ahead of him as Haydon stood back to let them in. They were gathered in an awkward little huddle before Christie rescued the situation. Haydon had yet to learn social graces and niceties.

'Come through to the kitchen,' she beckoned, leading the way. 'Haydon, bring the other chairs through, will you darling?' she called as she busied herself with the kettle and glanced at the reverend. He nodded knowingly at her and she drew her breath in, preparing herself for what was to come and wondering how it would unfold with Mrs Gilmore present.

Although it made a comical sight, the four of them squeezed around the tiny kitchen table, Christie could feel the tension in the room and knew it was up to her to do something to ease it. Hitting on a brainwave she put her hand on Cynthia's arm. 'I think we need cake, don't you? Shall we go and get some?'

'As you wish, my dear. I need to get a couple of things myself,' said Cynthia with some enthusiasm.

The two of them swiftly gathered themselves and left the cottage to walk along The Nip towards the High Street.

'How are you, Christie?' Cynthia asked after they'd walked in silence for a while. 'I was so sorry to hear about your ordeal. And I'm sorry about how I spoke to you when you came up to the vicarage. It was unfair of me and I've regretted it since.'

Christie waved the apology aside. 'So much has been happening over the past few months, Mrs Gilmore, that I really hadn't given it a thought. Anyway, you had every right to be suspicious of me: I was a bit forward! But that's me, I'm afraid,' she said, grinning at the older woman.

Meanwhile, Reverend Gilmore was beginning the most difficult conversation of his life. 'Haydon, I've come here today to tell you something …' Unable to go on, the reverend struggled to find the right words. Haydon was so vulnerable and the old vicar had no idea if what he was about to say would knock his grandson sideways. Although his heart went out to Haydon, however, he did not lose sight of the fact that his grandson was a man and should to be treated as such.

As usual, Haydon just waited, not making it any easier for the old vicar, who shifted awkwardly in his chair and took another sip of tea before continuing.

'Haydon, I'm truly sorry that I haven't told you this before, but the fact of the matter is that you're more to me than just a member of my parish. You are, in fact, part of my family. You're my grandson.'

Haydon's reaction was swift and unexpected. 'I know,' he said.

The old man was speechless and confused. This week was almost becoming too much for him. 'You already knew? My dear boy, how was that? How did you know?'

Haydon shrugged. 'I don't know. I just knew when I saw you here with Christie the other day.'

'Have you spoken to Christie about it? Did she tell you?'

Now it was Haydon's turn to look shocked. 'Christie knows!' he exclaimed.

Sensing a potential issue between the two young people, Reverend Gilmore quickly added, 'I asked her not to say anything. I needed to think things through and work out how best to tell you. But Haydon, I don't understand how all of a sudden you realised, after all this time.'

Again Haydon shrugged. 'I don't know. But there are lots of things in life that I just know and I don't know how I know them. I just feel them. Doesn't everyone?'

The vicar laughed and laid his hand on his grandson's arm. 'Maybe we would, Haydon, if we weren't all too busy to notice.'

It wasn't long before Christie and Cynthia returned and they all shared how everyone had already known, which presented rather an odd state of affairs in that it automatically redressed a balance in their relationships to one another. Reverend Gilmore was less stressed, now, but he was still fidgety. After a second cup of tea and more cake, the reason became clear.

'Er … ' The reverend cleared his throat uneasily as all eyes turned to him. 'As it's a day for things to come out in the open, there's something else that we want to tell you both,' he said, looking from Haydon to Christie and back again. 'Haydon, a few days ago I learned what happened to your mother. How I found out is another story, the main thing being that we know where she is and why she left you, dear boy.'

Shock registered on both young faces.

'Yes?' breathed Christie into the pause left by the vicar.

Taking a deep breath he continued. 'The day your mother left you, Haydon, she was having a complete mental breakdown. For some unknown reason, she must have got on a bus and she ended up wandering the streets in Hayle with just her dressing gown and slippers on. She didn't seem to know who she was or where she lived, and she had no form of identification on her, so the authorities found her a bed at a residential home, run by the Church in St Ives, where they care for people with those kinds of disorders. She's been there ever since, cared for by nuns. She has little recollection of the past thirty or so years of her life and is quite childlike, although apparently happy enough. She's well in body Haydon, but I'm afraid she's a different person to the mother you knew.'

Haydon's chair fell against the kitchen cupboard behind him as he abruptly stood up, his face ashen. Christie reached for his hand but he moved away and silently left the room. They could hear him on the stairs and Christie had no doubt about where he was going. His grandfather stood to follow him, but she laid a hand on his arm.

'Leave him, Reverend Gilmore. He just needs to take this in – as do I!'

Cynthia said nothing but looked gratefully at her husband for not involving her story. There was no need.

'Is she well enough to come home?' asked Christie.

The old man shook his head. 'Physically maybe, but mentally, no. She seems very content in the home and helps with looking after the other residents; in fact, the nuns say she's a real asset to them. To take her away from what's familiar could be disastrous for her, so she'll stay there. I did ask if she could come for visits, to see Haydon and, of course, meet you, Christie, and they seemed to think that was a good idea. I don't know if she'd know this place as she's suffering retrograde amnesia and can remember little if anything of her life before she went to the home, but you never know. So maybe we can think about arranging that.'

At his words Christie felt the now familiar heat rise through her, transmitting a comforting essence. Kathleen was coming home. It wasn't about coming to the cottage: she was coming back to a family who would love and support her. Christie reached across the table and squeezed the old man's hand. 'Thank you,' she said fervently. 'That couldn't have been easy.'

'No,' he replied, patting her hand affectionately, 'but I think it will all work out. Like Haydon says, I just *feel* that it will.'

'I'll just go up to him, now,' she said and the elderly couple nodded in understanding.

'We'll let ourselves out,' said Cynthia, 'and leave you both to recover from the shock of all this.'

'Thank you.' Christie smiled and left them to it, knowing they needed some recovery time of their own: the conversation had undoubtedly taken a lot out of Haydon's grandfather.

She pushed open the door of the pink bedroom to find Haydon standing straight and tall, arms folded, looking out of window into the far distance. She walked up and put her arms round him from behind.

'I can feel the heat in you,' he said.

She rested her cheek on his back, feeling him relax, and after a while he turned and took her in his arms.

'So much has happened,' he murmured into her hair.

'I know. Let's just take one day at a time, shall we?'

Chapter 25

In October of that year, Rosie shut up her house for the last time. The new owners were going to convert it into a holiday cottage so there would be no one living in it for a while. Her husband had been arrested the day she had led the police to the caravan, where he had, indeed, been hiding out. At first he'd denied everything, but changed his plea to guilty once forensic evidence proved that Christie had been in the white van. He'd already started his prison term of nine years and Rosie's new life was beginning.

She had visited Pete and Diane, one Sunday morning, while they were enjoying a cup of coffee in the late summer sun that was flooding their backyard. She'd told them that she was selling up and going travelling. She'd thanked Pete, telling him that meeting him had given her the confidence to step out after years of bullying and abuse. Pete and Diane, having re-kindled the romance and passion of the early years of their marriage, had happily responded with enthusiastic encouragement.

Now, as she walked away from the home in which she had never found true sanctuary, Pete was waiting to drive her to the coach station in Penzance. On the way, they chatted about nothing more personal than her plans. Christie's abduction had changed Pete: his wife and family now had his undivided love and loyalty and he would never again risk losing them. At the coach station, Rosie hugged him tightly and resolutely walked away; she could have loved him, but she knew he would always love another. As he waved her off, the thought struck her that he might remember her, but he would never miss her.

By Christmas, Christie and Haydon had made the little cottage a cosy home. Apart from the time when they were both at work, –

Haydon with Pete, Christie in her new job as manager of the tearooms on the harbour side – they spent all their time together. The recluse who used to haunt the fishing town was all but forgotten, and everyone who realised that Haydon had been that man was simply pleased to see him renewed – a man reborn.

Christie still had occasional nightmares about the abduction, but Haydon was always there to hold her until she recovered. She clung to him like a drowning person to a raft, but then calmed and slept, remembering little about them by morning.

It was Christmas Eve and they had decorated the cottage in bright gold and greens to celebrate their first Christmas together. A tree twinkled invitingly with white lights in the front window and a fire crackled in the hearth. Christie surveyed the room with a satisfied smile. It looked lovely. The new rug added warmth to the boarded floor and the old, second-hand sofa had been given a new lease of life with the richly coloured throw she had bought during the week.

Everything was ready. Today was the day that Kathleen was coming home to visit.

At the same time, Haydon was upstairs looking around his mother's room, lost in memories. He realised that his childhood had not been particularly happy: she had never been emotionally strong and he had picked up much of her anxiety. Nevertheless, she'd been all that he had, and he'd loved her. The loneliness when she had disappeared had been agonising, resulting in the downward spiral of which he was now ashamed. Christie had suggested he see a professional counsellor to help him get over those years, but Haydon had just shaken his head. He had everything he needed in *her*, and now he had a family around him for the first time. It felt good, and just knowing that he had not been abandoned or unwanted had made a huge difference to his confidence and how he felt about himself.

Understandably, he now realised, he had found his first visit with his mother difficult. Reverend Gilmore – or Alan, as they all now called him – had taken him to the residential home and he would never forget his initial shock at how much his mother had aged: it had taken him a while to relate to the tiny, bird-like woman she had become, and to adjust to her poor mental clarity, even though, every now and then, she had mentioned her baby boy or said something that made him think she still had memories from their past together. She had not, however, recognised that he was now with her as an adult, which had greatly saddened him.

'Dad's here, Haydon,' Christie shouted from the bottom of the stairs.

'Coming!' he called, taking one more look around the room and checking the thermostat on the storage heater before closing the door behind him.

Pete drove them to St Ives to pick up Haydon's mother. When they returned, Kathleen Rouse timidly walked up the garden path of the cottage she had left so many years before. Christie spotted the Critchleys peering out of their window and waving and she gaily waved back. They had become firm friends with Haydon and her over the past few months and had popped round regularly to see if they needed any help.

'Come and see your room, Kathleen,' invited Haydon, using her name, as it had been suggested he should, so as not to confuse her too much.

She smiled up at him and nodded. Like Haydon, she said very little, leaving the conversation to others and happy to just listen and watch. Opening the door, Haydon walked in first and then turned to watch his mother's reaction. She stood in the doorway and looked around her. Smiling at Haydon she first walked over to the wardrobe, opened the door and touched the clothes still hanging there. *They would swamp her now*, Haydon thought. She did the same with all the drawers, nodding contentedly as she closed each one, and then she went to the storage heater to feel its warmth, which she clearly enjoyed while looking out of the window to take in the view. Following that, she continued to inspect every item in her room, nodding to herself every now and again, and it seemed to Haydon that she was recognised things. He felt like a young boy again, and his throat constricted as he remembered how he had tried to watch over her, and worried about her while feeling powerless to do anything to help.

Kathleen concluded her examination of the room and came to Haydon, smiling and looking somehow different to him. She put her arms round his chest, cuddling into him as he returned her embrace. They stood like that for some moments, until she raised her head and smiled up at him.

'Thanks, son,' she said.

'That's okay, Mum,' he replied, allowing his tears to fall unchecked as she held him.

Christmas dinner, the next day, was being hosted by the Gilmores at the vicarage. The table was set for eight and with the help of her cleaning lady, Cynthia had been busy getting everything ready for weeks. Everyone arrived at the vicarage around ten o'clock for coffee, laden with presents, bottles and festive cheer. Kathleen's moment of recognition had not been sustained and she had returned to being childlike, but she was thoroughly enjoying herself. Alan had had to deliver the morning service but was back by midday, when everyone enjoyed festive drinks, and then came the traditional roast turkey dinner with all the trimmings; it was a noisy, joyous affair.

Afterwards, Diane, James and Christie cleared away and insisted that Cynthia sit down and relax. Meanwhile, Alan showed Pete and Haydon an old car he had begun restoring years before – a beautiful, rich burgundy coloured Jaguar. Haydon was all over it, inspecting every inch and stroking it lovingly. Knowing Haydon had an artistic streak and took great pleasure in tenderly restoring things to their former glory, Pete alerted Alan to the attention Haydon was paying the car. Alan picked up on the hint and promptly asked his grandson if he would like to get involved in the restoration with him. Haydon's face lit up and he enthusiastically agreed, which, in turn, made Alan's Christmas.

Following the exchange of presents, and the 'oohs' and 'ahhs' and copious thanks, Alan stood up and announced that he had a final gift for Haydon and Christie. Cynthia was grinning mischievously as her husband went off into the back of the house, returning some minutes later, slightly dishevelled and a bit hot and bothered, carrying a cardboard box topped with a bow.

'A gift from Cynthia and me to you both,' he announced. 'We thought you might like it to make your home complete.' He placed the box on the floor in front of Christie, who was sitting at Haydon's feet. As he did, she heard a faint mewing and immediately expected the sensation of inner heat to spread through her body, although she hadn't experienced it for a few months and she had generally been alone when it had happened before. It all seemed odd and out of whack, and the heat didn't develop, so she quickly undid the bow and opened the box, gasping with pleasure and surprise as she lifted out a tiny black and white kitten, which meowed at Christie and elicited merry laughter from everyone in the room.

'How sweet!' exclaimed Christie. 'Is it male or female?'

'Male,' Alan informed her with a broad grin.

'He's gorgeous!' gushed Christie, holding the little face up to her own and being rewarded with a scratchy lick on the end of her nose. 'We'll call him Eddie!'

'Eddie?' Diane said in surprise. 'Why Eddie?'

'It just feels right,' replied Christie, smiling to herself.

Kathleen was back at the cottage in The Nip and tucked up in bed by nine o'clock, recovering from a day that had worn her out in the best possible way. Haydon and Christie would take her back to the home on Boxing Day. After checking that she was peacefully sleeping, Christie went downstairs, poured wine into two glasses and joined Haydon in front of the fire, where he was playing with the newest member of the family.

'Oh Haydon, he's so cute!' she laughed as the kitten jumped onto her outstretched legs and then rolled off backwards.

'So, why Eddie?'

'It's the nearest thing to Edie.'

'That doesn't explain anything, my darling.'

'Let's just say that he's named after a friend of mine who helped me when I needed it most,' she said with a sly smile.

Haydon had no idea what she was talking about and even less interest as he looked at her face in the firelight and pulled her into his arms.

'Was that someone at the door?' Pete asked, as Diane came into the room with two cups of hot milk.

'I didn't hear anything, but I was out back. Go see!'

Heaving his tired body out of the chair, Pete ambled through to the hall and opened the front door. It creaked with the salty rust embedded in the hinges. A man with a large kitbag was standing at the bottom of the steps, his back to the street light, making it impossible to identify him.

'Hi, Pete! Long time, no see!'

Pete knew the voice. 'Vince, mate! What the…! Come in! Come in! I didn't even know you were in the country. Come in!'

Vince laughed as he came up the steps and hugged his old friend and employer. 'Good to see you, mate.' he said with a slight Australian twang.

'Di! Di! Look who's here!'

Diane popped her head out of the lounge door and beamed when she saw Vince's face.

'For heaven sake!' she laughed. 'I thought I recognised that voice! Come on in out of the cold, Vince. I'll put the kettle on. James will be so pleased to see you.

At that moment, James was sharing a final drink with Ollie before his friend left the following day. James and Vince had started talking online over the past couple of months and had both realised what they meant to each other. But, like his parents, James had no idea that Vince was in the country and that, after landing at Heathrow, he had hitch-hiked all the way to Cornwall to be with him and was now sitting in his home just yards away.

Ollie stood to go and James followed him out to his car, where Ollie pulled him into a tight embrace.

'Take care, Ollie mate,' James said from within the hug. 'Be true to yourself. It's the only way.'

Ollie drew back and nodded, unable to speak for the emotion closing his throat. He gave James another hug and then got into his car and drove off without looking back. James felt somewhat desolate but there was also relief that they had parted sooner rather than later and on good terms, as James knew a long term relationship with Ollie was never going to happen. As he made his way back home, a solitary figure came walking towards him and there was something in the man's gait that was familiar to James. His eyes widened in disbelief. It couldn't be, could it? The smile in the darkness said it all: Vince had come back to him.

An hour later, the two men, red cheeked and laughing after a tearful reunion followed by a couple of beers in the pub, eventually made their way back home to James' parents, having decided to take the 'sticky plaster route' and just tell everyone that they were 'an item'. The week between Christmas and New Year thus became yet another interesting time for the new patchwork family that had come together in just six months.

After a year of revelations, trauma, drama and change, Pete and Diane had thought nothing else could surprise or shock them, until James and Vince made their announcement. Pete was less than enthusiastic, at first, but after several trips to the pub with Vince and numerous walks round the lake with James, he managed to reach a level of understanding with which he could readily live. Diane just wanted her son to be happy. The fact that James was gay was neither a problem for her nor that much of a surprise; she was his mother, after all. The real shock was the relationship with Vince, but she knew that if James was with Vince – a man she liked and trusted – she could rest easy in her bed.

Christie simply laughed out loud with glee, when she heard, and hugged first her brother and then Vince, welcoming him to the family. Haydon stood by with a grin on his face and invited them to stay for lunch. He had a feeling he would get along well with Vince and a male friend of his own age was a novelty he thought he would like.

In the early hours of a frosty January morning, Christie woke suddenly, with an uneasy feeling in the pit of her stomach. Haydon was in a deep sleep beside her, and Eddie, curled up in the cosy space created by Haydon's legs being bent at the knee, was purring loudly. Without warning, the heat, which had not come to her for months, circulated in her body, bringing with it the urge to write again. Since Edith had been quiet and absent, Christie had assumed her job was done and Edith was happy with how it had all turned out. The present growing urge, however, was indicating that there was something else Edith wanted to say. So Christie quietly got out of bed, slipped on her dressing gown and slippers, and made her way downstairs. Her laptop lay open on the floor. Had she left it like that? *Unusual*, she thought, as it was her habit to close it.

After stoking the fire and adding more coals, she settled into the armchair, pulled a blanket round her and placed her fingers on the keypad as the laptop booted up and a smiling picture of Haydon and Kathleen – one she herself had taken at Christmas – came up on the screen. She wondered how it had got there; it seemed unlikely that Haydon would have done it. She left the question hanging, opened up a blank document and waited for the words to come.

My Darling,

Words cannot describe the sweet emotion that comes with knowing you are now surrounded by love and affection. Your life has been lost, but now you understand how much you were loved from the start and have been ever since. You have learned the hard way that sometimes we are not in possession of the truth: I know you felt unwanted, betrayed and abandoned, thinking you had been given away. But that was never the truth, my darling.

You spent your young life in a family who wanted you but didn't understand your delicate nature. They did not realise that deep down you needed to be with the ones who made you and whom you made. When your borrowed family went, you were free to take your loved one and go where your spirit took you. You were guided to choose the place where you were created: the magical town that was always your home.

Now, my darling, you are fully coming back to me and, at last, we will be together to go on side by side through eternity. I feel your presence in my soul. I see your face and hear your voice - no longer crying but now laughing and loving.

Those whom you leave behind will continue to love you, for it is true, that love never dies, whatever the circumstances. But now... here you are, my darling. You are with me. Now I can sleep. Now I can rest. Finally, you have come home.

The heat that had been consuming Christie dissipated, and with it the compulsion to write. Edith, she knew, would not be contacting her again. She noted the time on her laptop – 4am – and pulled the blanket more closely round her shoulders, staring into the fire for a few minutes before saving the document. When she switched back to her desktop in order to shut down the machine, she found the background image had changed back to the one of herself and Haydon. Unsurprised by the mysterious change of picture and what it was confirming, she smiled sadly, deciding there was no point in waking Haydon or calling the nuns at St Agatha's.

When the call came four hours later, she stood behind him as he listened on the phone and then she held him as he cried, loving him through his loss – and always.

*****

A few words from the author:

As with my first book, Beyond Fragile Boundaries, I have grown to love my characters. The minute I finish writing about them, I miss them. I know it sounds odd but there it is.

I wrote a lot of The Hidden Depths of Haydon Rouse whilst staying in my favourite holiday destination - Porthleven. The book is based there and I have been a constant visitor every year since 2000, always staying in the cottage that belongs to my dear friends, Nigel Smith and Jane Rutherford. Sadly, Jane died last year so it is my pleasure to be able to dedicate this book to her as without her and Nigel's generosity, I would not have had the material to write it.

I enjoy writing about people who seem so real even though they are fictitious. They could be anyone that we know. They have good and bad in them. They inspire and shock us. They are sometimes weak and frustrating and at other times loveable and fun. Just like us.

I hope you enjoyed reading about Christie and her newly extended family. I like to imagine that they are still there as I think of the craggy little Cornish fishing town.

I like to believe that most people are good inside, but I know that no one is perfect and I think this story illustrates that. I feel it shows that we should not judge others based on appearances and we should always speak the truth , even if it is hard to do so at times.

Thanks for reading. See you next time.

Jill

Book Club Questions.

Don't read these until you have finished the book. You might spoil it!

Which of the characters in the book did you find most interesting and why was that? Did they remind you of someone? Yourself perhaps.

What do you think were the reasons behind why Haydon had 'checked out of life' and allowed himself to become so undesirable?

What was your reaction to Pete's behaviour towards his new neighbour? Was he weak? Should he have not even started the relationship with Rosie?

How about Diane. Was she guilty of double standards? Or was it understandable due to the way her husband was acting?

How did you feel about the way that the writer dealt with James being gay?

Was there anything in the book that reminded you of a happening in your own life? What was that and why?

Was the ending expected? If not, what had you thought may happen?

Did you feel that the book was plot or character driven?

What sort of person is Steve, Rosie's husband? What do you think drove him to kidnap Christie?

Have you read Jill's other book(s)? If so, what are the similarities and differences?